A BILLION DOLLAR ARRANGEMENT

THE COMPLETE SERIES-A BILLIONAIRE ROMANCE

MICHELLE LOVE

HOT AND STEAMY ROMANCE

CONTENTS

About the Author v
Sign Up to Receive Free Books vii

	Blurb	1
1.	What She Wants Part 1	2
2.	Work Habits	9
3.	What She Craves Part 2	28
4.	Recovery	58
5.	What She Needs Part 3	66
6.	Relationships	86
7.	What She Feels Part 4	93
8.	The Game	98
9.	Dining and Teasing	101
10.	Redemption	105
11.	Girl Talk	109
12.	Plans	113
13.	Destination: Unknown	117
14.	Away For a Day	121
15.	Morning Sex	125
16.	Maxine to the Rescue	129
17.	What She Chose Part 5	132
	Sign Up to Receive Free Books	165
	Preview of Maelstrom Complete Series 1-4	166

Since Yesterday Part One 167
Other Books By This Author 251
About the Author 253

Made in "The United States" by:

Michelle Love

© Copyright 2020 – Michelle Love

ISBN: 978-1-64808-303-7

ALL RIGHTS RESERVED. No part of this publication may be reproduced or transmitted in any form whatsoever, electronic, or mechanical, including photocopying, recording, or by any informational storage or retrieval system without express written, dated and signed permission from the author

 Created with Vellum

ABOUT THE AUTHOR

Mrs. Love writes about smart, sexy women and the hot alpha billionaires who love them. She has found her own happily ever after with her dream husband and adorable 6 and 2 year old kids.
Currently, Michelle is hard at work on the next book in the series, and trying to stay off the Internet.
"Thank you for supporting an indie author. Anything you can do, whether it be writing a review, or even simply telling a fellow reader that you enjoyed this. Thanks

SIGN UP TO RECEIVE FREE BOOKS

Sign Up to Receive Free E-Books and Audiobook Codes.

Would you like to read **The Unexpected Nanny, Dirty Little Virgin** and **other romance books** for **free**?

You can sign up to receive these free e-books and audiobooks by typing this link into your browser:

https://www.steamyromance.info/free-books-and-audiobooks-hot-and-steamy/

Or this one:

https://www.steamyromance.info/the-unexpected-nanny-free/

BLURB

Angela Hayes is a beautiful city girl who longs for some excitement and fulfillment in her love life. She has a great job at a huge marketing company and she just learned that the company's billionaire CEO will be making an appearance at her branch.

Anderson Cromby is a sexy billionaire playboy who is every woman's fantasy. He's tall, dark, and handsome, and rich beyond words. He could have any woman he wanted, but he has his eyes on the vibrant young Angela.

Angela thought she was content having casual flings here and there, and she enjoys being in control of things. But when the billionaire Anderson brings his dominating personality and sexual possessiveness into her world, he turns it upside down—in a good way!

1

WHAT SHE WANTS PART 1

The bubble bath was piping hot. Angela had used the special bubble bath additive that her mother, Karen, had given her for her thirty-second birthday last month. It was delightful, and it smelled great as it moisturized. She glanced at the nozzle of her bath, the one that spewed forth high pressure hot water at the push of a button. She thought of the many lonely nights she'd had right here in her dingy little apartment, where that nozzle had been her best friend. The nozzle didn't cancel dates; it didn't give excuses. It just pleased you.

Angela Hayes was a young woman much like any other her age. She had been out of school for eight years and was working in the city as a law clerk. She hoped to one day make it through law school and become a full-fledged practicing lawyer in her own right. She was Italian-American by descent, and had a huge family that was scattered across the state. Her father had passed away on Christmas day two years before, and her mother lived alone in an apartment that was even smaller than hers, on the other side of town.

Angela felt bad for her mom, truly, and tried to visit her as often as her work and social life permitted. Her five younger brothers and two sisters were mostly all married off and had their own lives and careers. A few of them were businesspeople, and the rest were tradespeople— electricians and plumbers and the like. Overall, most of the people in her family seemed happy with their lives, and Angela was grateful for that. They usually all got together on the big holidays and Easter was coming up, so she looked forward to a nice reunion then.

As Angela lay back in her luxurious one-woman spa and glanced at the nozzle, she wondered when she would find a sweet man who could be with her, pleasure her, and share a life with her. Angela didn't date very often. She found most men her age were immature and just weren't ready for a serious commitment, which was strange because she was thirty-two and that was considered a fairly late point in a person's life to be settling down.

She had heard stories of couples hooking up through those online dating sites, and that seemed to be a fairly popular option these days, but Angela was just too much of a romantic to go down that route. All her friends were trying it, but she just had a different picture of how she was going to meet her soulmate. She was going to meet him at a benefit, for instance, and their eyes were going to lock from across the room. He was going to approach her from across the dance floor and hold out a hand. "Care to dance?" he would say. They would have a romantic dance; his hand would caress the small of her back; and they would get lost in each other's gaze.

That was how it was supposed to happen. That was how it would happen. She promised herself that night that she wouldn't settle for anything less than perfection in her romantic life, for it would be worth it when the time came. She reached for the nozzle and spread her legs, lowering it into position.

After her bath, she put on a beautiful silk robe and moved

into her living room. She plopped down on her comfortable couch and grabbed the remote. She flipped through the channels until she came to the news channel. Apparently there was a big takeover at the city's largest consulting firm and this bid would result in the largest company of its kind in the country. She could already imagine the share prices skyrocketing. Too bad she didn't own any of those shares, she thought.

After a few more minutes, it was revealed that Angela's law firm would be handling the majority of the legal work surrounding this takeover. It was Saturday today, so she had another day of rest ahead of her, but she knew that Monday would be chaotic. She could already picture her boss bellowing orders at her and the staff. She shuddered briefly.

Finally, she decided that it was time to turn off the TV and go to bed. She walked over to her bedroom, passing by the fridge to get a quick snack of a piece of cheese and some fruit, and then brushed her teeth and got into bed.

That night she dreamed of the merger, and of the new CEO, Anderson Cromby, who would be taking charge. He was a very handsome man who dressed well and had nothing but the finest tastes in the arts, sports, and whatever else he was passionate about. He also happened to be a billionaire, having made his fortune in investing in technology companies, and was only a little older than Angela. She had heard all of this through the grapevine at work. And now, perhaps, she might even get a chance to be in the same room as him—a chance to meet him!

Her dream was pleasant. She and Anderson were dancing together at a ball and he had some really smooth moves. Then he asked her to come back to his expensive penthouse in the city and they cuddled and watched movies together until the sun came up. When Angela woke in the morning, she was left with a longing in her core, for it was obvious to her, through the dream, that she needed a male companion. She needed one badly.

She showered, got dressed, and made herself breakfast. The clock only showed 7:30 a.m., so she had a couple of hours before she had to start getting ready for the day. She spent that extra time at the gym working out. She loved working out in the mornings. It made her feel good all day, and it also made her feel good about her already stunning body. She looked great for a woman her age. Men had even confused her for a twenty year old on several occasions.

Her plan for today, once she had finished her routine, was to meet Maxine for brunch at the Carlisle club across town. Maxine Palmer was her closest friend. They had known each other since college. Maxine was a professional tennis player and spent her time traveling from circuit to circuit. She made quite a lot of money doing that. She wasn't quite at the highest level yet, but she was getting there. She was also married, to an accountant named Henry Palmer. They were happily married and Maxine had recently told Angela that she was expecting. The two of them couldn't have been happier. They even said that they wanted Angela to be the kid's godmother when he was born.

Angela didn't drive, so she took a taxi all the way to the Carlisle club and entered the large wooden doors. She was greeted by a doorman who offered to show her the way to anywhere she needed to go.

"That's okay," said Angela. "I've been here before."

The doorman nodded and smiled pleasantly. Angela walked over to the dining area and approached the busboy.

"Angela, for two," she said. He showed her to a beautiful table by a large glass window overlooking the street below. Maxine was already seated and was engaged in smelling the floral decorations that adorned their table.

"Hiya, babe!" exclaimed Angela excitedly.

"Darling!" responded Maxine, rising to hug her dear friend,

who returned the loving embrace. "You look great, girlfriend!" she said.

"So do you!" responded Angela. "You are positively radiant!"

"Not bad for three months, eh?" said Maxine jovially, and she twirled around for her friend to see how great she looked.

"Let's order some seafood! And I'll get a sangria!" suggested Angela happily.

"You and your sangria. I'll get an orange juice, and I will enjoy it!"

They ordered their meals and within about fifteen minutes they arrived. They each had a shrimp cocktail, and an assortment of cheeses, crackers, and fruit was set out before them. They hungrily ate, all the while chitchatting about their respective lives.

Maxine was complaining that she was missing training time because of the pregnancy. Angela was saying how nervous she was about the big deal that was cooking in the merger world.

"I'm sure you'll knock them dead, Angela," said Maxine reassuringly.

"Thanks, buddy," said Angela, and forced herself to smile in return.

After their bill was paid and their bellies were full, they decided to go for a steam in the club's steam room. They walked up the stairs to the workout area and wandered into the changing room. They got undressed and Maxine's smooth black skin was positively radiant. Angela could see where her belly bulged out as only a woman who was just finishing her first trimester could.

Angela took off her clothes and hung them in one of the wooden cupboards. She draped a town around herself and the two friends walked to the steam room. It was very hot and moist inside the room, and they took a seat in the far corner. There were two other women sitting opposite of them engaged in a discussion. They were talking about the big merger and about Anderson Cromby, who would be the new CEO. Maxine was quiet, settling into the comforts of the steam room. So Angela listened.

"You know, he is just so dreamy. Most CEOs are old and unappealing," said the first woman.

"I know. You know, he looks a little bit like my husband, Ron. Minus the red hair, of course. Anderson's hair is so thick and brown. I would love to run my fingers through it. I would love to get ahold of him and do things to him," said the second woman.

"Tell me about it. I mean, I would just take his dick in my mouth and suck it like there's no tomorrow!" said the first woman.

"Erica!" said the second woman, embarrassed. "There are two other people here."

"Oh, I'm sorry. I didn't see you two. I hope we are not disturbing you," said Erica.

"No, it's okay," said Angela reassuringly. "Believe me, our mouths are much dirtier. This is my friend Maxine, and I'm Angela. Nice to meet you two."

After the steam room, the two friends went back to Angela's place and put in a DVD. They lounged there for a few hours watching the movie, until they decided it was time to do something different.

"So, what are you going to do if you actually get to meet Anderson Cromby?" asked Maxine.

"What do you mean, what will I do? I'll just play it cool, like I normally do. He wouldn't be the only man who was ever interested in me, by any stretch," replied Angela.

"No, but if you do meet him he will likely be the first billionaire you have ever met," retorted Maxine.

"That's true. Okay, so you want to know my honest feelings? I haven't made up my mind yet. He seems great, but what are the chances he would go for a woman like me? Who knows if he's really my type or not? There are just so many unanswerables."

"Well, I guess you're right. This is all just conjecture at this point. But it's fun to dream, huh?"

"I swear, Maxine, sometimes I think you are psychic. I actually had a dream about him last night."

"You don't say! I'd love to hear all about it."

The two friends spent the rest of the afternoon lounging about and talking about various things. Maxine kept reminding Angela that she might have the opportunity to meet Anderson. It was almost as if Maxine wanted Angela to get into a serious relationship. Angela wasn't sure if she wanted that or not. She just wanted a dreamy guy to fool around with. She didn't quite know if she was ready for a serious commitment or not.

2

WORK HABITS

The following morning at work, Angela settled into her regular routine. She answered some phone calls, sent out a few emails, and chatted with her coworkers. The main topic was clearly the firm's new acquisition of Anderson's new conglomerate file.

Handling the merger would be a big task, and there was lots of work to be done. It would take years to fully sort out all the paperwork, but Angela's firm was the best in the city at handling that sort of thing. In the afternoon there was a staff meeting in which Eric Taylor, the firm's president, laid out the details of the file, dispelled myths, and answered questions about what the new business would require. Apparently Anderson would be paying a visit to the firm the next day, as he wanted to see what kind of business theirs was.

Angela couldn't help but get goosebumps when Eric said that Anderson wanted to meet everybody. That meant he would be circulating around her part of the office and perhaps they would have a chance bump-in. Angela made a mental note to wear her best suit. She even decided that she would go for a hair appointment that evening and get a mani-pedi as well.

After the staff meeting, the rest of the day seemed to fly by. Everyone was abuzz about the news, and it seemed as though all the women in the office were already starting to swoon over Anderson's announced arrival.

That evening, as Angela was getting her manicure, she made small talk with her manicure artist. She was a short Asian lady with beautiful brown eyes and long black hair. She looked to be in her early twenties. She hadn't heard of Anderson Cromby, however. Angela tried to explain to her how important a man he was, but she didn't seem to be excited about him. Perhaps it was only businesswomen who understood exactly how much of a catch this bachelor was. Although, the fact that he was a billionaire probably should have set the manicure artist off.

What would I do if I was a billionaire? Angela thought. She realized that she could have whatever life she dreamed of if she was privy to that much money. She could imagine it now: skiing trips, lavish vacations in the Caribbean, expensive yachts, caviar and champagne ... the dream was endless. But she hadn't even met this guy yet, and already she was imagining what kind of lifestyle they would have together. Get a hold of yourself, Angela.

Angela paid the bill and left the spa. She was only a couple of blocks away from her home, so she decided to walk it. As she was walking, she bumped into an old acquaintance of hers.

It was Mark Stevenson. They had gone to college together. She had studied art history and he was a biology major. They had been great friends. There had always been a lot of flirting between them, but nothing had ever happened. She had thought he was cute; in fact, most of the girls back then thought he was cute. He was tall, about six-foot-one, and had a muscular build. He had well-kept thick black hair that was parted to one side. His face lit up when he recognized who he had bumped into.

"Angela!" he exclaimed very excitedly. "Fancy meeting you here!"

"Likewise! What are you doing in this part of the city?" asked Angela.

"Just going for a stroll. I am in real estate now, and I was just appraising a building not too far from here. Is this where you live? Gosh, Angela, you look great. We should go for a drink sometime. You know, to catch up, for old time's sake."

"How about right now?" she ventured.

Mark could see in her eyes that she was dead serious. He could also tell, past her fierce bravado, that she was incredibly horny. She needed to get laid, badly. And so he jumped all over it, as any warm-blooded heterosexual man would have.

She leaned into him and grabbed his crotch. He could smell her womanly scent and whatever mild eau-de-toilette she was wearing.

"I want you to fuck me, Mark." she whispered plainly in his ear. "Fuck me like you never did in college. I have learned a thing or two since then."

Mark got hard in his pants and her grip tightened. She could already tell he was a good size. She stroked him through the fabric of his linen suit-pants, and Mark let out a sigh of release.

"Where do you live?" he asked.

"A few blocks away."

They walked hand in hand to her apartment, took the elevator up to her floor, and immediately started undressing one another as they entered through the door. Their clothes were scattered all over Angela's apartment.

They worked their way to the bed, making out as they went. Angela took off her shirt, then her bra, and then her pants. In her red satin panties, she felt very naked—and loved it. Mark removed his shirt and pants and took off his underwear. His giant manhood bounced to attention and he had a full hard-on.

It looked as though he measured in the eight or nine inch range.

Angela grabbed him and pushed him down onto her bed. She stood there for a few moments, hovering above the bed, taking a moment before diving in.

He scanned her body. Her tits were even more perfect than he had imagined. They were full and round and hung in perfect teardrop fashion. He thought to himself wistfully that she could have been on the cover of Playboy. That was how perfect she looked.

When she slid out of her panties, he could see that she was completely shaved down there. She crawled onto the bed next to him and placed a hand on his erection.

She whispered into his ear, "I have dreamed of this ever since college. What is your fantasy?"

"I want to fuck you good, Angela," said Mark honestly. "I have always dreamed of ravaging that perfect body."

"Then let's get to it."

They fucked passionately for close to half an hour. Mark's rhythmic penetration was exactly what Angela had needed. She came a few times during their fuck session, and at last Mark said he was close. She sucked him off the rest of the way and swallowed his manly load. After they finished, they crawled under the covers next to each other and cuddled for what seemed like an eternity.

Later that evening, after a brief nap in which the two lovers lay nestled in each other's arms, Angela got up to take a shower. When she came back into her bedroom, there was no sign of Mark, just a note that he had jotted down and left on her unmade bed. It read:

Dear Angela,

I had a wonderful time this evening. I don't want this to turn into one of those 'things,' so I'll just say that I'll be around. You can reach me at the number on my business card, which I am leaving."

Angela could read between the lines. She'd had no notion that their engagement this evening would lead to a relationship. That's not what she wanted with him anyway. She had just wanted sex with a hot guy. And he had delivered.

A big smile made its way across her face as she crumpled up the note and tossed it in the trash. She took his card, which had his business address, telephone number, and email address on it and placed it in her purse. That night, as she lay in bed, thoughts of sex and romance made their way into her dreams. She had the distinct feeling that her life was going to take a drastic turn for the better. In many ways, it already had.

The next day at the office, Angela was very nervous and excited at the same time. This was when the big news was going to be released to the staff. She wore her best outfit and looked great. She even received some compliments from her co-workers on how great she looked. The morning passed by fairly quickly and after lunch she didn't have a lot of work to do, so she called up Maxine to check in and see how she was doing. Maxine had a tennis match that morning and at that point was at home icing her ankle, since she had twisted it.

"Have you seen him yet?" asked Maxine.

"No, replied Angela. Not yet."

Finally, at around 4:00 in the afternoon, her boss got the staff together and let them know that Anderson would be coming by the office to "check things out," so everyone was supposed to be on their best behavior and put their best foot forward.

When Anderson arrived with about four other lawyers as his entourage, Angela's heart skipped a beat. He was very attractive, about 6'0, and had thick, dark brown hair and blue eyes. He seemed to be walking very quickly and scanning the area, as if to get a quick impression on how things were done around the office. He didn't really spend time in any particular area, but just kind of perused around at his leisure. He then walked up to Eric and shook his hand. They discussed some matters for a few minutes. Angela couldn't really tell what they were talking about. But Eric kept nodding and smiling.

Anderson's eyes surveyed the room. At one point, Angela could have sworn that Anderson made eye contact with her, but it was sort of impossible to tell. Finally, Anderson turned around, walked back to the elevator, and took it back down to the ground floor with his entourage. That was as close as Angela got to Anderson that day. What a thrill.

After work, Maxine and Henry invited Angela over to their condo, which was on the other side of town. The plan was to have a nice seafood dinner and then watch a DVD from their extensive collection. The dinner went really well. Henry described in detail the challenges he was having at work. Apparently the accountants at work were changing some of the standards to be used in practice yet again, which meant that he would have to either go back to school or learn a ton of new information on his own. Angela and Maxine sympathized with him as much as possible. Then the discussion turned to Maxine's pregnancy once again.

"So when is the due date?" asked Angela.

"In exactly six months, as of yesterday. I am so excited! We both are!" Maxine held Henry's hand.

"And do you know the sex of the baby yet?"

"It is still a bit too soon to tell," said Henry. "We have names planned out though, regardless of the sex. We are thinking William if it's a boy and Tracy if it's a girl."

"Those are lovely names," said Angela. "Say, not to change the subject, but what movie do you guys want to watch tonight? I am soooo in a lounging type of mood. Today at work was so exciting."

"Did you see him?" asked Maxine.

"Wait—who are we talking about?" interrupted Henry.

"Oh," continued Maxine. "Angela's company is handing the legal work for a big takeover. Anderson Cromby's conglomerate is buying the biggest consulting firm in the city. It's really big news. Angela was hoping to get a glimpse of Anderson today."

"And I did!" exclaimed Angela.

"Congratulations, then!" said Henry, chuckling to himself.

"He was so dreamy, you guys," said Angela. "His eyes were amazing. They were so big and blue. You could tell that he had a really generous spirit. And it's no wonder that he is the CEO. I mean, I only caught one glimpse of him but he seemed really smart. And so attractive. I wonder where he works out."

"If you found out where his gym was maybe you could go work out there as well and 'accidentally' bump into him," suggested Maxine.

"Say, that's a good idea. I wonder how one would find out that kind of information," puzzled Angela.

"You could probably do some sleuthing," continued Maxine helpfully. "Call his assistant and pretend to be a staff member at a gym. Then just ask when he is planning on returning. Say he left a document in the changing room or something. If you ask to confirm which location he works out at, they are bound to give you that information."

It was a good idea. Angela mulled it over for a while and decided it was worth a shot. During their movie, which followed dinner, thoughts and ideas of what it might be like to bump into Anderson Cromby danced in her mind. She couldn't wait to get to work the next day.

After the evening was over, Angela thanked both Maxine and Henry for a wonderful time. She gave a special thanks to Maxine for her wonderful "sleuthing" suggestion. She left their condo, took a cab across downtown, and arrived at her own apartment. She got ready for bed and within moments was asleep.

The next morning, she skipped her early morning workout and went straight to work. She arrived at the office early and searched on the internet for Anderson Cromby. She was able to find the line to his assistant and saved it to her desktop. She was going to call around noon, when she knew that the assistant would be in the office.

An Occasional Meeting

Angela picked up the phone and dialed the number to Anderson's assistant. The phone rang several times, and no one was picking up. Angela's heart was pounding a mile a minute. Finally, a woman's voice came on the phone and said, "Anderson Cromby and Associates."

Angela wasted no time getting in the role. "Uh, yes, hi," she started. "My name is Rachel Goodale, calling from the Carlisle Club. It seems we have a document here with Mr. Cromby's name and phone number on it. He must have left it here during one of his workouts. Could you tell me which location he will be at next, so I can have the documents made available for him?"

"Sure thing," said the assistant. "He will be at the King Street location this evening. That's where Mr. Cromby always works out. And it's always in the evenings. He gets there at about 8:00 p.m."

"Thank you very much," continued Angela. "You have been very helpful. We will see to it that he gets these back. Cheers."

Angela hung up the phone and noticed that her heart was racing. Tonight was going to be her big chance to meet Anderson face-to-face. All she would have to do was find a way to bump into him, and then turn on her charm so that he fell for her. She decided that she would get there a bit early and scope out the premises.

7:00 a.m. should be good, she thought. She would have to

pay some consideration to what to wear. She thought she would go for a black leotard and Nike sneakers. She would wear her hair up, as if she had just been working out. A sports bra would also be a good idea, not that she needed it. Her breasts were full and large and looked great with or without that extra support. She wondered whether or not she should invite Maxine to tag along. She might get a thrill from watching Angela bump into Anderson. She decided she would call her and ask. At the very least they could have an early dinner at the club before she got into her workout attire and made plans to bump into him. She called Maxine at home.

"Hi, Maxine?" she asked after a few rings.

"Yes, hi, Angela. What's up? Did you call the gym?" asked Maxine.

"Yes, I did. Everything is going according to plan. He arrives at the club at 8:00 p.m. to work out. I am going to arrange to be there then and bump into him. I was wondering if you'd like to grab an early dinner beforehand. We could have some smoked salmon and cheese or something."

"That sounds wonderful. Should I meet you there at around 5:30 p.m., then?"

"Yes, that sounds good. And bring Henry if he wants to come. I've gotta get into my workout gear by 7:00 p.m. if I'm going to have a good chance of meeting him. Also, I wouldn't mind working out a little bit myself."

"Wonderful, see you then," said Maxine and she hung up the phone.

The rest of the day was spent in consternation for Angela. She realized that this was going to be a huge personal leap forward, if she could get into Anderson's life. It would also be a leap professionally. If she got in with Anderson, there might be new opportunities for her.

Finally, after the day finished, she made her way home and

got changed. She put her sweats on over her black leotard and sports bra and laced up her sneakers. She made her way over to the club at 5:30 p.m. to meet with Maxine and Henry. They hadn't arrived yet, so she sat down at one of the glass tables near a big window that overlooked the street below.

The table was adorned with beautiful flowers. A few minutes later, Maxine and Henry arrived and smile broadly at Angela. They shook hands and hugged and took their seats.

After they ordered the smoked salmon, crackers, and a cheese platter, the discussion turned to Angela's plans.

"So, are you really going through with this?" asked Henry.

"You bet," responded Angela. "I am really excited. I have seen the man from afar, but never up close and personal. This should be an exciting evening."

"It sounds like you've fallen for him already," mused Henry. "This must be quite the man, if the invincible Angela could have feelings for him."

Angela couldn't help but laugh. "Well, let's just say that I have had dreams about him."

"So he is literally the man of your dreams," said Maxine laughingly.

"I suppose so," said Angela. She seemed serious now, as if she was contemplating the turning of tides in her life.

Henry lit up a Cuban cigar and blew some smoke rings. They still had a few minutes before Angela was planning on heading for the gym. Henry offered Angela one of his cigars, but she declined. Then he passed his to her and she accepted. She blew a few smoke rings herself before passing it back. She had always loved the smell and taste of a nice cigar. She didn't smoke them often, but relished the opportunities to do so.

When it was time to head to the gym, Angela excused herself politely and said goodbye to her two friends. She made her way to the elevator and rode it down to the second floor. She entered the women's changing room and made her way to her locker. There was a beautiful young woman taking off her clothes next to her. She seemed to be of Mediterranean descent, with beautiful, olive-colored skin and thick black hair that fell all the way down to the small of her back. Her breasts were ripe and perky, her nipples standing erect.

Angela watched her out of the corner of her eye as she threw on a cotton robe and walked barefooted over to the steam room. Angela had never been sexually attracted to women, but she did appreciate their beauty. Angela got dressed and headed for the workout area. It was a quarter past seven.

Angela busied herself on one of the cardio bikes. She decided that getting in a workout before bumping into Anderson was probably a good idea. She spent about twenty minutes doing cardio, then moved over to free-weights. She believed in getting toned and always tried to incorporate the weights into her routine. They helped to burn off excess calories throughout the day, and Angela was the type of person who always ate what she wanted. She did not believe in yo-yo dieting.

Finally, at a few minutes before 8:00 p.m., Angela moved to the main doors. Then, lo and behold, Anderson Cromby opened the doors and stepped over the threshold of the gym. He was wearing a purple tank top and black shorts with white socks and blue sneakers. He made brief eye contact with Angela and gave her a brief smile.

He smiled at me!

Angela's gaze shifted towards Anderson's arms, which were very muscular. She realized that he must be a regular at the gym. It was time to act. Angela swiftly moved into her pre-rehearsed actions, and dropped her pink water bottle directly in front of him. Anderson made a move for the water bottle to help pick it up. At the same time, Angela leaned in for it and the two bumped into each other.

"Oh my gosh!" exclaimed Angela. "I am so sorry!"

"That's quite all right!" responded Anderson.

He picked up the water bottle and handed it to Angela. They made eye contact again for the second time. This time their gaze held on a little longer. Then Anderson sized her up briefly, his eyes making their way from her chest down to her legs and then back up again. She could see why he was so successful. She could tell he was really good at judging a person right off the bat. And, fortunately for Angela, his initial opinion of her was very positive.

"Say," he began. "I've never seen you before at this gym. Do you come here often to exercise?"

"Actually, I just come here to scope out the cute guys," she mused.

Anderson laughed. His laugh was a thing of beauty, medium-pitched and very masculine, right from the gut.

"Well, have you been successful?" asked Anderson, continuing on with the flirtatious joke.

"Not until now," replied Angela. Her voice had suddenly taken a more serious tone. She reached out, grabbed his upper arm, and squeezed it gently.

Anderson gulped. Then his face went completely serious.

"Well, perhaps you wouldn't mind if I invited you to dinner this Friday night?"

"That would be wonderful. My name's Angela Hayes."

"Anderson Cromby. The pleasure is all mine."

Angela withdrew her hand and put it up to her mouth, tracing her full pouty lips and staring at him longingly, giving him her sexiest look. She didn't even have to fake it; she was truly horny about this amazing man.

"Carolina's is a beautiful new Italian place that just opened up on 7th. I have been meaning to check it out. Give my friend here your address and I'll pick you up at 6:00 p.m." And with that, Anderson gave her another smile and wandered over to the weight machines.

Angela gave her information to his friend, who was a huge black guy who obviously lifted weights. She wondered if he was his friend or his bodyguard. Not wanting to jinx the moment any further, she quickly made her way back into the changing room.

That night she watched TV and dreamed about what was to come. She couldn't believe how perfectly her plan had been carried out. Friday was just two days away! She did not know how she was going to wait that long. Her phone beeped and she checked it. It was Mark Stevenson, sending her a text. It read:

Hi Angela. Was thinking of you the other day. I am around your area again tonight looking at a new condo. Was wondering if I could stop by with a DVD and some popcorn.

Angela had had a lot of fun with Mark the last time they got together. She decided that seeing Mark tonight might be a good idea. After all, it was still early. So she messaged him back, telling him that it was okay if he came over.

Angela got in the tub and waited for Mark to send her another message, letting her know that he was there. She looked at her nozzle and, not for the first time, wondered if she should use it to make herself feel better. She also wondered if she should use it to make herself warmed up for Mark. She added some bath bubbles and leaned back. Her bathtub was fully outfitted with jets, which were currently massaging her back. She leaned back and let the botanical extracts seep into her skin.

Several minutes went by. She let thoughts of Anderson creep through her mind. She was not sure when she was actually going to be able to sleep with him. Perhaps sleeping with Mark tonight might just be the next best thing. All of a sudden, her phone beeped again. She checked the message. Mark had arrived. She told him to come on upstairs and to come straight to the bathroom. She didn't hear any argument from Mark's end.

A few moments later, Mark opened the door to her apartment and let himself in. He was dressed in an overcoat and a fine Italian gray suit. The sounds of his loafers on the hardwood floors reverberated throughout the small apartment. He entered the bathroom and leaned against the door frame. He was carrying a bottle of champagne in one hand and a DVD and some popcorn in the other.

"Where should I put my jacket?" he asked.

"What's the matter, Mark? No 'hello'?" responded Angela coyly.

"A thousand pardons, miss. Hello, greetings, and salutations to the nicest piece of ass I have ever known."

Angela laughed despite herself. "That's better. Now come over here so I can get a better look at you. I want to feel that suit. It looks like it was really expensive."

"If the deal that I'm currently working on goes through, I will be able to buy many like it. And I will be able to take you out to any restaurant you want. Any restaurant in town that you deserve. Hell, I can already do that."

"Yes, but it is our dates here that I enjoy the most," said Angela.

Mark approached the tub and sat on its edge. "I can barely see you through all the bubbles,'" he said.

"I look about the same as I did last time we hooked up. Or have you forgotten?"

"I could never forget what you look like."

Mark cupped his hands into the bath and took some of the bubbles into his palm. He flicked them at Angela playfully. Then Angela grabbed his hand, spread her knees wide apart, and directed it down into the bath between her thighs. Mark's powerful hand grazed the inside of one of her thighs and found its way to her snatch. He inserted a finger and began fucking her in the water.

Angela leaned her head back and moaned. It felt really good. Almost as good as it would feel when Anderson eventually inserted more than just a finger in there.

After a few moments, Mark stood up and removed his coat, hanging it on a hook that was conveniently positioned on the back of the bathroom door. He stood up and took in the beautiful sight of Angela—naked except for bubbles.

"What are you doing, Mark?" asked Angela.

"Admiring you," he replied.

"How do I look?" asked Angela playfully.

"You look like a lot of things. You look like a Greek goddess. You look like an Italian-American beauty. You look like the paintings I see of naked women at the Art Gallery. You look like Angela Hayes."

"Do I look like someone who is going to get fucked tonight?"

"It is definitely possible. Any room in that bath for a second person?"

"Not in this bath, no. But I am just about to get out."

Angela rose to her knees in the tub and then placed one of her feet on the outside tiles, bringing herself to a standing position. She then turned off the tub's jets and opened up the drain. She beckoned to Mark to hand her one of the towels that was hanging on the hook. He handed it to her, noticing how soft and supple it was in his hand. She tied it around herself and then left the bathroom, making her way to her bedroom. Mark followed obediently, unable to take his eyes off of her.

Metropolitan Fun

Angela chose her most comfortable pajamas from her drawer. They felt really good on her smooth skin. She let the towel drop and then bent over at the waist. She knew that Mark was scanning her body all the while, and that he was getting a great view of her pussy from behind. The thought of him looking at her and getting aroused got her aroused as well. She felt herself getting wet.

Once dressed in her pajamas, she grabbed Mark by the hand and led him over to the couch, which was positioned in front of her large flat-screen TV.

"What movie did you get?" she asked.

"Forrest Gump," he said. "I hope that's okay with you."

"It absolutely is. I love that movie. Tom Hanks is one of my favorite actors," responded Angela.

"Perfect," he said. "You look great in those PJs, by the way. You also looked great without them on."

Angela looked over at Mark, who was sitting beside her, and winked. She moved her hand over to his lap and massaged him through the fabric of his suit pants.

"Why don't you get more comfortable? Take off that jacket."

Mark took off his jacket and placed it on one of the chairs in the living room. He then loosened his tie and draped it over the same chair. He sat back down on the couch. Angela noticed that there was a significant bulge in his trousers. She decided she wanted to do something about it.

She slowly unzipped his fly and then released his erect member. She remembered this penis so well from the last time they were together. It was a fine looking cock, cut, muscular, throbbing, and dying to have some release. She knelt down in front of him and gazed into his eyes. He looked back at her and smiled.

She then removed his pants completely and slid down his boxers. She cupped his testicles with one hand and placed her mouth on the tip of his manhood. She kissed his cock, working her way from the tip all the way to the base. She then used her tongue to dance circles around his balls, and lick back up the shaft. Then she took him in her mouth and began bobbing her head, fucking his cock with her wet mouth.

A few minutes of this and Mark grabbed the back of her head. He was ready to explode. He let loose in her mouth and she hungrily swallowed up all his cum. Having finished what she thought was a fine blowjob, and scooting back onto the couch beside him, she cuddled up next to his chest.

The movie was half over before Mark turned his head and kissed the top of Angela's thick, brown hair.

"God, you are beautiful," he said in a very sincere tone. "I could get used to this."

"I love you coming over here as well. But you haven't made do with your promise yet. You said you were going to fuck me."

Angela tilted her head up and gazed into Mark's big blue eyes. Mark leaned in for a kiss, and Angela also kissed him back. She slid her fingers through Mark's black hair and began passionately making out with him. Then he leaned into her, and she leaned back onto the couch. He positioned himself on top of her and slid down her pajama bottoms.

"Condoms are in the dresser over there," she said matter-of-factly.

Mark grabbed a condom and put it on. He then entered her and they began making love. Ten minutes into their lovemaking, Angela was on the cusp of an orgasm. She began panting and screaming his name.

"Mark! Mark! Oh, yes," she exclaimed.

Mark was ready to come at the same moment, and the two of them climaxed in ecstasy together. Then Mark withdrew and disposed of the used condom. They lay together in each other's arms, cuddling and watching the rest of the movie. That night, they slept together in her large bed.

Mark had to get up early, at around 6:00 a.m., to go home and get dressed for a sales meeting. Angela kissed him goodbye and lazed in bed for another hour. She couldn't seem to get a foolish high school girlish grin off her face. Between the sex with Mark and her date with Anderson coming up, things were going pretty well in her life.

Angela decided to call Maxine before work. Whenever she felt happy, she felt the need to share the feeling with her best friend. Maxine picked up after a few rings.

"Girlfriend!" she stated excitedly.

"I just had to call you!" exclaimed Angela. "I have so much good news. I have a date with Anderson for Friday at Carolina's, and I slept with Mark last night."

"You're on a roll, girlfriend!" Maxine exclaimed. "Share some of those good vibes with me!"

"Oh, you are doing great too," said Angela sympathetically. "You've got a great husband. And a baby on the way!"

"I bet soon you and Mr. Cromby will be able to say the same thing. Any idea what you are going to name the child?"

Angela laughed. "Don't start with me, Maxine! Anyway, have a great day. I am going to somehow make it through mine, even though I am very excited about Friday. I'll talk to you later."

That day at the office, Angela went through some basic paperwork. She had to touch base with some of her clients' offices to make sure their timelines were in sync. Eric stopped by her cubicle to see how things were going. They chatted for a while.

Angela had always been able to get along well with Eric. He was a very good boss, very fair and reasonable. Today, he seemed extra excited given the merger and the fact that Anderson's conglomerate would now be their major client.

"This is big stuff, Angela," he said. "Once everything gets finalized, there are going to be a lot of new positions opening up. Keep working hard; there could be some new opportunities for you. You are one of our hardest workers."

Angela could only smile and respond with a heartfelt, "Thank you, sir."

During her lunch break, Angela decided to call her mother. It had been a week or two since they had last spoken, and she wanted to get an update about how her life was going. Angela loved her mother with all her heart. Ever since her Dad had passed away, Karen was basically the only immediate family that she had. Her closest sister, Rosalie, was off getting her Master's degree at the other end of the country, and could only afford to visit home on special occasions. Since Karen lived in the city as well, Angela always tried to make the most of their proximity and keep close ties with her.

Angela picked up her phone and dialed her mother's number.

"Hello?" Karen answered.

"Hi, Mom!" exclaimed Angela excitedly.

"Darling! How are you? It's been a week since I've heard from you! I've been seeing your law firm in the news. Looks like some exciting stuff is happening."

"You bet, Mom! Things couldn't be better. I just had a talk with Eric, who says there will be a whole bunch of new opportunities now that we are getting such a major client."

"Such wonderful news, Angela. Any other news? Anything with a new boyfriend, perhaps?" Angela's mother was always very curious about whether or not Angela was settling down. She wanted to see her oldest daughter happy. And she often said that she wanted to have grandchildren some day.

"Oh, Mom, you know I will tell you the minute I get into a relationship. I just love being single for the time being. But I do have a big date this Friday with Anderson Cromby."

3
WHAT SHE CRAVES PART 2

The Big Date

As Friday night approached, Angela thought of all the ways in which her date with Anderson could end in a booming success. She pictured them having champagne and arriving at the restaurant in a black stretch limousine. She thought about what would happen after dinner and how she would go back to his place. Then she realized that she didn't yet know where he lived. She would have to make a point to ask him. She pictured him having several exquisite houses around the city and in the country.

Finally, as 6:00 p.m. approached on Friday night, she had to decide on which dress to wear. She looked in her closet and saw a few different options. There was a showy black, sleeveless dress that was sleek and sexy. There was a midnight blue dress that was low cut and accentuated her supple breasts. There was also a beautiful yellow dress that had a sexy slit up the leg. In the end, she chose the black sleeveless dress that looked both sophisticated and sexy at the same time.

A few minutes after 6:00 p.m., her phone rang. It was

Anderson's driver, calling to let her know that he was downstairs and ready to go. Angela took the elevator down and walked up to the big stretch limousine. The driver opened the door in the back and Angela slid onto the comfortable leather seats. Anderson was sitting inside reading a newspaper and wearing a stylish black Armani suit. He put the paper down as soon as she entered and gave her a sensual smile.

"Hi, Angela!" he said. "It's great to see you again! You look absolutely breathtaking."

"Thanks, Anderson. You look very nice as well. I really love the suit."

"Oh, why, thanks for the compliment. I have dozens of these. When I find a suit I like, I get my tailor to custom-make a lot of them. I've never been one to take an interest in picking out a new outfit each day."

"I had about three options for tonight," said Angela, laughing a little. "I'm glad I went with this black dress. Now, we match!"

Anderson laughed and grabbed a bottle of champagne. He uncorked it and filled two wine glasses.

"Would you mind if we start with some champagne?" asked Anderson.

"Sounds wonderful," said Angela. "Say, how's business, by the way? I noticed you were reading the financial section."

"Oh, yes, I always try to stay on top of the financial news. As the head of a conglomerate that is currently undergoing a merger, I kind of have to. It's my job. Which reminds me, your firm is doing some great work. I'll have to talk to Eric about getting you a promotion. He mentioned your name to me personally."

"Well, that would be great," said Angela. "You know, I have actually been working very hard on your file. Our whole team is going to represent the legal work of the merger very well. You can count on that."

"Wonderful. Let's not talk about business, though. That's not why I asked you on a date."

"Why did you ask me on a date, Anderson, if I may ask?" Angela asked, raising an eyebrow at Anderson.

"Well, because of this."

Anderson positioned himself closer to Angela so that he was next to her on the comfortable leather. He then put a hand on her leg. Angela raised her head and made eye contact with him. Their gaze lasted a few moments. Then Anderson slowly leaned into her and held the moment even longer. Finally, he closed the distance and kissed her softly on the lips. They held the kiss for a while and then Anderson withdrew.

It was the sexiest kiss Angela had ever experienced. She figured it was just a sign of things to come. If Anderson was already kissing her, she could only imagine how bold he would be later in the evening.

Angela decided to give Anderson a little taste of things to come.

"Look what I can do," she said.

Then she took the gum that she had been chewing out of her mouth and discarded it. She went onto her knees in front of Anderson and slowly unzipped his fly. She could feel that he was already getting stiff beneath his pants. Then she took out his cock. It was semi-erect. It was a beautiful cock. It bulged like a love-muscle and begged to be serviced.

Angela took Anderson's cock in her mouth and slowly twirled her tongue around it. She grabbed his balls firmly with the other hand, cupping them and playing with them. Anderson leaned back in his seat and sighed, stretching his hands up over his head. Pretty soon, his cock was hard as steel, and fully erect. Angela bobbed her pretty head up and down his shaft, paying special attention to the tip with her tongue. She licked at his precum and played with his balls. Anderson could only stand a few minutes of this. Pretty soon, he was ready to come.

"I am going to cum, Angela," he said while panting, a bead of sweat trickling down his forehead.

"Come in my mouth, baby," she said in a sexy, sensuous voice.

Anderson began to move his hips up and down, a sign that he was on the verge. Then his cock squirted hot semen into her mouth and down her throat. With every pulse, more and more cum made its way into Angela's mouth. She savored the taste and made a special effort to swallow all of it.

She brought herself back up to the seat by his side and kissed him on the cheek. She ran a couple fingers through his hair.

"How was that, baby?" she asked.

"That was the best blow job I've had in a long while," stated Anderson.

Angela enjoyed the compliment. As they drove throughout the streets, Angela looked out the window. It was a busy night in the city. There were a lot of hot girls and guys going clubbing. She thought back fondly to the memories she had as a young woman in her twenties. When she was in college she would often go out partying with her friends. Now, she was riding past the clubs, in the back of a limo with the richest man in the city.

Angela and Anderson talked about various things. They discussed how the local sports teams were doing. Then, Anderson mentioned his latest trip to Africa.

"I was in South Africa on business, examining one of our new offices and getting feedback. We ended up going on a safari and saw some really interesting animals. One of the perks of owning a conglomerate, I suppose."

"That sounds wonderful. I don't often get the chance to

travel, but when I do I like to go all over the place. I have a soft spot in my heart for Paris. I went there in my twenties and I've been dying to go back. I also like Hawaii."

"Paris is great. We don't have any operations located in France, currently, but we are thinking of expanding our economic base to include it. A lot of our competitors do business over there."

As their conversation became more engrossing, they were interrupted by the driver, who announced that they had arrived at Carolina's. The driver opened the door for Angela, who exited the vehicle and then took Anderson's arm. He led her up to the glass front doors of the restaurant and approached the reception area. Angela had never been to this restaurant before, but she had read about it. Nothing on the menu was under $100, and the bottles of wine averaged in the thousands of dollars.

"This place looks great!" exclaimed Angela. "Thanks so much for picking it out and taking me here."

"It's one of my favorite restaurants," responded Anderson. "I'm glad to have the opportunity to introduce you to it."

They walked past the clientele to the far end of the restaurant. Their table was positioned in front of set of large windows. The night-time ambiance was palpable. A few tables away, there was a jazz band playing a Miles Davis cover. There was a dance floor, but it didn't look as if anyone had gravitated towards it yet. Anderson decided to get the ball rolling.

"Come, let's have a dance before our drinks arrive," he said.

Angela felt somewhat nervous. She loved to dance, but it had been a while since she had done it. She decided to let Anderson take charge and lead her on the dance floor. She stood up and followed him towards it.

"We're going to have to get close," he said, and put one hand on the small of her back, bringing her in closer so that there were only a few inches between them. Then, with his other hand, Anderson grabbed her ass. He squeezed forcefully, spreading her buttocks with his powerful hand. His fingers worked their way through the thin fabric of her dress and probed her crack.

Angela could smell his expensive cologne. It was an intoxicating fragrance. She couldn't pinpoint what it was, but if she had to, she would have guessed that it was Hugo Boss. Either way, he smelled great. His strong arms held her very firmly and confidently.

They danced together for several songs. When they had first set foot on the floor they were the only ones dancing. After a few moments, several other couples joined them. Angela looked around. The other dancers were mostly wearing expensive tuxedos and suits. The women were dressed very extravagantly as well, in fine eveningwear.

"Do you know anyone else at this restaurant?" asked Angela. She wasn't sure why she asked that question. She just figured that Anderson might have known people here, since it was a place that he frequented quite often. Someone in his position was likely very well connected, and so it was quite possible that he recognized a few faces.

"Actually, yes, I have already made eye contact with a few acquaintances. Mostly bankers come to this place. It is a hot spot for financial-type people. Our firm is a client of a few investment banks in the city. The head of the national treasury also happens to be here tonight as well. His name is Frank Edwards. He is a great guy. After we are done dancing, I'll introduce you to him and his wife."

"That would be wonderful. Thank you!" exclaimed Angela.

They danced a few more songs together and then retreated back to their tables. A bottle of wine had been uncorked and left there by their waiter. Their wine glasses had already been filled as well.

"A toast!" said Anderson. "To new relationships!"

"To new relationships!" repeated Angela, and they leaned in for a kiss. His lips were once again very soft and she found it impossible not to get excited. She felt a yearning in her core every time his lips touched hers.

They sipped their wine for a few minutes, not really engaging in any conversation. His eye contact made her feel like she was the only woman in the room. She had never felt sexier. As she reached for a breadstick that was in the middle of the table, Anderson also brought his hand forth and they grazed hands. Then Anderson clasped her hand confidently and they held hands for a while.

Anderson and Angela were engaged in some small talk when Frank Edwards, a tall man with a round belly and strong limbs, approached their table. He was accompanied by his wife, an elegantly dressed woman in her forties, wearing an exquisite blue satin dress and high heels.

"Frank!" exclaimed Anderson. "So good to see you!"

Anderson reached out his hand and grasped Frank's in a firm handshake.

"I see you have brought your lovely wife," continued Anderson. "Amanda, how lovely to see you."

"Likewise," responded Amanda. Angela could detect a faint English accent in her tone.

Anderson wasted no time in introducing Angela to the high-ranking couple.

"Frank, Amanda, let me introduce to you my date. This is Angela Hayes. We met just the other day at our gym. She works for the legal firm that is doing the paperwork for our merger."

"It is such a pleasure to meet you both," said Angela. "I have seen you on the news very frequently, Mr. Edwards. Your wife is just lovely."

"Please, call me Frank," said Frank. "I saw you two on the

dance floor just now. You make a very fine-looking couple. Say, after your date, perhaps you two would care to join my wife and me for a nightcap at our new condo? It is actually only a few blocks to the north of here. Just head up Montgomery Street and it is the tall silver building on the left. You can find our name in the directory and we'll let you up."

"A great suggestion," said Anderson. "I'll get in touch with you if we decide to do that."

"Well, it was wonderful bumping into you," said Frank sincerely. "Enjoy the rest of your evening."

Frank and his wife walked back over to their table at the other end of the room.

"Would you like to hang out with them afterwards?" asked Anderson, rather directly.

"Sure, but perhaps we could drive around in your limo a bit beforehand and have some more champagne and talk."

As Angela said this, underneath the table she grazed Anderson's leg and slowly moved up his pant leg to his crotch area, moving her sole in circles in the area. Anderson gulped. Then Angela's toes moved around his cock, playing with his balls and shaft. She traced the outline of his cock with her foot, quickly feeling it harden as a result of her touch.

Their meal arrived moments later. It consisted of shrimp cocktail and sirloin steak, cooked to medium-rare. The wine kept coming as well and by the end of their second bottle, Angela was getting quite tipsy.

"You know, I have a confession to make," said Angela.

"Oh?"

"I thought you were cute the moment I saw you on TV. I talked about you with my girlfriend, Maxine. From the first time that I saw you, I just knew I had to make an excuse to meet you."

Anderson laughed.

"When I saw you at the gym, I knew instantly that I wanted

you in my life. I didn't know how or to what capacity, but I just knew that I wanted to date you!"

Angela was very pleased to hear him say that.

After the Date

Her meal was one of the most delicious meals in recent memory. She devoured the perfectly cooked steak and steamed vegetables, and they made it through a third bottle of the finest French cabernet. Angela was ready to get positively flirtatious. Anderson paid the bill on one of his many credit cards and stood up, helping Angela up from her seat.

"I am tipsy!" said Angela, and she giggled to herself.

"Good! I am feeling it too. Let's drive around a little. We don't have to visit Frank. But if you want to, we can."

"Can I call Maxine from the limo? I want her to know how much fun we are having."

"Of course!"

They left the beautiful restaurant and got into Anderson's limo.

"While you are calling Maxine, I am just going to send off a few work emails. Pat! Can you just drive us around a little? We need to calm down from dinner. Thanks."

Pat, the limo driver, nodded in response. Angela took out her cell phone and called Maxine.

"Girlfriend! Guess where I am? That's right! In the back of the limo with the sexiest man in the city! No, wait, the sexiest man in the world!"

Anderson laughed again. It was a nice, deep, masculine laugh. Angela and Maxine chatted for a bit. It turned out that Maxine wasn't feeling very well lately. She had a bit of a cold. She had already been to the doctor and it turned out there was nothing she could really do about it but wait out the symptoms and take some Tylenol.

Angela scooted over to Anderson and sat on his lap. He put his phone away and wrapped his arms around her waist. They engaged in a deep, passionate kiss. They made out for a good long while as the driver drove them around various sites of the city. Anderson reached into the top of her dress and felt one of her firm, large breasts. He massaged it fervently, feeling the weight it had and enjoying how good it felt in his hand. Angela moaned in pleasure.

Then Anderson was on top of Angela. He slid up her evening skirt and began playing with her pussy with his right hand. She was already getting wet from his touch. He rubbed her clit until she was nice and wet and then slid two fingers inside of her. Angela sighed as his fingers moved in and out of her, pressing against her G-spot with each thrust.

His left hand removed the top of her dress entirely, exposing her pert, milky-white breasts. Angela raised her hips and slid her red, satin panties down her legs, exposing her moist mound. Anderson's eyes lit up with desire at the sight of her cleanly-shaven pussy.

He took off his pants, spread her legs wide, and positioned his stiff cock directly in front of her pussy. He moaned as he teased around the lips and the opening of her slit with the tip of his dick. Angela was so turned on, her juices of arousal were soaking the head of his cock.

Finally, Anderson couldn't take anymore and with one forceful entry he was inside of her. As he thrust himself deeply into her, over and over again, he licked and sucked on her supple breasts and kissed his way from her nipples back up to her lips. Every time Anderson penetrated her, she felt closer and closer to ecstasy. As Angela began to reach her climax, her body stiffened, and she raised her hips upward, forcing Anderson's cock deeper into her as her legs began to shake. She cried out Anderson's name as her orgasm wracked through her body, grabbing Anderson's ass and holding him there inside her. She breathed deeply as her climax began to subside and her body went limp.

Anderson picked up the pace, pounding away at her tight, wet pussy until he, too, came in a monumental orgasm. He moaned loudly as he shot a huge, hot load of cum into Angela, squeezing her ass cheeks as his orgasm took control. As his climax subsided, he fell back into his seat, panting heavily. Without exchanging any more words, they got into their clothes again, and holding hands, they giggled wildly at each other.

After driving around for a while, Angela glanced at her phone and saw that it was already 11:00 p.m. She told Anderson, and they decided it was time to visit Frank and Amanda. Pat took them back around the city and into the neighborhood where they'd just had dinner. He pulled up to Frank's condo and, opening the door for them, let them out on the sidewalk.

"Thanks, Pat," said Anderson.

"Thanks," echoed Angela.

Angela was smiling giddily from the drinking. She took Anderson's arm and, still giggling to herself, walked with him up to the condo entrance. Anderson kissed her on the forehead in a loving, compassionate way.

The happy couple buzzed up and took the elevator up to the thirty-second floor and entered Frank and Amanda's condo. It was a beautifully decorated place with hardwood floors, a grand piano, a beautiful, large kitchen, and several bathrooms and bedrooms.

Amanda walked up to Angela and hugged her warmly.

"So great to see you! We were hoping you'd decide to stop by," said Amanda. "Can I offer you a drink? We have wine, spirits, beer, juice, or my personal favorite, Spanish coffee."

"I'll take one of those coffee thingies," said Amanda, still awestruck at the beauty of the condo and the quality of the company.

The foursome sat down on one of the comfortable leather sofas that were positioned to face the breathtaking view of the city streets and lights.

"So, Angela, tell us about your current job," said Frank in a non-threatening, fatherly-type way.

"Well, I have been there for about five years. My boss, Eric, is wonderful. I do a lot of the legal work and fact checking whenever a big client joins with us. I am one of the head people on the team that is handling Anderson's merger. I look forward to doing some great work on that file."

"She is already doing a great job," interjected Anderson. "We are very pleased with the level of legal support that our merger is receiving. It has barely been a few weeks but we can tell that it is going to be a smooth process, thank God."

"Has anyone ever made you any other job offers?" asked Frank of Angela.

"Um, I'm not sure what you mean, sir. Work has been steady for me ever since I joined up with our firm. I do like it there."

"I'll tell you what I mean, Angela. Our office has a position opening up for a head legal counsel within the treasury. I was wondering if you'd like to interview for it. I am one of the people on the hiring committee, so there would be at least one friendly face. I think you might be perfect for it."

Angela could tell that Frank was really good at sizing people up. He had not known her for very long, but this type of opportunity was something that Angela coveted. After all, she had been with her firm for five years and things were getting kind of stagnant. Her raises over that term had been pretty underwhelming. She made good money, of course, but it was not as glamorous as working for Frank would be.

"I am definitely going to consider that, Mr. Edwards—I mean, Frank. Can you leave me your card, please?"

Frank got up and walked across the room to the other end of the leather sofa. He sat down next to Angela, took out a card from his wallet, and gave it to her. Angela read the card.

Frank Edwards
Head of National Treasury
(416) 555-8232
f.edward@gov.org

"Thank you very much, sir," she said.

"Just get in touch with me next week and we'll arrange for you to come visit us. If you decide to stay at your current job, there will be no hard feelings. It's just something to consider. I am pretty good at judging the merits of a person, and I think you'd fit in greatly with our team."

"Now," interjected Amanda. "Who wants some tequila? Don't get soft on me now, Anderson. Are you enjoying your Spanish coffee, dear?"

"Very much so," said Angela. She took another sip. It was very warm and tasted like strong whisky. It was the kind of beverage that could sneak up on you and make you even drunker than you were. Of course, tequila did that too.

Amanda lined up some shots and the four of them downed a few rounds each. When it came time to take his first shot, Anderson sprinkled some salt on Angela's cleavage, licked it off before downing his shot, and then sucked on a lime wedge to chase the effects. Angela was giddy and laughed very hard.

"Who wants to see Angela's panties?" asked Anderson.

"I do!" cried Frank.

Before Angela knew it, Anderson was lifting up her dress. Not only that, but he was taking her over his knee and spanking her ass. Then he decided it would be appropriate for the three of them to get a look at Angela's bare ass. So he yanked down her panties and spread her cheeks, exposing her cunt and asshole to the welcoming crowd.

"No fair!" exclaimed Angela. "I'm drunk!"

"That's not an excuse," said Amanda.

All of a sudden, Amanda brought her hand down onto Angela's bare cheek, swatting it in a spanking motion. She did this a couple more times, gently squeezing her cheek every time she brought it down.

"I wanna see her cunt!" said Amanda. "Up close, that is."

Angela was just at the right state of being drunk where she didn't really care to put up a fight any more. Besides, they all had been drinking, so what was the harm in getting a little playful?

Angela leaned back on the sofa and, raising her hips, spread her cunt for all to see. Amanda wasted no time in getting a closer look. She lay down in front of her and licked a line going from her ass-crack all the way to the top of her pussy. She paused on her clit, licking circles around it, before going back down.

Anderson, who was getting hard, wondered how he could enter the playful mix. Frank had already gotten behind Amanda and was undoing his trousers, getting ready to fuck her from behind.

"Fuck my face, Anderson," said Angela. "I want to taste your balls and dick."

The evening progressed into a scene of completely steamy sex. The drinks kept coming and the four of them got all the more adventurous. Anderson ended up fucking Amanda for a while, who let her husband, Frank, fuck Angela. The rest of the evening, for Angela, was a bit of a blur.

∼

THE FOLLOWING MORNING, Angela's head ached. It took her a few moments to figure out where she was. Evidently, upon surveying the area, she figured out she was not in her apartment. The condo that she was in looked much nicer. Then she remembered the events of the night.

She remembered Anderson, and the Edwards, and the dancing, and the Spanish coffee, and the tequila. She was naked except for her bra and panties. She looked over to her side but found the bed empty. Then she heard some noises coming from the kitchen. It sounded as if someone was making something using a blender. That must have been Anderson.

"Anderson?" she called out.

"Yes, honey? Glad you're up. I'm making us the breakfast of champions. Eggs, bacon, sausage, pancakes, waffles, and my own special fruit smoothie, that has won many an honorary award."

"Did last night really happen?" asked Angela. "How many drinks did we have?"

"I lost count after that second round of tequila," said Anderson. "It was a lot."

"Don't we have to be at work? What time is it?" asked Angela.

Anderson laughed. She remembered that sexy laugh from the night before.

"It's Saturday, silly. Aside from answering emails, I never work on Saturdays. Especially when I have someone as sexy as you to spend time with."

Anderson walked over to the bed and planted a soft, tender kiss on Angela's forehead. She surprised him by grabbing him by the wrinkled shirt and pulling him onto the bed. Then she flipped him around and mounted him, pinning his hands in place above his hand.

"Ha!" she exclaimed. "You see, now I have the upper hand!"

"Don't get too excited there, tiger," said Anderson. "Say, have you given any thought to Frank's offer last night? I thought that that was incredibly generous and astute of him, offering you an interview like that. It could be a big step up for you, if it worked out."

The memories came back to her, like a bubble being popped, and the offer that Frank had made her settled into her mind.

"Oh yeah!" said Angela, trailing off a little bit to herself. "I do remember that. He gave me his card, right?"

Anderson nodded.

"He seemed most impressed by you, and who could blame him?"

"All right there, Mr. Suck-up. Say, did we have sex last night?"

"No," said Anderson matter-of-factly. "We were way too drunk for that."

Angela smiled at Anderson warmly. He smiled back.

"Come get some of this breakfast!" said Anderson. "It took me forty-five minutes to make!"

"Sounds delish," said Angela.

The two of them made their way to the kitchen and sat down at a high marble table. Anderson served some pancakes and bacon. Angela ate hungrily.

"You know what would make this breakfast even more enticing?" ventured Anderson. "If we ate topless."

Angela laughed so hard that orange juice almost came through her nose.

"That is maybe the cheesiest line I've ever heard! I think we can arrange something."

Angela took off her bra and let it fall to the floor. Her large, voluptuous breasts popped loose. Anderson's eyes became glued to her chest.

"I think I may have trouble finishing the meal. There is too much eye candy in front of me. As hard as it is for me to have an actual discussion while you look as amazing as you do, what do you think you are going to do about Frank's offer?"

"Well, I think I may learn more about it. It sounded very tempting. Frank seemed like a great guy to work for. He is so senior, and quite the gentleman. I also really liked Amanda."

"What do you think Eric will say? Surely, he won't want to lose you."

"I will mention it to him only if I'm serious about the job. Perhaps he can give me a counter offer if he's that eager to keep me. We'll have to wait and see."

Angela put another mouthful of bacon into her mouth.

"Well, Anderson," she began. "I think I should be going. I have to get back to my place and freshen up. I was hoping to get a workout in today or tomorrow, and I want to see Maxine as well. Thanks for the wonderful time."

They kissed one last time and Angela got dressed and took the elevator down to the main floor. She hopped in a cab and headed back to her apartment. There, she showered and got into a new outfit. She called Maxine to tell her about all that had happened. About the drinks, the company, meeting Frank and Amanda, and about the delicious breakfast that Anderson had prepared. She spent the rest of the day lounging about her place, contemplating the interview offer, and then finally going to the gym.

In the evening, at about 10:00 p.m., Angela's mother called with some news. Apparently, her sister, Rosalie, was going to be in town this week to visit. Also, apparently, she had a new boyfriend, Sam Harris. They were fellow Master's students. He was getting his degree in archeology. Karen laid out plans for them to go to an Italian restaurant on Wednesday.

NEW OPPORTUNITIES

At work on Monday, Angela decided to give Frank a call to follow up on their discussion. She wanted to reaffirm that she was interested in interviewing for the position, and to showcase her enthusiasm once again. She and Frank had a detailed conversation regarding the opportunity and it sounded as though she was a perfect match. She resolved to discuss the idea with Eric later that day.

After lunch, she made her way to Eric's office and knocked on the door. Eric was on the phone, but she let herself in and sat down on the couch in her office. He was just finishing up talking with Anderson and finalizing some legal details. He hung up the phone and then focused his attention on Angela.

"What can I do for you, Ms. Hayes?" he asked, shuffling some papers on his desk.

"Well, Eric, I just wanted to let you know that I am going on an interview for the office of the treasury. Frank Edwards asked me over the weekend. I only thought it would be fair to let you know that I was considering it."

"Angela, you've worked for me for five years. I have always supported you and given you opportunities to grow. I don't want to lose you now. Anderson's business is going to present huge opportunities for you, myself, the rest of my team, and the firm. What can I do to keep you?"

"Well, Frank has offered me almost twice my current salary. Plus, I would have a staff of four clerks working under me. So it would be a real opportunity to grow my career. Plus, I have always wanted to work in government. I did take some finance classes in college, so I could combine what I learned there with the legal know-how I learned working for you."

"We can talk about that. I can match the salary that they are offering you and we can hire some staff to support you. We could create a new position for you, higher up in the firm. You could even sit in on some board meetings."

"That sounds very intriguing, sir. I will think about it over the next week."

Angela had already decided that she was leaning towards interviewing for the job working for Frank. At the very least she could apply for the job and then decide later which one she would take. Eric was making a very generous offer.

Later that afternoon, Angela sent an email to Frank. In it, she said that she would like to go to the interview. His assistant got back to her at around 4:00 p.m., offering to see her on Wednesday. Angela's meeting with Karen, Rosalie, and Sam was at 6:30 p.m., so the timing would work out.

When the interview rolled around, Angela was nervous. She wore her best suit and had gotten a manicure and pedicure the previous day. She had gotten a number of compliments at work that day. Also, Anderson had texted her telling her "good luck." She had replied thanking him and telling him that she would get in touch soon about their second date. Also, Mark had texted her, but she hadn't replied to that one just yet. She didn't know what she was going to do about Mark. She had a feeling that if things progressed with Anderson, she would have to give some thought to seeing both of them at the same time.

"Good afternoon, Ms. Hayes," said the assistant as she walked into Frank's section of the office. "Please have a seat. Mr. Edwards will be with you shortly."

Angela couldn't help but feel relieved that it would be Frank who was interviewing her. Although, probably, he wouldn't be alone. After about five minutes of waiting, Frank opened the door to his office and came out, surrounded by about five or six Japanese businessmen. He said a few words to them in Japanese, and then they all bowed and made their way across the office and towards the elevators.

"Ah, there you are!" exclaimed Frank, focusing his attention on Angela.

"I didn't know you spoke Japanese, sir," said Angela, not having to feign her deep respect.

"It's one of the requirements of my job. I deal with Japan on an almost weekly basis. I also speak several other European languages and I'm learning Mandarin on the side. Don't worry, languages aren't really a huge requirement of the job you will be interviewing for."

"I speak French," said Angeles with a laugh. "I have always wanted to vacation some more in Paris."

"Anderson goes there from time to time and is hoping to expand there. Speak with him. Maybe he'd like to take you along. Care to step into my office?"

Angela walked into Frank's office, which was sparsely but elegantly decorated. There were leather chairs, impressionist paintings, a fridge with many different types of beverages in it, and a collection of bonsai trees lined up on a mahogany table and positioned next to a large glass window. Two other staff members, one female, the other male, were sitting holding binders and clipboards.

"Can I offer you a beverage?" asked Frank. "We have Evian, San Pellegrino, Perrier, and, of course, Snapple."

"I'll take a Snapple, thanks," replied Angela.

Frank introduced the two other staff members who were sitting in on the meeting. They were both senior members of the office of the treasury.

The interview lasted a half hour and went quite well. Or so Angela thought. At the end of it, she shook hands with the three of them and then left the building. She went straight to the Italian restaurant and arrived a full half hour before the reservation. She was excited to see Rosalie and Karen. She also could not wait to meet Sam.

Rosalie had always been particular about the guys she dated. She was highly independent and had gone long years without the comforts of a boyfriend. So, Angela reasoned, this one must be a keeper. They arrived exactly on time, the three of them, and walked happily to Angela, who had been sitting by herself nursing a glass of wine. She rose to greet them.

"Mom! Hi, Rosalie. You must be Sam," said Angela happily.

"Angela, you look wonderful," said Karen.

"I just came from a big job interview. I'll tell you more about that later. Rosalie, you look wonderful. It's been almost a year since I saw you. How is your Master's going?"

"It's going great, thanks. Got almost a year left. Let me introduce you to my boyfriend, Sam. Sam, say hello to my adoring sister, Angela."

Sam was a tall, attractive, dark-haired young man in a blazer and jeans. He looked like he was part of academia. He looked smart. Angela was glad for her sister.

"It's a pleasure," said Angela, shaking his hand. "Let's have a seat and eat!"

The four of them sat down at a square wooden table and a large-bellied Italian waiter served them. First, he brought bread and a bottle of red wine. Then he brought their dishes. Angela and Karen had ordered pasta, whereas Sam and Rosalie had ordered a pizza each. The food was delectable. After they had finished most of their meal, Angela decided to ask the young couple about how they were doing in school.

"I'm getting straight As. So is Sam," said Rosalie. "Some of the professors have actually been kind of encouraging us to do our PhDs. We might become professors one day ourselves."

"I'm jealous that you got all the brains in the family, Rosalie," said Angela with a laugh. "No fair!"

"Yeah, but you're making the big bucks," said Rosalie, reminding her. "Speaking of which, tell us about this new opportunity that is opening up for you."

"Well, it's for the office of the treasury. My pay would be significantly higher than it is now, although my current boss, Eric, says that he would match any offer that I got from them. It would be a glamorous post. I'd be working in government, which means I'd actually be doing something very meaningful. Kind of like a public service. The job stability and prestige would be through the roof, at least in comparison to what I'm doing now, working for Eric. I just had my interview this afternoon."

"How did it go, dear?" asked Karen.

"It went really well, as far as I can tell. I could sort of tell that Frank (who would be my new boss) has taken a liking to me, for whatever reason. I got the interview through my connection with Anderson Cromby."

Sam almost spat out his Diet Coke when he heard that name.

"You know Anderson Cromby?" he said, completely floored and impressed.

"Yes, we went on a date last Friday."

"Jesus, Angie," said Rosalie. "If you get in with him, you'll never have to work another day in your life. He's got so many billions."

"I know that. Well, you know, he's not my boyfriend, yet. We've just been on one date. Plus, I don't want to stop working. I enjoy being independent and making my own money."

"Wait until the first baby arrives," mused Karen. "That might all change in a heartbeat."

"Wait a second, Mom. We have only been on one date and already you have us having our first baby? Let's try to stay a little more real here."

There was a pause. The four of them considered the conversation until finally Karen broke the silence.

"Yes, you're right, dear. I don't mean to be jumping the gun.

He's just such a prominent person though. Being with him could change your life. So, how's Maxine?"

"She's doing well overall, but she has some kind of a sickness. She thinks it might be a cold. The doctors say they don't recognize anything severe, but there is nothing they can do for her at the same time."

"I hope she's okay," said Rosalie and Sam together.

"Me too. I am going to see if I can visit her tonight and bring her anything."

The foursome wrapped up their dinner. Karen offered to pay the bill, but Angela said that she was more than happy to pay it. The three of them thanked her, and then they all went their separate ways.

Back at her apartment, Angela got into some comfortable clothes—sweatpants and a hoodie— and helped herself to some of the good ice cream that she kept on hand so that she could indulge from time to time. It was already getting pretty late, so she decided to see if she could visit Maxine the following day. She sent her a text as much, and also asked how she was doing.

Maxine replied that she seemed to be getting even sicker, but that Henry was being great about it. He was taking some time off work to stay with her and comfort her. Maxine said that Angela could visit tomorrow evening after work. They could make it a girls' night and watch movies and gossip. Angela said that she thought that was a really good idea.

The following day at work, Angela was busy fact checking the latest request for a proposal for one of their clients when Eric stopped by her cubicle. He wanted to know how the interview went, and to reaffirm his enthusiasm in keeping her on.

"Well," she said. "The interview went really well. They are going to get back to me next week."

"How much are they offering you?" he inquired.

"They haven't said yet, actually. I'll let you know as soon as I find out."

"Good," he said, and then walked off.

Angela honestly didn't know what she was going to do. She liked working for Eric, but a new opportunity was a new opportunity. She knew she could grow and thrive working for the government.

A Friend Fallen Ill

The following day, after work, Angela stopped by the flower shop and picked up a bouquet of chrysanthemums for her best friend. She also grabbed a DVD (this time, Titanic, a movie they both loved) and some ice cream. She made her way to their apartment and opened the door, to see crumpled up tissues everywhere, dirty dishes, and empty medicine bottles.

It looked as if Maxine was in trouble. Where was Henry? Angela thought that her husband was supposed to be taking care of her.

"Oh my gosh, Maxine," said Angela as she walked through the door.

Maxine was lying on her back on the couch, sipping diet ginger ale through a straw and watching the news.

"Where is Henry, Maxine?" asked Angela.

In a coarse, raspy, and weak voice, Maxine replied, "He went out to get some food. Chicken noodle soup, I think. Come in. You look positively radiant."

Maxine chuckled hoarsely. Even in her emaciated state, she hadn't lost part of her sense of humor.

"My gosh, Maxine, let me have a look at you," said Angela, who took off her shoes, hung up her jacket, and walked hurriedly over to the couch, putting one hand on her forehead.

"You are burning up!" cried Angela. "This is not good; we need to get you to a hospital right away."

"I've already been to the hospital, dear," said Maxine with as much courage as she could muster. "There is nothing they can do for me there. They just said it was a really bad strain of the common cold, that's it."

"All right," replied Angela. "If you are not a lot better by tomorrow afternoon, I am ordering a cab and dragging you to the hospital."

"Fair enough," said Maxine. "How did your date with Anderson go?"

"It went so well, Maxine," said Angela. "I wish you could have been there. He took me to the most amazing restaurant in his private limo. The meal was so good. We drank such good wine. Then we actually bumped into another couple. Frank and Amanda Edwards. We ended up hanging out at their place for late night drinks. I got really drunk, but it was the most fun I've had in a while."

"Did you put out?" asked Maxine, rather directly.

Angela laughed at the forwardness of Maxine's question. They were best friends. They were allowed to be forward.

"No. I really like him, so I kind of want to wait to have sex, plus we were just way too drunk. It was one of those fun party nights. Like the kind we used to have in high school."

Their conversation was interrupted by a round of hoarse coughing on Maxine's part. She coughed up some phlegm and then went back to lying down on her back on the couch, one hand over her forehead.

"I don't want to be sick, Angela. I can't miss any practice sessions. My game has to be on point. I am going to a tournament later on in the month."

"Which is why we've got to get you better as soon as possible," said Angela seriously. "Let's watch Titanic and eat some ice cream. I brought your favorite, Ben and Jerry's."

The two of them settled into the movie. Angela sat on the

couch beside her best friend, who propped her head up on her lap. Angela massaged Maxine's arm and back. That's the kind of friends they were. They were very close physically and emotionally. She was like a sister to Angela. Maxine, who had no siblings, considered Angela to be like a sister as well.

Halfway through the movie, at about the part where the Titanic hit the ice berg, Henry walked in the door bearing goodies. He had chicken noodle soup and some panini sandwiches which he said he would heat up and serve. He was happy to see Angela there, for he knew that Maxine needed as much care as possible.

Henry heated up the sandwiches and cut them into pieces for the girls and himself. They watched the rest of the movie, and then Angela said she should get home. Tomorrow was Friday and she needed to be up early. There was a lot of work to be done at the office.

As she rose, her phone buzzed and she saw that she had a text from Anderson. He wanted to meet up for drinks after work at the Carlisle Club. She wondered why he chose that location, since he could afford any club in the city. The Carlisle Club was a medium-range hangout. Maybe he wanted to get a workout in beforehand. In any case, she replied that she would see him there at 6:00 p.m., but that she might not be able to stay out that late because she wanted to check in with Maxine again. Anderson said that he would come with her to see Maxine. He seemed genuinely concerned about her welfare.

That night, Angela had some strange dreams. She dreamed that she was in the middle of a tug of war between Frank and Eric, and that they were both competing for her employment. No one was winning, however, and she was being pulled in either direction. Then, all of a sudden, she was on a yacht with Anderson and he was feeding her fresh, juicy grapes as she reclined on a lounge chair, basking in the sun. For some reason, it was in the middle of summer and the day was beautiful. When she awoke at 6:00 a.m., she wished she could be there with Anderson.

The work day went by relatively quickly, and by the time it was over, Angela was positively giddy to be meeting Anderson at the club. She didn't have time for a workout, however, and arrived just a few minutes before 6:00 p.m.

Anderson was with a business colleague named Francis Cole. He was a vice president at Anderson's firm, and Anderson considered him to be his "right hand man" for all his operations. He was a well-built, medium-height man of about thirty-five, with curly brown hair and piercing hazel eyes. When Angela approached their table, both men stood up to greet her.

"Hey, darling," said Anderson first. "You look great this afternoon. I am glad you could meet me here. Let me introduce to you one of my most trusted colleagues at the firm, Francis."

"Charmed," said Francis, extending a hand for her to shake.

The three of them sat down and ordered some food. Anderson was in the mood for fresh Atlantic lobster, and so ordered three of those. Angela adored lobster and was eager to have one. She had always found it difficult to eat a lobster, as the shell was hard to break and so much of it you couldn't eat, but the parts that were for eating just tasted so delicious. The lobsters they had here were large enough to be considered a full meal. She reached for a slice of sourdough bread and spread some butter on it, eating it hungrily.

"Anderson has told me a lot about you," said Francis. "I am glad to be having the chance to meet you."

"Well, Anderson has great taste in people," joked Angela. "No, but in all honesty, if you are his friend and colleague, then the pleasure is all mine. Anderson introduced me to Frank and Amanda Edwards last week, and that actually might be turning into a new job for me. Say, Francis, help me decide on this. All else being equal, should I go to work for the government, or keep my current job as a senior legal clerk at the firm?"

"I think you need to do what's in your heart, dear," said Anderson.

"Don't interrupt!" exclaimed Angela, half-jokingly. "I wanted to hear Francis' opinion."

"Well, of course I agree with Anderson. Doing what's in your heart is the best strategy. You have to figure out where you'll be happiest. You'll potentially be at this job for a number of years, at least. Are you ready for a new challenge at a new workplace? Or do you want more of the same? Both jobs seem to offer money and stability. In a sense, you can't really lose."

Angela took a long pause to consider the very talented advice that she was receiving. She knew she did have to do what was in her heart. At that moment, it sort of seemed that going to work with Frank would offer her more excitement, as well as a change of pace. She had always been somewhat of a risk-taker, and the allure of the unknown was always so tempting. Now that she was with Anderson, she felt that working for one of his close friends might be a solid idea. It was almost as if she was rising in the world. It was as if she was entering a whole new social strata.

"You guys give great advice. Honestly," said Angela. "Thank you."

"You'll do fantastically, hon," said Anderson. "Just remember that you earned all of these opportunities for yourself. I didn't even have to put in a good word for you with Frank. He realized all by himself what a catch you were. So congratulations. Now, if you two will excuse me, I have to use the restroom."

Anderson got up and made his way to the men's bathroom. Angela also excused herself, and then stealthily followed him in there. She quietly locked the door behind them and then snuck up behind Anderson and grabbed his package through his thin trousers.

"Hey sexy," said Angela.

"Hey, what are you doing in here?" asked Anderson, although by the look on his face it seemed as though he was pleasantly surprised.

"I just had to surprise you and get a look at your magnificent cock again."

Then Angela undid his belt and dropped his trousers to the floor. She quickly slid her hand into his boxers and felt around for his cock, which was rapidly becoming harder.

"Okay, but we had better be quick!" said Anderson.

"Don't worry," responded Angela. "What I have in mind will only take a couple of minutes."

Angela dropped to her knees quickly and started to suck on Anderson's balls. She put one in her mouth, then the other. Then both at the same time. Meanwhile, she was jerking his cock off with her left hand. Through Anderson's moans she could tell that he was getting ready climax. So she licked up his shaft and put her pouty lips around the tip of his cock. She was just in time to receive a hot load in her mouth. As she was apt to do, she swallowed.

"That was amazing," said Anderson.

At that point there was a line outside the restroom waiting to get in, so the two of them scurried out and made their way back to the table.

They finished off their meal and then ordered some coffee. Angela had to apologize to Anderson and Francis for having to dine and dash. When she explained that her friend was very ill, they understood completely.

When Angela arrived at Maxine's apartment, she noticed right off the bat that her dear friend had taken a turn for the worse. Her face was extremely pale and she seemed weak. She could barely acknowledge the entrance of her friend.

Henry was absolutely frantic. He was on the phone with the

hospital trying to see if they had a bed available so that she could go in. Henry had never seen her that sick before. Neither had Angela.

"I know, goddammit. Her regular doctor already said that there was nothing that could be done," barked Henry angrily on the phone. "The situation has changed. She is much worse. Yes, she has a fever, for Pete's sake. Don't you think I checked that already? You've got to let her in. I have insurance up the yin-yang."

Angela walked over to Maxine and looked into her eyes. All Maxine could do was stare through her.

"Maxine, it's me, Angela. Do you recognize me?" she asked.

Maxine moaned in response, but she managed to nod her head.

"We're going to get you into a hospital as soon as possible. I'll get your clothes ready and help you put them on. Stay put. I'll be right back."

Angela entered Maxine's room and came out with a duffle bag and a bunch of clothes. She packed the bag to the best of her ability, trying not to forget anything. She packed her toothbrush, toothpaste, floss, and other miscellaneous toiletries. Then she raced over to Maxine and felt her forehead again. She seemed to be burning up even worse than before.

"What's going on, Henry?" asked Angela seriously.

"I think I found a hospital that will take her. It's on the other end of town. I can get us there, so let's walk Maxine to the parking lot and get her in my car."

"I am going to come with you and make sure that everything is all right," stated Angela.

"Fine," replied Henry.

The three of them got to the hospital as quickly as possible. It only took them about twenty minutes, because of light traffic. Angela thanked her lucky stars that it didn't take longer.

4
RECOVERY

The wait time in the hospital lobby was excruciating to both Angela and Henry. They wanted their loved one to be seen as soon as possible. Finally, after about an hour's wait, the insurance went through and a nurse came to the waiting area with a stretcher. Two other nurses helped put Maxine on the stretcher. Maxine seemed very incoherent and was probably only barely aware of what was going on. Angela was positively petrified. This was not how she imagined her Friday night going.

Angela and Henry insisted on accompanying Maxine into the main hospital. They followed the nurses and the stretcher until they came to a small private room where Maxine was going to be treated. Angela got a text from Anderson asking how Maxine was doing. Angela had to reply that she had no clue as of yet.

Angela and Henry waited with Maxine until the doctor came, at which point he recommended that Angela and Henry go home. They were going to keep Maxine there overnight so they could run some tests and be sure of what was ailing her.

Angela arrived back at her apartment but could not sleep.

She was much too concerned about her friend. So she put on the news and lay back in her bed. The clock showed 11:30 p.m. She was just in time to catch a rerun of Anderson's press conference that had evidently happened earlier that day. He was talking about exporting some of his customer service jobs to India. He maintained that he was not cutting jobs at his firm in general. In fact, the merger was actually going to add jobs, which would be paid for through increased international revenue, as a result of economies of scale.

Angela thought he looked very handsome on TV. She wished she didn't have to be with Maxine that evening, for she really had wanted to go on another date with her dreamy Anderson. There was always time for that. Both Anderson and Angela were extremely busy people, so it was to be expected that their dates would suffer. She resolved to call him in the morning. Surely he didn't have to go into work on a Saturday.

That night was another restless one for Angela. She was very worried about her friend. When she woke up at 7:30 a.m., by force of habit, she made herself some breakfast and decided to go for a workout. Her workout was intense and she felt much better afterwards. On the taxi ride home, she called Henry. Henry had some news for her.

Apparently, Maxine had come down with a rare strain of the flu, one that the doctors hadn't had much experience with. They had seen other cases of it over the past year or so. So Maxine was in treatment, and expected to recover within about a week or so. It was just important that she had plenty of rest, drank lots of fluids, ate when possible, and had plenty of positive support around her.

That evening, Angela had dinner with Henry at a small coffee shop near the hospital. Most of the dinner was passed in silence as they were worried sick about Maxine and didn't have much to say. After the dinner, they stopped by the hospital to visit Maxine. She actually seemed to be doing better. Her head was propped up and she was able to watch TV. Some of the pallor in her face was gone. It appeared as though she had been able to eat, however minimally. Angela approached the bed.

"Honey," she began. "We are here for you, one hundred percent. How are you feeling?"

Maxine groaned, but then she added, "Thanks, you guys. I'm sorry."

"You have no reason to apologize to us," said Henry. "I just wish I had gotten you into the hospital sooner. We might have been able to nip this in the bud a bit earlier."

"You're going to get a lot better, I promise," said Angela, and she stroked a lock of Maxine's hair away from her face.

"I feel like my insides are on fire," said Maxine, who then let out another groan.

"The doctor said it should take about a week for you to get out of here. Two weeks, at the most. I bet you'll be back out on the courts before the month is up," said Henry optimistically.

"I hope so too," uttered Maxine.

Angela, Maxine, and Henry waited around for a bit more. Visiting hours wouldn't be done for another half hour. So they watched TV and tried to be as cheerful as possible, given the gravity of the situation. When it was time to go, Henry and Angela shared a cab back to their respective destinations. Angela said that she would visit Maxine again and again—as often as possible. Henry thanked her for the gesture.

When Angela got home, she kicked off her shoes and collapsed on the couch. Then her phone rang. It was Mark.

"Hey, Mark!" said Angela.

"Hey, baby doll," he said. "I was in the area. Thought I'd drop by for one of our movie nights."

"Sure, you can drop by. Just know that I am feeling kind of bummed. Maxine is in the hospital; she is really sick."

"Feeling bummed? I bet I can cheer you up, princess."

"Yeah, maybe," said Angela. "Come on up. I'll be here. I'm just watching TV."

Mark opened up her door and came right into the living room, plopping down on the couch next to her. Then he planted a kiss on her cheek and gave her shoulders a quick massage.

"You're right, baby. You do look kind of sad. I am so sorry about Maxine."

"That's all right. It's just a major bummer, is all. The doctors are optimistic. They say she'll be out in a week. Two weeks, tops."

"That's good," said Mark. "She has to keep on her game if she is going to compete in any tournaments."

"That's what she is most worried about," said Angela.

Angela leaned on Mark. It was comforting for her to have a close personal friend at a time when she was most worried about Maxine. She cared for Mark deeply, just as she cared for Anderson. With Anderson, all sorts of doors were opening up for her. With Mark, she took comfort in the familiar. His hands were familiar, as were his lips, and his masculine aroma.

Mark put one of his long arms around her and pulled her tight. Then he kissed the top of her head, before working his way down to her forehead, then her nose, and then finally her lips. She kissed him back. Pretty soon they were making out again. She climbed on top of him and took off her shirt. Then she unhooked her bra. Mark kissed her large, milky-white breasts and she pushed them onto his face. His hands gravitated down towards her ass. He cupped each cheek in one hand and gave them a squeeze.

Angela felt electricity once again running through her entire body. At that point, she was unequivocally turned on. Then she grabbed his hand and led him towards the bed. They lay down on the soft bed. He took off his clothes with her help and then positioned himself on top of her.

He slid off her pants, exposing her naked body. His powerful hand grazed her belly on its way down to her womanhood. He then positioned his head between her legs. He took in the full aroma of her moist vagina. He then licked her lips, parting them with his fingers. As his tongue danced and swirled about her clit, he inserted two fingers and then began to rhythmically finger-fuck her into ecstasy.

As she cried out with her first orgasm, Mark took delight in being able to give her that much pleasure. He then kissed his way back up to her mouth and they shared a long, passionate kiss.

"I'm ready for you," said Angela softly, still breathing heavily.

"Good, so am I," responded Mark.

He then proceeded to make love to her. With every fervent thrust, he sent both himself and Angela into a deep state of bliss. It only took about three or four minutes until he was ready to come. When they reached climax together, she dug her nails into his back and called out his name. Afterwards, they laid next to each other, cuddling and laughing to themselves.

Angela reached into a cupboard and took out a large, 12-inch vibrating dildo.

"Have you ever used one of these on a woman?" asked Angela.

"No, I can't say as I have. Have you used that on yourself?"

"I do sometimes, but I love being fucked with it. Mark, I want you to put it in my ass. I want to feel fucked in both holes."

Mark took the dildo and squeezed some lube onto it. Angela got on all fours and spread her knees apart, arching her back so that her ass was in full view. It was a beautiful ass, so curvaceous and fresh-looking. Mark leaned in and kissed her right between the cheeks, leaving a trail of saliva that dripped its way down her crack to her cunt.

"Fuck me with it, Mark," said Angela. "I'm ready."

Mark lubed up her ass again for good measure and then slowly inserted the length of the dildo into her butt. As it went in almost all the way, Angela gave a moan in pleasure.

"Keep fucking me," instructed Angela.

Mark slid the dildo into her ass, then out again, then back in. He continued this for several minutes. He began to become stiff again himself, as this sight was quite beautiful. With his free hand he began massaging her clit, which sent Angela to the moon and back. Angela came several times, each time screaming out Mark's name.

Finally, as her final orgasm wound down, Mark took out the dildo and tossed it onto the bed. He gave her cunt another playful massage, fingering her vagina a bit, and then withdrew. He kissed up her back and neck, followed by her cheek and lips. They lay next to each other silently for a while.

"You are so great in bed, Mark," said Angela.

"Thanks, so are you," said Mark.

"I hope we can continue these meetings," said Angela.

"Why shouldn't we?" asked Mark.

"No reason."

Angela felt bad about not telling Mark about Anderson. She wasn't the type to two-time anybody. She just felt that it was not time yet to share her relationship details with the man. She and Anderson had only been on one date, really. She did not consider herself to be his girlfriend, just yet. So making love to Mark seemed normal. Their relationship came with no strings attached.

Mark spent the night, and the following morning they went out for breakfast. They ate at a brunch place only a few blocks from her apartment. Mark told her all about his new real estate deals that were going down. Apparently, he was very close to securing a major client that would bring in hundreds of thousands of dollars. He was excited, and said that he would finally be able to afford a really nice condo with the proceeds.

Angela told Mark about the new job possibility working for the government. To Angela, the idea of working for Frank was sort of becoming more and more like the preferred route to take. She wondered to herself how she was going to break the news to Eric. Mark was very supportive, and told Angela that it was a good idea and that she should go for it.

After Mark left to go home, Angela walked back to her apartment and got on the phone with Henry. Maxine was doing a lot better that morning, and was almost fully coherent. The medicine that they had been giving her was, apparently, working well. The doctors even estimated that she might be ready to go home in under a week.

"Do you want me to stop by the hospital this afternoon?" asked Angela.

"You can if you want," replied Henry. "She might enjoy seeing you. Absolutely no pressure. If you're busy, then we totally understand."

"Nonsense," said Angela. "I was just going to go for a workout, but I can do that any time. I'll take a cab over right now. I want to see my best friend."

When Angela arrived at the hospital and made her way into Maxine's room, her friend was very happy to see her.

"Girlfriend!" exclaimed Maxine. "You look great. How was your night last night?"

"I met up with Mark," said Angela. "Don't focus on me. The important thing is your recovery. How do you feel? You look a lot better."

"I think the medicine is working. The doctors, at first, weren't sure what to do. Apparently that strain of flu that I had was really rare. They got their act together, and just in time. I was afraid that my illness was fatal. I sure as heck wasn't getting any better."

"No, you weren't," agreed Angela. "You gave us all a fright. Promise me you'll never do that again!"

Angela squeezed Maxine's hand.

"I promise, dear," said Maxine.

"Thanks for being here for us," said Henry. "It really has meant the world to us to have you by our side in this time of need."

"As if there were any two ways about it!" cried Angela.

Angela gave Maxine a hug. Then she walked up to Henry and hugged him as well. She remained for a few more minutes and then took her leave. She headed back to her apartment to start deciding on ways to let Eric know that she had chosen to go to work for Frank.

5

WHAT SHE NEEDS PART 3

Paving the Way

Angela had been overwhelmed with the amount of stuff that was going on in her life. There were her relationships, her interview, Maxine getting sick, and the romance with Anderson. She loved her life, but even she had to admit that things were getting a bit busy. It was Sunday night, and she knew that tomorrow she would have to break the news to her boss, Eric, that she was accepting Frank Edwards' offer to go and work for him. She dreaded this conversation, for Eric had been a great boss for the entire time that she had worked for him. But she counted on him understanding that this move was only to advance her career. It was nothing personal.

Since it was Sunday night and the rest of the world was getting ready for the workweek, Angela decided to have a relaxing night alone. As she was wont to do, she decided to have a bath and then watch Netflix. As she got into her robe, she started preparing the bath by adding bubbles as well as essential oils. Her bath was one of the best things about her apartment. It was large, had jets for massaging her tender muscles, and plenty of room to move around. The faucet was a heavy, thick stream, and filled up the bath quickly.

Angela dropped her robe and put one foot into the bath. It was piping hot. Then she slid in comfortably, swinging her other leg over the edge of the bath and fully submerging herself into the relaxing, pulsating jets. She closed her eyes and let out a long, drawn-out sigh of relief.

Whenever she took a long bath like this, her mind always went to how her life was doing. This evening, her mind was filled with positive emotions. She was moving up in her career. She had great relationships. Anderson, the hottest billionaire in town, was treating her like a downright queen. She had been having great sex with some great people. In fact, Angela thought merrily, she was turning into quite the little slut. She had had several sexual encounters with different people in the past week alone. But she knew those encounters were safe, and as long as she wasn't careless in letting the wrong people find out, she figured, what was the harm?

She thought of the last blowjob she had given Anderson. Angela had seen a lot of cocks in her life, but none of them were quite as nice as Anderson's. She loved everything about it. She wasn't one to love blowjobs all that much, but she had to admit that going down on Anderson was downright fun. He seemed to appreciate it so much.

As she thought of Anderson's dick, she grabbed the nozzle of her bath and lowered it just in front of her pussy. She spread her knees and brought the stream of water in close. It was amazing how much it felt as though she was receiving head. The nozzle pulsated and stimulated her clit, massaging around her outer lips. She kept the nozzle there for a few minutes.

She was rapidly becoming very turned on. She rubbed the nipple of one of her massive tits, circling it with her thumb and forefinger. She was on the brink of orgasm. She then dropped the nozzle and began rubbing her lips with her free hand. In a few more moments she was rocked to her core by an explosive orgasm. It felt wonderful.

Afterwards, she got out of the tub and opened the drain, letting the water dissipate. She threw on her robe and made her way to the TV. She turned on the news. There was more stuff going on with Anderson's firm. They were expanding their human resources and hiring all kinds of new people from around the world. After the merger, Anderson's firm would be the largest consulting company in the world, with operations on all the continents.

"Oh, Anderson," she murmured to herself. "You are one powerful man. And I am your woman."

The next day at the office it was Monday morning, and everyone seemed a little groggy. Eric came to her desk and brought her some fresh coffee. Double cream, double sugar. Just the way she liked it. She accepted happily and then mentioned to Eric that there was something she wanted to talk to him about when he had the chance.

"Just give me a few hours, Angela. I need to review some documents. Anderson Cromby wants feedback by the end of the day. Come to me at around lunch. Maybe we can go out and grab a bite together."

Angela spent the rest of the morning performing some menial tasks. She had a few spreadsheets to look over, and a deck or two to begin. When it came time for lunch, Eric reappeared at her desk and suggested that they go to Folocia's. It was a new Italian restaurant that had just opened up down the block.

"You know that I am Italian-American, right?" asked Angela.

"I think I did know that," responded Eric. "So in honor of that fact, we can enjoy the food of your people."

At the restaurant, Eric ordered seafood linguini and a Perrier. Angela just had a salad.

"So, Angela," began Eric. "What is it that you wanted to talk to me about?"

"Well, first of all, let me just say that I have given this some very deep thought. As you know, I have been entertaining the idea of going to work for Frank Edwards. As much as I regret leaving your company, for I have spent many rewarding years working for you, I have to say that I am going to accept Frank's offer. I hope you can understand why."

"Well, it will be difficult for us to replace you. You have created quite the niche for yourself at our firm. You know my thoughts on your work performance. You have always over-delivered. However, I suppose that I have to respect your decision. If things don't end up working for you over at the government, know that you'll always have a place back here on my team."

Angela was heart-warmed to hear Eric's very reasonable response to her decision.

"I want us to keep in touch, Eric," said Angela. "You were a great boss, and I hope that now we can start being friends."

"That would be great."

"Let's have dinner again next week, after I have finished moving my stuff out of the office. I want to show you the club that I belong to. It's called the Carlisle Club. Since we are friends now, I want us to develop the relationship."

"Sounds great. Here's my cell number. Just give me a call when you want to get together and we'll work it out."

That evening, Angela decided to pay a visit to her mother. She took a cab directly from the office to her apartment on the far end of town. Approaching the entrance, she found her name on the buzzer and pressed the button.

"Yes?" came Karen's voice through the intercom.

"It's Angela. I just wanted to stop by and see how you were doing."

"Come on up."

Angela entered Karen's apartment. It was medium-sized, with some basic furniture. There was a couch, a TV, a dining table, a large kitchen with many appliances, and a bedroom with a double bed and some book shelves.

Angela walked over to the couch, took off her bag, and had a seat.

"Can I get you anything, dear?" asked Karen. "A cup of tea, perhaps?"

"Yes, that would be wonderful, Mom," said Angela.

As Karen was preparing the tea, Angela took out her phone and went over some work emails. She was in the process of letting her contacts know that she would be switching jobs. Eric had found a replacement for her, a young woman by the name of Tina Tupinski, who had just graduated with her MBA from an Ivy League school. Over the coming week, it would be Angela's job to orient Tina to her position so that the transition would be as smooth as possible.

When Karen reentered the living room, she had a tray with a teapot on it and two ceramic mugs. She placed it on the coffee table and sat down next to Angela. She poured tea into the two mugs and then offered Angela sugar, but Angela preferred to take hers plain. They drank in silence for several minutes.

"How's everything at work, dear?" asked Karen. "Are you going to be accepting Frank's offer?"

"Yes, as a matter of fact, I am. I just told Eric, who is rather sad to see me go. Apparently I am pretty valuable at the firm."

"Well, I always knew that. You have always been smart and good in business environments. I have always said that."

"What about you, Mom? What's new in your life?"

"You won't believe it, but I actually met someone. His name

is Ben Taylor. He's sixty-three years old, and he's a retired banker. We met at bingo the other night. He is so kind, Angela."

Angela was truly happy for her mom. Ever since her father had died, Karen had been single. Karen was an attractive lady. She was slim, with long hair, and a good body for a woman her age. There was no reason why she shouldn't be able to attract a boyfriend.

"Wonderful, Mom!" exclaimed Angela. "And you are both retired, so you will be able to spend a lot of time together. Do I hear wedding bells?"

Karen laughed so hard she had to put down her tea.

"No, Angie. Not yet. We only just met! But he is taking me to the movies this Friday. Speaking of which, since Rosalie is still in town with Sam, perhaps the five of us could do something. Perhaps bowling might be fun?"

Angela wondered to herself if she could bring Anderson along. That would make it six people on the outing. A good number. Three couples.

"That is a good idea, Mom," said Angela. "I am really busy this week. I have to teach the new girl to my position. But on the weekend I should be free. Let's try to do something then. And I can bring Anderson."

Karen's eyes lit up.

"Do you think he would want to go to a dingy bowling alley? I mean, a man of his position ... don't you think he would a bit embarrassed to be seen at a place like that?"

"I think he loves me, Mom. Plus, he'd love to meet my family. All of us."

Just at that moment, Angela's phone vibrated. She checked the display and it was Anderson. The text simply said:

Hey babe, thinking of you. Today was a killer day. Very busy. I need some Angela time. Can I swing by your place tonight at around 8:00 p.m.?

Karen and Angela finished their tea. Angela stayed a bit longer. She wanted to find out more about Ben. It turned out he had had a very interesting career. He had worked his way high up in his firm as an investment banker. Then he joined the army as a senior officer and served two terms overseas. Now, he was retired. As Karen said, he was going nuts with all the time that he had on his hands. Bingo was just one of the activities that he occupied himself with. He was also an avid sailor and collected rare first-edition books. He was extremely well read and highly educated. Angela was very happy for her mother.

When it came time to go, Angela excused herself and thanked Karen for the tea. She said she would try to see if Anderson wanted to go bowling on the weekend. This got Karen very excited. They hugged goodbye, and Angela left the apartment.

Romance in the Air

During her cab ride home, she texted Anderson to let him know he could come over whenever he wanted. She got a message back that he would be there in half an hour.

Back at her apartment, Angela decided to get ready for Anderson. She dimmed the lights, put on some low-volume jazz (she was partial to Miles Davis), and set out some scented candles. Then she walked over to her closet and looked for something sexy to put on.

There were a number of dresses that would have been perfect. They were all very revealing and sexy, but she decided to go with some lingerie instead. She picked a pretty red number out of her closet and held it up against herself in front of the mirror. The lingerie, complementing her beautiful, dark hair and Mediterranean complexion, was perfect.

The red-laced bra was skimpy, revealing a lot of skin and was see-through enough to expose her brown nipples. The panties were crotchless and rode up her ass in the back, exposing her perfectly round buttocks. She got into the lingerie and looked at herself in the mirror. She twirled about, getting a three-hundred-and-sixty degree view of her perfect body. She smiled to herself. She knew that Anderson would love this surprise.

She threw on a silk robe, tied it around her waist, and made her way to the kitchen. She rummaged through her fridge and found an unopened bottle of champagne. She placed the bottle into a metal bucket full of ice and brought it out to her dining room, placing the bucket on the table. Everything was perfect.

She sat down on the couch and turned her attention to her phone. As she waited for Anderson to arrive, she went through some more of her contacts, taking note of the ones she would have to call at work.

When she heard a knock at the door, her heart leapt. She walked over to the door and playfully asked who it was.

"It's the police," was the answer.

Anderson's voice was unmistakable.

"Have I been bad?" she asked playfully.

"You have been very naughty. Now open up so that you can receive your punishment."

"I hope that it is a very big, hard punishment."

Angela opened the door and Anderson was standing there, wearing a dark blue suit and a beige overcoat. He was carrying some Styrofoam containers which, by the looks of them, had sushi in them.

"May I come in?" he asked.

Angela grabbed him by the overcoat and pulled him in. Anderson barely had time to close the door before Angela stood up her tiptoes and kissed his lips passionately. She pushed him up against the door and, taking off his overcoat, ran her hands all over his body and through his hair. She began to take off his clothes very deliberately, throwing them onto a lounge chair that was in the living room.

Anderson's hands were all over Angela's body. First they were gliding their way through her hair. Then they traced the outline of her back. He stopped to feel one magnificent boob in his strong hand. Then he brought his hands down to her butt. He could tell through the robe that there was hardly anything beneath.

"Come with me," ordered Angela to a nearly-naked Anderson.

They walked over to the couch and sat down. Angela uncorked the ice-cold champagne and poured each of them a glass. Then she took the food that Anderson had brought and laid it out onto the table. They each ate for a while, not really wanting to speak or to spoil the moment. When they had had their fill, Angela cleared the food away and sat back on the couch, directly opposite to Anderson. She leaned back and let her robe fall to the floor. Her legs were spread just enough so that Anderson got a view of her beautiful, pink pussy.

"So how was your day, honey?" asked Angela.

Anderson gulped. He was rapidly becoming red in the face and turned on beyond measure.

"Uh, it was fine. I am going to be making preparations to visit France. There is some business that we need to settle in Paris. New offices opening up and all that. How was your day?"

Angela reached down and started playing with her pussy.

"It was fine," said Angela casually. "I told Eric that I'd be leaving the firm to go to work for Frank. He seemed to take it well enough, although I think they are going to have a hard time replacing me."

Angela's fingers danced across her pussy, now spreading her lips, now rubbing her clit. She started to notice a bulge forming in Anderson's trousers.

"And how's your mother doing?" asked Anderson, trying to sound nonchalant.

"She has a new boyfriend," replied Angela in a monotone voice.

"Oh, good for her!"

"Come here," Angela ordered.

Anderson crawled over to her and kissed her on the lips. Then Angela directed his head down, fingers running through his hair, until he was directly in front of her pussy lips.

Anderson didn't have to ask what Angela wanted. He licked around her lips, spending time on her clit. His tongue probed around her pussy, entering her hole and then dancing back out to softly massage her inner lips. He brought a hand up and spread her lips, so that he could more accurately reach the inner folds of her vagina.

Angela moaned in pleasure. She started grinding her hips, pushing her pussy into Anderson's face. Anderson savored the taste, not wasting any time kissing and making out with her vulva. This went on for a solid fifteen minutes.

Then Angela lifted her hips and slid her panties down so that they dangled on one ankle. She turned around and pushed her ass into the air. Anderson got a wonderful view of her pussy and ass, and still kneeling before her, began licking her pussy from behind. His face was positioned directly in front of her private area. He reached up and spread her cheeks. He kissed her asshole, and then licked her pussy some more. Angela cried out in pleasure.

"Fuck me, Anderson," Angela whispered. "I want you inside me now."

Anderson took off his pants and knelt directly behind her. He pushed his rock-hard cock into her pussy, softly at first. Then he began fucking her harder and harder. His thrusts were tender and deliberate. They weren't forced. He never broke the rhythm, as Angela was sent deeper and deeper into ecstasy.

"Touch my ass," Angela ordered now. "I want to feel your hands all over my ass."

Anderson didn't waste any time squeezing her cheeks and separating them. He placed a finger over her hole and kept it there, still fucking Angela rhythmically.

"Oh yes, Anderson, that feels so good. You are such a big, strong man. Fuck me harder. Your cock feels so good."

Then Angela noticed that Anderson began panting harder and harder. It appeared as though he was ready to come. Angela wanted Anderson to come inside her. She pushed her ass against his torso, trying to get him deeper and deeper inside her.

Anderson exploded semen into her vagina, his orgasm lasting a full thirty seconds. As he came, Angela screamed in pleasure.

They collapsed together onto the couch, exhausted. Angela felt fully satisfied with their lovemaking. From the look on Anderson's face, so did he.

They moved to the bed and crawled under the covers. They both wanted to take a quick nap. When they awoke, it was almost midnight.

"My mom wanted me to invite you to go bowling this weekend. My sister and her boyfriend, as well as my mom's boyfriend, will be there. Want to come?"

"Saturday?"

"Yes. Do you like bowling?"

"I was on the bowling team in college. I haven't practiced in forever, but that sounds like a fun idea."

There was a long pause. Angela cuddled closer to Anderson, and pushed her ass into his crotch. She couldn't tell if it was just her imagination, but she thought she felt something becoming stiff there.

Anderson had to leave to go back to his place, and so couldn't spend the night. His day tomorrow would start at 5:00 a.m. He needed to make arrangements for their expansion into Paris. Angela had to be up at her usual 7:00 a.m.

The rest of the week went by relatively smoothly. Angela spent each day working with Tina, getting her acclimatized to the office. She transferred her computer files onto a disk for Tina to use.

On Friday, Angela invited Tina and Eric to go for drinks at a nearby bar to celebrate the end of the work week, and Tina's successful transition to the team. Both Eric and Tina thought that it was a wonderful idea. The afternoon flew by, at which point the three of them walked over to the Flaming Eagle, which was a pretty ordinary sports bar. They served the best martinis in the neighborhood.

Eric, Angela, and Tina found a table by the window. Eric bought the first round of martinis.

"To new opportunities! To old friendships!" Eric toasted.

The three of them raised their glasses and, making eye contact with one another, performed the "cheers."

"Are you excited to be part of our team, Tina?" asked Eric. "I know you have some big shoes to fill, but you are a smart and talented woman; it shouldn't be any problem for you."

The conversation went on along those lines and as the drinks kept coming, the three of them started to have more and more fun.

"I always thought Angela was cute," admitted Tina with a girlish giggle.

Angela's jaw dropped.

"I don't know what to say, Tina," said Angela.

Then Eric, feeling the effects of the martinis, said something that also surprised Angela.

"Don't you think Tina's cute too, Angela?"

Then Angela had an idea. She took out her phone and called Anderson. She hoped that he would pick up. He usually worked late on Fridays, but maybe he could make an exception for her and her friends.

"Hello?" said Anderson.

"Anderson! I am here with Eric and the new girl, Tina. Say hi, guys!"

Eric and Tina said hi.

"Anyway," Angela continued, "we are just having drinks right now at the Flaming Eagle and I was wondering if you could stop by at some point in your limo and take us for a cruise. That is, if Pat wouldn't mind."

"I am just finishing up at the office now. But drinks sound good. I can be by there in about an hour."

"Sounds good, babe. See ya soon," said Angela, as she hung up the phone. "You know, Tina, the more I look at you, the more I am reminded of my roommate when I was a college freshmen. You are just as pretty as her. You both have blonde hair. And a nice rack."

The expression on Eric's face turned from embarrassment to intrigue in a heartbeat.

The three of them made small talk and ordered a few more rounds of martinis before heading out onto the sidewalk to wait for Anderson's limo. Eric had paid the bill, which was very nice of him, because it wasn't cheap. As they waited, Tina slid her hand down Angela's arm and clasped her hand. They stood together, holding hands, for the better part of ten minutes, until finally Anderson's limo pulled up and Pat came around to open the doors.

Eric, Tina, and Angela got in and made themselves comfortable on the black leather. Anderson kissed Angela on the lips, then gave a solid handshake to Eric. He hugged Tina as well and said it was nice to meet her.

"How were drinks?" asked Anderson, addressing no one in particular.

"They were good," said Tina, hiccupping. Out of the three of them, she had the least experience drinking. She was a very fun drunk. She was about to get even more fun.

Wild Times

Anderson told Pat to drive around a while until they figured out what they wanted to do. It was Friday night, and they were bound by nothing. Anderson had nothing but cash, and the four of them felt like doing something fun. They considered going to a club. Or to another bar. Or to a fancy restaurant. Then Tina said that she wanted to see Anderson's apartment. It was at this point that Angela realized that she hadn't really been spending a whole lot of time there. She and Anderson were partial to hanging out at her place, for some reason.

"I think that's a good idea. Let's hang out at Anderson's," said Angela.

"You don't want to go to a club first, babe?" asked Anderson.

"I think—hiccup—we should go dancing and then go to Anderson's. The night is still fresh and young," said Tina.

Then Eric piped up,

"Anderson, Mr. Cromby, I just wanted to say what a pleasure it is to be hanging out with you outside of a business environment. Our firm is still delighted to be taking you on as a client, and having this opportunity to see you outside of the office is priceless."

Anderson appreciated the compliment.

"I have the highest respect for you, Mr. Taylor, as I do for Ms. Hayes over here. If things go well, maybe we could do things as a threesome more often. And, of course, we can hang out with your wife as well."

Then Tina hiccupped again very loudly.

"Those were great martinis," she said.

"Okay," said Angela, interrupting the moment. "Let's go to a club, then to Anderson's. We can make this a very fun evening. Now, onto an important matter. Should we invite Mr. and Mrs. Edwards?"

"I'll give them a call," said Anderson.

Anderson called the Edwards, but they didn't answer. So he sent them a text message to get in touch with them. In the meantime, they were going to have to find a way to have fun without them.

"I think I have some tequila in the fridge in here," said Anderson, who pulled out a bottle of expensive Mexican tequila and started lining up shots at the bar in his limo for the four of them to take.

"I want to lick salt off of Angela's ass," said Tina suddenly.

The three of them laughed at that suggestion, but they thought it was a great idea. Tina really knew how to get the ball rolling. Angela bent over and lifted up her skirt. Then she pulled down her panties. She was acutely aware that everyone around her was able to stare at her pink snatch.

Eric found a saltshaker in one of the limo cupboards and sprinkled some salt on Angela's bare ass. There happened to be a few sliced limes as well, so Tina picked one of those up to use as a chaser. She downed the shot of tequila expertly and then quickly licked up the salt. Then she sucked the lime wedge dry and discarded it.

"Who's next?" asked Tina.

It was Eric's turn. He performed the same task as Tina, except this time, instead of sprinkling the salt on Angela's ass cheek, he sprinkled it over her hole. Then he downed the shot and unflinchingly licked up the salt off her ass. This sent shivers up and down Angela's spine. It felt so good. And she loved being the center of attention.

Finally, it was Anderson's turn. Before sprinkling the salt and pouring himself a shot, he rubbed Angela's pussy a bit, getting it nice and wet. But Anderson decided not to use salt after all. He drank his shot and then licked Angela's pussy for the better part of minute, before sucking back on his lime wedge.

"No one else? No seconds?" asked Angela.

"I want to see what everybody's dick looks like," said Tina, again surprising the rest of them.

It seemed as though Eric felt a bit embarrassed about taking off his clothes. Anderson, on the other hand, was all over it. After Eric saw how easily Anderson had loosened his pants and dropped his boxers, Eric decided to follow suit. His cock wasn't quite as big as Anderson's, but it had a nice girth and was a nice appendage for the girls to look at all the same.

Tina moved over to Eric and sat on his lap. With one hand, she supported herself on his shoulder, and with the other hand she stroked his erection. She jerked him off expertly, and then began kissing his mouth. Their tongues twirled about one another as they made out passionately. The sight of them fooling around made Angela even more aroused.

Angela positioned herself onto Anderson's lap, but this time, instead of gliding his dick into her pussy, she pushed her ass onto his cock, until the head slipped into her asshole.

"We haven't done this before, I don't think," she whispered into Anderson's ear.

Then she rode him, his cock gliding in and out of her asshole. Anderson brought his hands around to her front and circled her tits, playing with their weight, and making a special effort to pinch and play with her perfect nipples.

Tina took her free hand, the one that wasn't stroking Eric's cock, and reached over to Angela's cunt and began feeling around. Angela's clit was hard, and Tina brought her hand up to Angela's mouth. Angela sucked on Tina's fingers. This was the lubrication that Tina needed. She began twirling her fingers around Angela's clit, making sure to massage her pussy at the same time.

The feeling of Anderson's cock in her ass made Angela scream in pleasure. She wanted to feel him fill up her ass with hot semen. Just then, Eric exploded in an orgasm, drenching Tina's hand with cum. A few moments later, Anderson also came and filled up Angela's ass.

A few moments of silence passed. The four of them felt completely satisfied, and now shared a level of intimacy that only those who had engaged in sex together could feel.

Pat continued to drive them around the city streets. The group switched from tequila to wine, as Anderson brought out a very expensive vintage of French cabernet. Tina gazed at Anderson, her eyes at once innocent and doe-like. Angela wondered if Anderson thought about fucking her. She wondered if Anderson had a thing for cute blondes.

Anderson's phone rang. It was Frank Edwards. He and his wife had just finished up at a benefit for a philanthropic organization that he was involved in, and apparently they wanted to celebrate with a night out on the town. There was plenty of room in the limo.

Anderson directed Pat to swing by the benefit and pick up their new companions. Eric was very enthusiastic to meet Frank and Amanda. Part of him wanted to meet the person who was taking away one of his best employees. Of course, as Eric had stated many times, there were no hard feelings.

Frank and Amanda entered the limo. They were dressed in beautiful and elegant eveningwear. Frank was wearing a black and white tuxedo, and Amanda was dressed in a beautiful and sexy evening gown, which showed off her natural, beautiful figure. She looked great for a woman in her forties.

"It smells like sex in here," Frank said at once, to a chorus of laughter from everyone else.

Tina winked at Frank and then extended her hand.

"I'm Tina!" she said enthusiastically. Frank saw at once that she was both the youngest and the most inexperienced in the group. But she was damn hot.

Anderson jumped in.

"Frank, you know Angela. This is Eric. He's Angela's soon-to-be ex-boss."

"Thanks to you!" said Eric, in a kidding way.

"I suppose I should thank you, Eric. You have groomed a very well put-together businesswoman. If what she tells me is true, then you are a very fine manager as well. Maybe someday we can talk about taking you on and bringing you into the government."

"Maybe," said Eric, who liked his current job. The offer flattered him, however.

"The night is young, my friends," said Anderson. "What shall we do?"

"Let's go for drinks at Castle Winery," suggested Frank. "They have the best selection of exotic wines in the city. Does that sound okay to everybody?"

Everyone seemed to be in agreement that that was an excellent suggestion. Angela, herself, thought it was a good idea especially since it would be Anderson that would be paying. A bill at that place for the six of them could easily run in the tens of thousands.

It took Pat about twenty minutes to wind his way across town and park in front of the prestigious bar. All kinds of high society was flocking towards the entrance. Anderson told Angela that he recognized at least half a dozen work colleagues just from glancing around the outside alone.

They took turns exiting the vehicle until the six of them stood in front of the luxurious entrance. There was a long line. Anderson wasn't going to see them wait for an hour just to get in. He handed the doorman several hundred-dollar bills, and the grateful doorman cleared the way for them to enter.

Upon getting in, Angela was overwhelmed by the classiness of the place. In the center of the main room there was a large mahogany bar with several well-dressed couples sitting around it. All across the back wall were square tables with white cloths on them. A live band that consisted of a cello player, a pianist, a classical guitarist, and a drummer was playing a jazz tune that made Angela want to dance.

"Where shall we sit?" asked Anderson. "I usually like to hang out by the corner over there, so we can get a good view of the band and can talk amongst ourselves privately."

"Sounds good to me," said Frank, and the rest of the group agreed.

A maître d' escorted them to their desire table and helped them sit down. He brought over an extensive wine list and a few food menus. Anderson made some observations about the various types of wines offered, and in the end, conferring with Frank and Eric, made a few selections. The server brought the drinks over a few moments later and poured six glasses.

Angela was lost in the overwhelmingly enchanting music. She looked over at Anderson, who was also paying attention to the live band. She reached for his hand underneath the table and squeezed it. Anderson turned towards Angela and leaned in for a kiss. The two of them noticed that Frank and Amanda were also holding hands. Eric was talking softly to Tina, and Angela couldn't hear what they were saying. That was okay with her, because she was having such a good time getting lost in the moment.

"Is anyone hungry?" asked Anderson.

"I am, a little," said Tina.

"What would you like?" said Anderson, "I recommend the filet mignon, personally. It tastes great when cooked to medium-rare."

"Okay, I'll have that. Am I the only one eating?"

The others just ordered some hors d'oeuvres. They had roast squid, a rack of lamb, and several dozen raw oysters. It was the perfect amount of food and it satisfied everyone immeasurably.

"I wish they had dancing here," said Angela.

"We can always go somewhere after this that does," replied Anderson. "We don't have to stay here all night."

The group finished the bottle of wine that they were working on, and then ordered several more. Angela was getting more than tipsy. Between the shots in the limo and the wine, it was a wonder that she could see straight.

"Is everyone else as buzzed as I am?" asked Angela.

"I am getting there," said Eric, "but I could still have a few more drinks. Maybe a scotch or a brandy."

6

RELATIONSHIPS

The rest of the evening was fun and engrossing for everyone involved. As the evening wound down, Angela started drinking a lot of water so as to minimize the next day's hangover. When she awoke at 11:00 a.m., she was surprised to find herself in Anderson's apartment. As she sat up and looked around, she realized to herself that she had never really fully explored it. If it were anyone else's apartment, she wouldn't really have been so interested. But what did the apartment of a multi-billionaire look like?

Anderson was fast asleep next to her, lying on his stomach, and snoring softly. He was naked from the waist up. Angela got out of bed and walked around. The first room she noticed, apart from the bedroom, was the kitchen. It was positively enormous. The entire condo had over eight separate rooms. Three of them were bedrooms. The rest were giant closets, living rooms, and lounge areas.

There were three extremely large flat-screen TVs, and the sofas were of the finest Italian leather. She made her way back to the kitchen and opened up the freezer. She took out a tub of Ben & Jerry's vanilla ice cream and walked over to one of the living rooms, sitting down, and picking up the remote. She watched TV for about an hour. Anderson was still asleep. She decided to go wake him up.

She entered his bedroom, and then, pulling down his boxers, started to jerk off his erect cock. The cock hardened even further in her hands till eventually Anderson turned and woke up.

"I dreamed that I was being jerked off by a beautiful goddess. And that dream was accurate," said Anderson.

Angela threw off her bra and panties and climbed on top of him. They began making out and, as Anderson's hands felt their way all over her body, Angela could feel herself getting wet again. But she didn't want to have sex just then. She wanted Anderson to give her the complete tour.

"I poked around your place," she said. "It is quite lovely. Would you like to give me a more comprehensive tour?"

Anderson threw on a robe and walked into his huge closet. He found a blue cotton robe for Angela and handed it to her. Anderson proceeded to give her a tour of the entire condo. He explained the purpose of all the different rooms and drew her attention to the technology behind each room. Apparently there were voice commands that controlled things like dimming the lights and setting the temperature of each particular room.

"You are a wonder, my love," said Angela. "Say, Mom wants us to go bowling tonight. Are you still up for it?"

"Sure am," said Anderson, "but I need a few hours this afternoon to get some work done, so I will have to go into the office. You can have Pat drive you around to wherever you need in the meantime."

"Maybe I'll go visit Maxine and Henry and surprise them. I should probably check to see how Maxine is doing anyway. To make sure that she is recovering fully."

"Sounds like a plan."

Angela showered in one of Anderson's lavish bathrooms.

The shower itself was magnificent. The water pressure was very strong and the temperature controls were very subtle. Her shower was long and hot, and when she got out, her skin felt clean and moisturized (she had found some lotions in the shower to use).

She got dressed in the clothes that she had worn the night before and, kissing Anderson goodbye, made her way down to the sidewalk. Anderson had called Pat, who was waiting out front. He was leaning against the limo smoking a cigarette. When he spotted Angela, he promptly put it out and opened the door for her.

"Thank you," said Angela.

She directed Pat to Maxine's apartment. When she arrived, she buzzed up, and Maxine let her in. Angela could tell right away that Maxine was doing a lot better. It even looked as though she could start training again as quickly as possible.

"Are you feeling all better, then?" asked Angela.

"A million times better! Thanks again for helping to take care of me. I spoke to my trainer on the phone yesterday, and we are going to start preparations for the next tournament. It is going to be held in Paris."

"That's funny. Anderson is always talking about how they are expanding into France. They are going to be opening up a big office in Paris. Maybe the two of you could meet up there, or something."

"Maybe all of us could? If you could take time off work, it would be fun to see you over there. You should ask Frank. By the way, when do you start working for him?"

"I have one more week at the firm and by Monday of the following week I will be at the office of the treasury."

"Sounds great. I am so proud of you, Angela."

"How is Henry doing? I know he had to take some time off

work to take care of you, but is his practice getting back up to speed?"

"He had some subordinates take care of his projects while he was helping me. So I don't think it was much of a big deal."

Angela and Maxine gabbed away for a few more hours. They talked about romance, news, their careers, and families. Angela mentioned how she was going bowling that evening with her mom, Ben, Rosalie, and Sam. She invited Maxine to go too, but she couldn't come because she had a practice tennis session at the courts with her trainer. She needed to make up for lost time by training extra hard.

Angela called her mom to see when they were meeting for bowling. Karen told her that she thought 6:00 p.m. would be a reasonable time. That was when Rosalie and Sam were planning on being there. Angela realized that she was going to have to get home if she was going to change into more comfortable clothes, as she was still wearing her eveningwear.

Angela hugged and kissed Maxine, then left her apartment. Pat was gone, so she took a cab back home to her place. When she got out of the cab in front of her building, she ran into none other than Mark Stevenson.

"Okay, this is getting creepy," mused Angela. "I can't believe I am bumping into you here again! Get over here!"

Angela gave Mark a big, tight hug. Mark hugged back, his strong arms enveloping Angela's curvy frame.

"How are you, Angela? Are you busy?"

"I have bowling in a few hours with my family, but you can come up for a drink or a movie or something."

Mark nodded, and Angela took him by the hand and led him through the doors of her apartment building. When they got up to her room, Angela took off all her clothes.

"You aren't wasting any time, are you?" asked Mark.

"I need to get changed for bowling, silly. Did you think I was going to wear a dress to the bowling alley?"

"Why not? You'd attract every guy's attention there."

"I don't need to attract them. I have your attention. Don't I?"

Angela winked at Mark.

"Make yourself at home. Lounge on the couch, I am just going to throw a few things on. There are beers and some cheese in the fridge which you can help yourself to. How's business?"

"We are working on some exciting deals. Commission this year is going to be juicy. I'll probably clear well over six figures. And by well over, I mean at least two hundred to three hundred thousand. But I don't like to talk about business. Let's talk about how great your ass looks in those jeans."

Angela entered the living room wearing a pair of faded blue jeans and a dark purple hoodie. She was happy that Mark noticed how good she looked in regular, casual clothes, in addition to fancy garments.

"You think my ass looks great?" asked Angela rhetorically.

"You are the best fuck I've ever had. Honest truth."

Angela smiled to herself. That was one other thing she could pride herself on doing well. She scooted over to Mark and sat on his lap. She picked up the remote and started changing channels.

Mark's hands began to wander. They slipped under her hoodie casually and cupped both breasts. They were exactly as heavy and as perfectly shaped as he remembered. He kept them there for a while, squeezing and feeling their tenderness.

Angela began to rub Mark's penis through his pants. She loved the feel of his cock through his trousers. As she rubbed and tugged on it, it became ever harder. She undid his fly and let his cock fall loose. She continued to rub it for a while. Just as Mark was about to come, Angela fell to her knees and, placing her head on his lap, swallowed the full length of his shaft. Mark gripped the back of her head as he exploded into a monumental orgasm. There was so much cum, Angela didn't know if she could bear swallowing it all. But somehow she managed. She thought it tasted good.

She got up and sat down beside Mark on the couch. She looked over at Mark, who had a rather sleepy expression on his face. Angela let Mark lounge on the couch while she got up and did a few quick chores around the apartment. Her laundry needed to be folded and there were some dishes in the kitchen that needed to be done. It took about twenty minutes to finish up what she was doing, then she turned her attention to Mark.

"I am going to have to kick you out, hun," she said. "It's bowling time."

"No worries. I've got to get back to my place and do some paperwork. All these deal deadlines are coming up pretty fast. It was great seeing you though. You look just as beautiful as you always do."

Angela kissed Mark goodbye, then got on her phone and called her mom. She told her that she was on her way and should get to the bowling alley in good time. When she got there, she found Rosalie and Sam, who had already begun bowling and were halfway through their round. Rosalie was leading by a few points. When they saw Angela arrive, they put the game on pause and came over to give her a warm hug.

"I guess Mom and Ben haven't arrived yet?" asked Angela.

"Not just yet," replied Rosalie. "We got here about an hour early so we have just been playing some games. You know, to warm up. I hope you don't expect to kick our butts!"

Angela laughed.

"If you think I wouldn't expect such a thing, then you don't know me very well."

Sam laughed pretty hard, as did Rosalie, who punched her sister playfully in the arm.

"Come on," ventured Rosalie. "Let's add you to the game."

The three of them played for some time, until Karen and Ben arrived. Angela was very happy to meet Ben, who seemed like a great guy. As they bowled, Angela and Ben shared a special bond, as he told her a bunch of adventure stories from his exciting path. She concluded, as did Rosalie, that he was the perfect match for their deserving mother. Angela was also thrilled to see that he was a pretty good bowler. He came in first place in every round they played. After the fourth round, everyone became tired and decided to call it a day. They made their way to the restaurant that was in the bowling alley and ordered some soft drinks and fries.

Just then, Anderson showed up, wearing a loose-fitting white cotton shirt, some slightly baggy dark blue jeans, and tennis shoes.

7
WHAT SHE FEELS PART 4

The Meeting

Angela walked through the hall of her new office building. It was a gorgeous building; the carpets were brand new and a deep gray color. The exterior of the building was covered in floor to ceiling windows that were kept spotless by the two window cleaners on staff.

Her high heeled shoes were silent as she nonchalantly walked down the hall toward the conference room that was seldom used. The building had three conference rooms, each one grander and more lavishly decorated than the one before. She was going to the last conference room, the one that was outfitted with an oak table and ugly blue rolling computer chairs.

Twenty minutes ago, Anderson had sent her a text message that said only "Conference room C-20 minutes. Don't be late." Anderson was a very close friend of Frank's, her boss, and could sometimes get special permission around Angela's office building.

She reached the heavy mahogany door and wrapped her

thin fingers around the cold handle. She took a moment and wondered what Anderson had planned for her and why he wanted to meet with her in the middle of their workday. She and Anderson were both very busy people, and it was difficult enough for them to get away and meet after work, let alone at 12:00 p.m. on a Thursday.

She took a breath and swung the door open. Sitting across the table was Anderson. He was dressed in an exquisite navy blue suit, with a gray tie. Angela wasn't sure that she had ever seen him look quite as handsome as he did in that moment. His eyes seemed to shimmer in the light that streamed in through the windows, giving an impression that he was up to something.

"Hello, Angela." Anderson spoke. His voice had a tone that Angela had never heard him use with her. It was sexy and raspy, yet dominant and demanding.

"Hey, Anderson," Angela responded, trying to contrast his serious tone with a light and playful tone.

"Sit," he said.

Angela could tell that it was a command, not a question. She did as he asked and took a seat across from him. The chair seemed rickety and moved underneath the weight of her body. It made her slightly nervous to be sitting across from Anderson on a chair that she didn't trust. She imagined herself talking with him one moment, and the next sprawled out in a very unflattering way on the floor.

"Do you know why I've brought you here?"

"Not really, no."

"I would like to ask you a very serious question. This is not to be taken lightly, Angela."

"Okay, what is it?" Angela asked. Her heart sank into her stomach, but it seemed to light up at the same time. The question could be very good, or very bad. Anderson gave no clue with his facial expression. He was stoic and stared directly at Angela, making her feel that it was indeed a serious question.

"Would you like to go to dinner tomorrow night?" Anderson said. His face instantly split into a wide grin, knowing that he had fooled Angela.

"You jerk! You had me so worried. Of course I want to go to dinner with you. I'm thinking lobster." Angela said. Her harsh words were lessened in effect by the giggles that were emanating from her throat. She loved Anderson's sense of humor. Even though he was a multi-billionaire, he didn't let that get to him; he acted just like any man would.

"I could go for some lobster. That does sound nice. I'll let you know where we are going later. Pat and I will pick you up at eight. Be ready, Angela. I don't like to wait," Anderson said. The last two sentences were ringed with the same dominant tone as before.

She couldn't deny the fact that Anderson taking control of her made her panties start to grow wet with her delicious juices. She had always had a thing for being submissive to a strong, powerful man, and Anderson fit that description perfectly.

"Yes, sir!" Angela said in a joking tone.

In response to her words, Anderson's eyes fluttered to the back of his skull. He let out a sigh that hinted at his strong desire to have Angela.

Apparently he likes that, Angela thought to herself. She would have to remember that.

Without warning, Anderson rose from his chair. He pushed the chair away from him as he stood, sending it flying back into the wall behind him. A loud bang was audible throughout the room, and possible throughout the entire floor.

He walked around the table to Angela. He walked with purpose, taking long, powerful strides as he approached her.

When he was close enough for Angela to see the detail on his expensive suit buttons, he stopped abruptly.

"Get on your knees," he said. Just as before, it was a command; it wasn't a question.

Angela obeyed and sank to her knees, thankful for the thick walls surrounding them, except for the windows that made up the back wall. She could hear the sound of his zipper descending, losing the fight against containing the hard rod of his excitement.

He took a step closer, holding his throbbing cock in his hand. He entwined his hand in her long, thick, dark-colored hair and pulled her head closer to his manhood. She wrapped her soft, voluptuous lips around him and sucked gently. Apparently that wasn't enough for Anderson. He held her still as he rocked his hips in a gentle, rhythmic motion as he fucked her face.

Angela loved sucking Anderson's cock. She knew that she was starting to become his little whore, and she loved that fact. He had awoken a hidden sexuality that Angela hadn't known she had. It was as if he had reached into her soul and awoken the woman waiting there.

Anderson's long, thick cock hit the back of her throat, making her gag slightly. Not to the point of wanting to vomit; it was still a slightly uncomfortable feeling. Anderson withdrew his thick manhood from her mouth and gently slapped her cheek with his tool.

"That's my good girl," he cooed.

Without giving her a chance to reply, he silenced her with his thick cock once more. Angela let her tongue graze along the underside of his cock as he pushed into her mouth and subsequently withdrew, only to slam into her again.

Angela felt the heat of his milky white juice squirt into her mouth without warning. It felt thick and warm with a slightly salty taste as it sat on her tongue. She swirled her tongue around, savoring the taste and texture before she let it fall down the back of her throat. She looked at Anderson and smiled.

"Good girl. Get back to work, my little slut," Anderson said as he stroked her cheek gently with his hand.

Angela rose to her feet and felt the blood rush back into her legs. She glanced at her knees and saw the imprint of the carpet as red as lipstick on her knees. She knew that everyone in the office would know exactly what she had done in the conference room, and that fact turned her on even more. She kissed Anderson's lips and walked out without saying a word. The heavy door closed with an audible thud.

She walked back down the hallway, letting her hips sway with each step. The short, flirty skirt of her royal blue dress swished against her thighs. The silky fabric felt wonderful as it grazed her soft skin. She saw her coworkers looking at her, but she didn't care. She really liked Anderson, and was proud to be the one to give him a midday blowjob. She smiled and remembered the taste of his cum on her throat.

8

THE GAME

The vibrator buzzed in her pussy. There were two prongs: one in her tight pussy and one firmly placed against her clit. With every vibration, waves of pleasure radiated throughout her body.

"Which way, Angela?" Anderson demanded.

"Right, go right!" she exclaimed.

It was a game they were playing in the back of Anderson's brand-new Rolls Royce. Every time they approached an intersection, Angela had to guess which way they needed to go in order to get to the restaurant. It wasn't a fair game, in Angela's opinion, since Anderson had never told her where they were going. When she guessed correctly, he would reward her with a strong pulse of the vibrator that he was controlling from his cellphone. If she guessed incorrectly, he would withdraw the sensation to a low hum. If she happened to miss two turns in a row, Anderson would completely turn off the device, leaving her begging for more.

Anderson pulled Angela onto his lap with his strong arms. Angela could feel the ripples of muscle on his arms and abdomen as she sat on top of him. Of course, he had already pulled his thick cock out of the confines of his slacks. Angela could feel the hot liquid precum against her skin. She was already soaking wet, and her pussy was begging to have Anderson inside her.

"Angela, we are going to add something to our little game. I'm going to put my cock inside your ass. You must make me cum by the time we get to the restaurant. If you don't, I will keep teasing you all night, but I won't let you cum. I'll bring you right to the edge of ecstasy, my dear, only to snatch it away from your grasp."

Angela's reply was only a surprised moan as she felt the tip of Anderson's cock slip inside her ass. He spent no time warming her up before thrusting inside her. Angela's high heels dug into the black carpet as she thrust herself down onto Anderson's body, trying to bring him to orgasm before they arrived. She wanted to feel the sweet release of an orgasm, to be carried away on the tide of bliss.

"Which way?!" Anderson shouted.

"Straight." Angela moaned. The feeling of the vibrator mixed with the feeling of his thick cock stretching her walls with every thrust had firmly planted itself in her mind and temporarily took control of her cognitive function.

She felt the vibrator slow down to a low hum as the car turned to the left. She wished she could turn the vibrator back up to its fullest power, but that was up to Anderson. She was left to his mercy; she was completely under his spell. The vibrator thrummed gently against her clit, just enough to tease her but not give her the intense pleasure she craved.

She thrust herself harder and faster on Anderson's cock. It was slightly painful, but that only made her enjoy it more. Anderson moaned with each thrust on Angela's perfect ass, but he didn't sound close to an orgasm. She squeezed her muscles around his cock, attempting to milk the juice from him. She fucked him like it was the secret to eternal life. In this case, it was the key to having the orgasm she so desperately desired. It was kind of the same thing, in her mind.

Anderson pushed her hair away from her neck. He kissed her neck gently as he placed his hands on Angela's thighs, stopping her rhythmic thrusts.

"I'm sorry, darling. You failed. It looks like there will be no orgasm for you tonight. Maybe, if I feel generous, we can try again on the ride home. We will see if you truly deserve an orgasm."

Angela's heart sank. She felt that she needed to orgasm. Her clit throbbed and her pussy ached to be filled with his throbbing cock. She wanted to feel the ridge underneath the tip of his manhood slide inside her.

She lifted her ass from Anderson's lap and adjusted her panties. She went to take out the vibrating device, but Anderson demanded she leave it inside her. He turned it on to its fullest potential once more, making Angela moan accidentally.

Pat came around and opened her door. She looked at Anderson pleadingly.

"Get out of the car, Angela," he said sternly.

She obliged and stood on wobbly legs, the type that would be found on a baby deer instead of a grown woman. She took slow steps toward the restaurant, feeling the buzz against her clit with every step. She tried to walk normally and not give away her dirty secret. It was hard not to moan. She enjoyed the vibrations inside her, the eyes of all of the dinner guests, and the handsome man holding her hand and grinning madly beside her. They walked arm-in-arm together and walked underneath the awning of the expensive steak house.

9

DINING AND TEASING

As Angela sat down on the soft chair of the restaurant, the vibrator made it hard for her to sit down without moaning. There was something about the combination of sitting, movement, and the vibrator that was buzzing fullforce against her clit that made it difficult not to utter a sound of pleasure.

While Angela was struggling to contain herself, Anderson merely sat across the table with a content smile spread across his handsome face. It was obvious to Angela that he was enjoying watching her struggle to contain herself while he gave her a secret pleasure that only they knew was happening.

Angela had to admit that it was really an erotic situation. The vibrator thrumming against her clit sent shivers up and down her spine. She had to speak to the waiter without making any moans or sounds that might betray their secret. Couple that with Anderson sitting across from her and her ass still hurting from the game they had played in the Rolls Royce earlier, and it was a wonder that Angela was able to speak at all.

There was so much stimulation taking over her body. Every

sensation, every orifice, every pore of her body begged to be released into the sweet bliss of an orgasm. That decision was up to Anderson, however. There was nothing she could do to convince him to let her cum, unless she won the game on the way back to her apartment.

Anderson had started to become more dominant in their relationship, and Angela loved every moment of it. She had always had a fetish for being submissive to a man, but had never expressed that urge to anyone before now. She had always kept it buried down inside her like it was one of her vital organs—safe and protected from the eyes of the world.

With Anderson, however, she felt free to make her wants known. It seemed that he didn't need her to verbalize her desires; he just seemed to know what she wanted. He had a power over her, and it was beginning to seem that she had one over him.

"Hey!" Angela cried as the buzzing against her clit slowed to a medium hum.

"You weren't paying attention to me. That's what you get," Anderson said. His eyes looked like they had been forged from steel, and yet they were still gentle in a way.

"I'm sorry. I was just thinking."

"About what?" he asked.

"Maxine," she lied.

Anderson nodded. She could tell that he knew she was lying by the way one corner of his mouth tilted up as his head moved with the nodding motion. She hated lying to him, but this wasn't the time or the place to tell him about her desires.

The waiter came by their table to take their drink order. Angela had never been to a restaurant where the wait staff wore black suits the covered pristine white shirts. Anderson ordered a bottle of wine that was foreign to Angela.

The light from the candle on the center of the table flickered against Anderson's eyes, making them shine. With each flash of light, Angela could see the playful glint in his eye. Angela could tell that there was something rolling around inside Anderson's mind. He was thinking of something, but his facial expression gave no indication of what might be going on inside his mind. He just wore a pleasant, easy expression. His lips were curled into a smile that he seemed to be trying to conceal, and his eyes were wrinkled at the corners.

The thrum inside her wet pussy shot up from a hum that was low and gentle to a strong vibration that made her muscles clench the moment it shot up. Angela couldn't hold back the quiet moan that escaped her lips.

The waiter came back to their table holding a bottle of wine. The bottle seemed black in the dim lighting of the restaurant. The blackness of the bottle was split in half by a dark green label that was accented by cursive words that were written in a recessed gold font. The words shimmered in the flickers of the candle light.

The waiter placed the wine into a metal bucket full of ice and rolled it back and forth between his palms, making the ice clink against the bottle and the metal bucket. The entire time the waiter stood next to their table, Anderson kept playing with the controls. He had it set at a sort of wave pattern. The intensity would slowly rise until it was at full force. It would stay at that intensity for a few moments and then it would begin to decrease, leaving Angela wishing the sensation wouldn't leave her clit.

After the waiter left their table, Anderson reached for the bottle and pulled it out of the bucket. Ice cascaded off the glass surface of the bottle and made a tinkling sound as it filled in the space where the bottle had been just seconds before.

He lifted the bottle and poured himself a glass. He asked Angela to lift her glass so that he could pour the sweet wine into her glass. With the vibration thrumming inside her body, she was unable to hold the glass still. Instead, her hand shook uncontrollably. The impact of the glass against the bottle made a distinct clinking sound. Anderson had a mischievous smile, knowing exactly the effect he was having on Angela.

10

REDEMPTION

As soon as Pat closed the door of the Rolls Royce, Angela lifted her skirt and pulled down her silky panties. She could see that Anderson had not lost his erection from the car ride earlier. It could have been the control he had held over her body as well as her mind, or it could have been the anticipation of the ride home. Angela wasn't sure what had caused it, but she honestly didn't care. She had been fantasizing about getting on his cock the second they got back into the car.

Now that her panties were lying on the floor of the car, she focused her attention on Anderson. She slowly undid the various fastenings of his slacks. The fabric felt smooth and expensive as she slid her palms across the slick fabric. She hooked her fingers underneath the waistband and pulled them until they were lying in a crumpled pile on the floor of the car.

Her mouth was instantly wrapped around the tip of his thick cock. She pushed her head down until her nose touched the skin that covered his pubic mound. She sucked hard; it was as if she were trying to milk his cock with her mouth. She had a quick, easy rhythm with her sucks. She took turns focusing on the head and the base. At first, she would suck the tip of his cock until her lips wrapped around the shaft, making him utter a loud moan. Then she would press her head down onto the base of his cock, taking him into her mouth until the entire length of his cock was inside her lips and the tip was down the back of her throat.

Anderson entangled his fingers inside Angela's dark hair. She could feel his tight grip that pulled her hair, sending a slightly painful sensation radiating through her nerves. The pain only served to arouse her more. Anderson pushed her head down and then pulled it back up so that her lips were soft against the tip.

Without warning, Angela rose from the carpet. Her knees found the leather of the seat as she straddled Anderson's lap. She wrapped her arms around his neck and kissed him passionately as she teased his cock with her pussy. Her fingers traced his muscles as she worked her way down his chest and abdomen. When her hand found the swell of his cock, she wrapped her fingers around the tool and rubbed the tip across her wet slit.

Anderson looked at her with pleading eyes. It was as if the tables had turned. He was the one begging for an orgasm. When Angela felt that they had both had enough teasing, she held his cock still and slammed herself down onto his cock. Their moans resonated in unison. Anderson turned the vibrator to a medium speed and kept it inside her.

Angela held onto Anderson's shoulders as she rose and fell on Anderson's stiff erection. She felt him stretching the walls of her pussy and hitting her cervix with each movement. She squeezed her pelvic muscles and heard a low moan escape his lips. She kissed him in the middle of his moan, silencing him.

She enjoyed being in control for the time she had the power, but it was short-lived. Anderson took control of her body as he lifted her and set her down on the seat next to him.

"Lie down," he commanded.

Angela did as he said. She sat against the cold leather of the seat and spread her legs wide open with the vibrator that started in her pussy and wrapped to her clit still firmly in place. Anderson wasted no time inserting himself into her soaking wet orifice.

"You were a very good girl during dinner, so I'm going to change the rules a little bit. I'm going to let you cum."

With that, he began to fuck Angela like she had never been fucked before. It felt like there was a deep-seated hunger inside him that could not be satiated until he shot his semen inside her. His hands felt hot against her skin as he held her thighs to his chest, opening her up even more.

Angela started to feel the familiar feeling of an orgasm welling up inside her. It felt like a warm wave that started in her toes and flew through every nerve, making their synapses fire rapidly. She felt that she wouldn't be able to hold back the orgasm that had been building inside her body for hours. She longed to feel the orgasm take control of her mind and her body, to feel as if she were floating on a loud of bliss for a few moments.

Anderson gave her a few more thrusts that were strong and forceful and enough to send Angela spiraling into the oblivion of the most intense orgasm she had felt thus far in her life. The orgasm completely consumed her, making her incapable of thought or focusing on anything but the waves of pleasure full sensations that were rolling through her body.

It seemed that sending Angela over the edge was just enough to bring Anderson to orgasm as well. Angela felt as the hot liquid filled her orifice. Anderson's eyes rolled to the top of his eyelids, making it apparent that he was feeling the same sensations that Angela had felt moments before. She could feel his thighs tremble against her own.

Anderson leaned down and kissed Angela lightly. He laughed and kissed her again. She felt his hand travel up her body, tickling her skin in the process. Anderson ran his fingers through Angela's silky hair. Angela's eyes closed as she enjoyed the gentle sensation. She felt more content and happy than she ever had before. Even with Mark, there had always been something missing. She could never figure out exactly what was lacking, but it was undeniable that there was something missing.

With Anderson, she had never felt that anything was missing. Their sex was incredible. He treated her like a lady in the streets and his personal slut in the sheets. He was very kind and generous toward her. He treated her like she was the only woman in the world, let alone in the room.

11

GIRL TALK

Angela sat down on the couch. The velvety fabric felt nice against the parts of her legs that weren't covered by her denim shorts. Maxine held her arm out and offered Angela the bowl of popcorn. She indulged and took a large handful of the fluffy popped kernels that were slathered with butter. As she ate them, they melted on her tongue with a slightly salty tang.

On the television was a movie about a woman who had been locked in an insane asylum against her will. It was on one of those women's entertainment channels. The girls were only half paying attention to the melodrama, however. The topic of conversation was how Angela felt about Anderson and about Mark.

"I don't know, Maxine. They really are great men."

"Except one is your ex. Ex's are ex's for a reason, Angela."

"I know, but he feels different somehow."

"Does he really, or do you just want him to be different this time?"

Angela had no answer. She was stunned by the truth that her friend might have revealed. It was as if Maxine had stumbled onto a part of Angela's mind that she hadn't been aware existed. Her words went right to her soul.

"I wish I had an answer, Maxine. I really do."

"I think you do know. I think you just don't want to admit it to yourself. I think you know that you need to stop seeing Mark. You have a really good thing going with Anderson. Why not throw out the old and welcome the new? I know that's what is holding you back from fully committing to him."

"I don't know, Maxine. I really do like Anderson, but I can't shake the feeling that there might still be something there with Mark."

"That's your choice; I can't make it for you," Maxine said quietly, "Pass the popcorn, please."

Angela moved the bowl closer to Maxine. She had to admit that she had been clutching the bowl of popcorn like she was somewhat of a popcorn hoarder. Maxine was her best friend, and she knew that she was only looking out for Angela. Nonetheless, she couldn't help but feel that she was trying to force Angela into making a decision that she wasn't sure she wanted to make.

She couldn't deny that there was at least a little bit of truth in what Maxine had said. It could be entirely possible that Mark truly was holding her back from fully committing to Anderson. She didn't hold back sexually, but she had to admit to herself that she was actually holding out emotionally. She wanted to have Anderson in every way possible, and she was pretty certain that he felt exactly the same way.

Angela trusted Maxine more than she trusted herself at times, but it was hard to trust her about whether or not she should give up on Mark. Mark hadn't been the worst boyfriend, but he definitely wasn't the best either. Sure, she felt strongly for Anderson, but she also had some remaining feelings for Mark.

It was glaringly apparent to her that soon she would have to make a decision about which man she would choose, and she would have to choose soon. It wasn't fair to the men to keep them in limbo like they were at that moment. Mark was lingering in her heart, and Anderson was quickly forging his way into her heart and her mind.

"How are you feeling?" Angela asked Maxine.

"I'm really feeling a lot better. I'm still not completely better, but the doctors say I have nothing to worry about and I am on my way to a complete and full recovery."

"That's good! I'm glad to hear that."

"Well, I am too, but I just can't shake the feeling that they're either lying to me or they're wrong."

"Why?"

"I'm really not sure, Angela. I just feel like the sickness is hibernating. Like it isn't really gone."

"I'm sure you'll be fine."

"I really hope so, Angela. I really do," Maxine said with tears beginning to well behind her eyes.

Angela's heart felt that it was in the grip of a very strong clamp. She could tell how worried Maxine was about her illness returning. Her worry inspired worry in Angela. She wondered what would happen if Maxine fell ill again. She wasn't sure if she could really handle that again. She had been so worried about her friend when she was sick before, and she knew that it would only be magnified if she fell sick once again.

She tried to put the worry out of her mind and enjoy the time she had with Maxine. It wasn't often that they were able to just have a girls' night in and watch television and eat fattening foods together. They were both very busy women, and it could be hard to make time for each other. She made a promise to herself right there in that moment that she would make a decision about the men in her life, and she would spend a lot more time with Maxine.

"Well, I have to get going," Maxine said.

"Oh, so soon? Come on, stay a little longer."

"I really can't! I've got to go home and start dinner."

"Oh, all right. Just leave me to stew in my misery."

"What misery? You seem pretty happy to me."

"I'm miserable because I want Chinese food for dinner, but I don't like any places that deliver. Leaving my apartment is completely out of the question. The couch has accepted me as one of its own and I just can't betray that trust right now."

Maxine threw a pillow at Angela. They both stood up from the couch and walked toward the door. They shared an embrace that was more than just a hug. It seemed that both of the girls were holding on to each other as if it they the only thing keeping each other alive. Angela kissed her friend on the cheek and told her that she loved her. Maxine pulled away and took Angela's hand. She squeezed it gently and walked out of the open door.

12

PLANS

Angela heard the tell-tale sound of the upbeat music radiating from the drawer of her desk. She slid the door open and pulled out her cellphone. She smiled when she saw that it was Anderson calling her.

"Hello?"

"Hey, beautiful. What are you doing?"

"I'm just working. What are you doing, flying around the world?"

"No, no, no," Anderson laughed. "Certainly not flying anywhere. I'm sitting in my office being buried by a stack of papers and thinking about this amazing, beautiful, sexy woman I've been seeing."

"Who is she? I'll fight her." Angela said. She was playing coy; she knew that Anderson was talking about her.

"Whoa there, tiger. She's you," Anderson laughed. "Here's the reason I called: what are you doing tomorrow?"

"I'm just working."

"Not anymore. I have already spoken with Frank and he is going to give you paid time off tomorrow. He is really impressed with you, Angela."

"He's given me time off? Why?"

"Because I asked."

"Well, what are we going to do?"

"I thought we could have a date with our clothes on for once. I'm going to pick you up at 9 in the morning, and then the rest of the day will be a complete surprise."

"That does sound nice. I'm not sure I'll be able to keep my hands off of you, though."

"We can always make up for lost time after the date."

"That's true. Oh, Anderson, I have to go. My work phone is ringing and I really have to answer it."

"That's why Frank loves you! I understand, doll. I'll see you in the morning."

Anderson hung up the phone, and Angela answered her. It was a boring business call. A client wanted to ask her if they had received her fax of an inconsequential document that they really didn't need.

The moment she hung up the phone, her mind instantly began churning the conversation and dissecting it into little tiny parts. She was sure that Anderson had something in his mind, and that it would be something to remember. He had said that he wanted to have a date with her with their clothes still on their bodies.

She had really been wanting to get to know Anderson on a deeper level, and she guessed that he felt the same. She had gotten to know Anderson's body more than his mind, and she really wanted to know more about him. Whatever Anderson had in mind for her, she knew she would enjoy. He was a billionaire, after all.

The rest of the day seemed to drag on; her mind was consumed by Anderson and his plan for the next day. Every time she faxed a paper or answered her phone, she did it with only half of her mind. Sure, she made a few mistakes, but nothing anyone would notice. She corrected her errors quickly. The rest of her wandered to what the next day would bring.

She imagined them going to a different city than where they lived. She could almost smell the salty air that would blow against her skin and through her hair. The restaurant would have a pot-bellied man singing sweet, gentle music in thick Italian language.

Of course, that was only her dream. She knew that what Anderson had planned would probably not be quite as lavish as her imagination, but it probably wasn't far off. She knew that the next day would be full of fun and excitement.

LATER THAT NIGHT, Angela climbed into her bed. The foam mattress cupped her body and made her feel cradled. Her dark blue satin sheets felt luxurious against her tanned skin. Her pillow only added to her comfort. She wasn't sure that she had ever felt more comfortable in all of her life. As she burrowed into her nest of sheets and blankets, she thought that only one thing would make her more comfortable.

She wanted Anderson in bed next to her. She wanted to feel his strong arms wrapped tightly around her chest. She didn't necessarily want him in a sexual way (not that she would mind that), but instead she just longed to feel him next to her. She wanted Anderson in every way possible. She wanted him to take control of her body and her mind; she wanted him to take all of her and leave her completely speechless.

She wondered if Anderson was thinking of her, too. She really wished that they were able to see each other more, but she knew that that just wasn't possible for them at that moment. Anderson had a busy life with his company, and things were just picking up for Angela.

Of course, now her time would be even tighter with Maxine

not feeling well again. The way Maxine had spoken the other day had really worried her about her friend. She hoped that nothing bad would happen to her, but nonetheless, Angela worried that her friend might be right. That terrified her.

Angela readjusted her head on her pillow. She found just the right spot where her head was at the perfect angle and in perfect alignment with her body. In that moment, all of her stress and her worries melted away. She was carefree and blissfully happy.

The last thought Angela had as she was falling asleep was of Anderson holding a bouquet of flowers. She drifted off to a deep, restful sleep, with not a care in the world.

13

DESTINATION: UNKNOWN

The next morning, Angela woke up before the sun. She pulled the blankets tighter around her body and tried to squeeze out a few more moments of sleep. Her mind, however, had different plans for her. Her mind fired rapidly with thoughts of what the day held in store for her. She knew that the day would be great and exciting, of course, but she was really excited to spend the day with Anderson away from the hustle and bustle of the city.

After about an hour of fighting for more sleep, Angela gave up trying. She pushed back her cocoon of blankets and silk sheets and felt the cold rush of morning air surround her skin. She rubbed her eyes sleepily and stretched her arms behind her head.

After her shower, Angela walked to her closet. She looked through the racks of clothing that were expensive by her standards and pauper clothes by Anderson's. She knew that Anderson really wouldn't care what she wore, but she wanted to look nice regardless.

She chose a pair of denim shorts with a triangular white lace cutout that went up to mid-thigh. She always felt cute and flirty in them. She wasn't trying to be overly sexy in the outfit; she really wanted this to be a day that she and Anderson would look back on and have fond memories of in the future.

Her feet slid into the soft faux leather of the strappy sandals with small, delicate white beads sewn onto the straps that wrapped around her ankles and down the middle of her foot until it met the faux leather between her toes. Of course, she had had a pedicure a few days ago that had left her feet feeling smooth and soft, and her toenails were painted a bright blue.

She walked down the hallway of her apartment; her footfalls were silenced by the soft, luxurious carpet covering the hard surface underneath until her foot found the hard beige tile of the kitchen. She walked over to the pantry and removed the loaf of bread. She put one piece of bread inside each slot and pressed the plastic slider.

While she waited for her breakfast to pop out of the small metal toaster, she jumped up and slid onto the counter top. She softly swung her freshly-waxed legs—tanned to look like she spent her days on an island—against the cabinets below her. She couldn't get her mind off Mark and Anderson.

Mark had only sent her one text in the last week, and Anderson had called her a few times each day, taken her to dinner, and was now taking her to a mysterious location. She still had feelings for Mark, she had to admit, but she started to feel that Anderson was quickly beginning to dominate her feelings, her mind, and her time. The thing that scared her the most was that she was perfectly okay with that.

The sound of the toast popping up from the toaster caught her off-guard and made her jump slightly. Angela hopped off of the counter where she had been sitting and went to the toaster. The toast felt very hot against her thin, freshly-manicured fingers as she laid it on the counter. She opened the refrigerator that was next to the counter and pulled out the butter and jelly.

While she ate her breakfast, she started to become more nervous about the day than she'd been when she had been getting dressed. She couldn't help but wonder what Anderson had planned for her.

Am I dressed in the wrong clothes? Is he going to take me somewhere nice, have a great day, and then tell me that he isn't interested in me any longer? Will we be going to the next state over and see the mountains, or will we go to the beach? Maybe we will go to a different city, Angela thought, the questions racing through her mind one right after another.

There came a point in the morning where she decided that she would just have to turn off her mind and just embrace whatever the day would bring. If she knew Anderson, which she did, she had a feeling that he would ensure that she had a really great day that was full of fun and laughter.

She heard Pat arrive outside of her apartment. She knew that in just a few seconds, he would walk to her door and she would hear his signature light knock. His knocks were always easy and light, with a sort of rhythmic melody behind them.

The knocks came just as Angela had expected. It seemed that Pat was always in a hurry, but he never appeared that way. He was always easy and gentle with a calm presence. His knocks were gentle; he took the time to help Angela into the car; and he was always extremely careful when driving. He was definitely on a tight schedule, though. He always arrived at exactly the right moment. If he was told to arrive at nine in the morning, he would pull up at 8:59 a.m. every time.

Angela threaded her arm though the faux-leather strap of her purse and felt the weight rest on her shoulder. She walked around the corner to her living room and examined herself one last time in the floor-length mirrors that were on the wall behind her dining table.

She really liked what she saw in her reflection. Her dark hair fell around her shoulders in perfect, easy waves. It looked like she had spent very little time on her hair; it was effortless and flowing. Her cleavage peeked over the top of her coral tank-top, giving just a hint of sexuality. Her thin frame truly looked great in the outfit. The shorts clung to her slender hips, accentuating her hourglass figure. Her tanned legs traveled down to the simple sandals.

She really hoped that she was dressed properly for wherever Anderson was taking her. They could be going somewhere slightly colder, or they could be going somewhere warmer. She had dressed hoping that they would be going somewhere warm, and not going to the mountains. Sure, the mountains were beautiful, but Angela longed to feel the rays of the sun warming her skin.

She decided that she had spent enough time looking at herself in the mirror. She turned and walked toward the door where Pat had knocked moments before. She flipped the light switch to the off position and opened the door.

"Hello, Pat."

"Hello, Miss Angela. Are you ready to go?"

"Yeah, I am. Hey, Pat, can you tell me where we are going?"

"No, I can't. Mr. Anderson has specifically told me not to disclose any information about the day. I will tell you, however, that you will have a really great time."

"Darn. Well, okay. Let's go."

Angela stepped outside and pulled the door shut behind her. She fastened the lock, and then placed her hand on top of Pat's waiting palm.

14

AWAY FOR A DAY

The warm breeze blew through her hair. She could smell the salt from the sea as she inhaled. The sound of the waves crashing against the sand mingled with the laughter of children and the live band that was playing a lively Spanish song. The hot sand felt wonderful beneath her feet as she scrunched and relaxed her toes. She lifted her margarita and took a sip, tasting the sweet alcoholic drink as it filled her mouth. She looked out into the water and saw Anderson enjoying the water. The waves licked his body and receded, leaving his skin glistening in the process. Every ridge of muscle was accentuated, every ray of sunshine shining off of his tanned skin.

The blue bikini looked great on her body. When they had arrived at the beach, Anderson had immediately taken her to a bikini shop that Angela could never have afforded on her own. The shop had smelled of coconut, and she had been sure that all of the employees were models.

She had tried on several bikinis and showed each one to Anderson. Every bikini that she tried was more expensive than the last. Of course, to Anderson, money was absolutely no problem. They had finally chosen a bikini that was blue lace over beige cups. The bottom of the set matched the top, but the sides had slits that ran from the top to the bottom. It was a bikini that radiated sexuality.

Anderson stepped out of the ocean and dripped water. He ran his hand through his hair in a seductive way and kept walking toward Angela. He didn't say a word when he reached her chair; he just bent down and picked her up.

Angela shrieked playfully and told him to put her down as Anderson carried her toward the water. The ocean water was crystal clear beneath her when they reached the shore line. When Anderson got to an area that was about waist deep, he stopped suddenly. The water was cold as Anderson dropped Angela into the ocean. She held her breath as her head was submerged.

As she rose to her feet, her hair felt wet and stringy down her back. Anderson looked at her as he laughed a full-bellied laugh. His smile crept into his eyes, making him look truly happy.

"You jerk!" Angela said. As she ran her fingers through her hair, she could feel the salt from the sea water.

Anderson didn't say anything. He just lifted Angela and pulled her to his body. She wrapped her legs around his hips and her arms encircled his neck. She kissed his lips gently amid their shared laughter. It was really a great feeling, being pressed against the man who was taking over her heart while the sun of the beach warmed her skin. She wasn't sure that she had ever felt as content as she was in that moment. It was as if everything in her life was absolutely perfect.

Anderson started walking deeper into the ocean. His grip around her waist tightened as she tried to get away. She was laughing, and he was grinning. They both knew what was coming. Anderson's legs flew out beneath him as he sank to the bottom of the ocean, submerging both of them in the process.

Later that evening, Angela took a sip of her sweet red wine. Anderson sat on the other side of the table and looked at her as if she were the only woman on Earth. The ocean air filled her nostrils, and the soft music of the Italian band enchanted her ears. Angela was glad she had put her clothing back on. As the sun sank behind the ocean, the air turned slightly chilly.

There was a red and white table cloth spread over the table, giving it the feel of a traditional Italian restaurant. In the center of the table, on top of a square mirror, was a tall white candle. It gave the restaurant a very romantic atmosphere.

Woven among the wooden planks that held up the awning were some white twinkle lights. It continued down to the railing and wove around the railing and around the spindles that ran to the ground. It was one of the most romantic restaurants she had ever seen.

Anderson smiled at her from across the table and placed his hand on the table. Angela placed her hand in Anderson's. The feeling of his thumb running across the skin on the back of her hand felt like it was made of a charged electric wire. She couldn't help the smile that spread across her face.

Suddenly Anderson bolted up from his seat and walked around to where Angela was sitting. He held out his hand and asked Angela to dance. Of course, she accepted the offer and allowed herself to be pulled onto the dance floor.

They embraced each other as they danced slowly underneath the twinkling lights that were woven through the ceiling. Anderson looked deeply into Angela's eyes, making her feel like she was an absolute treasure that Anderson had spent his life searching for.

As they twirled around the dance floor, Angela felt that her heart might burst right out of her chest. She felt so full of affection for Anderson, but she wasn't sure if she was ready to say that she loved him. He reached up and pushed a wayward strand away from her face and tucked it behind her ear. As he withdrew his hand, he gently ran his fingers down her cheek.

Angela leaned toward Anderson and kissed him deeply. It was as if their kisses were what were keeping them alive. They were deep and passionate. She laid her head on Anderson's chest as they swayed to the music of the band.

IN THE CAR, Anderson wrapped his arm around Angela. The arm was behind her shoulder and traced gentle patterns on her shoulder with light touches. Her head was nuzzled against the base of his neck. She felt safe and protected with Anderson, like he would never allow anything bad to happen to her. Until this point in time, she had never been treated so well by any man that she had dated.

Anderson gently kissed the top of her head. Angela started to feel the sweet lullaby of sleep edging slowly into her mind. She knew that it was pointless to fight it off; she would succumb whether she wanted to or not. The rocking motion of the car certainly didn't help matters, either.

15

MORNING SEX

The next morning, Angela woke up in a bed that was not hers. The luxurious sheets felt soft against her skin, and the white down comforter felt heavy and thick against her skin. The light streaming in through the curtains illuminated the room, making it apparent that she was in Anderson's bedroom.

She heard noises coming from the kitchen, but she couldn't hear if it was Anderson or one of his staff members. She pushed the comforter off of her and placed her feet on the floor. She recognized the clothes she was wearing; she had pointed at them once when Anderson had taken her shopping.

It was a simple pink nightie that came just to the bottom of her perfect ass. Underneath, she had the matching pink silk shorts. They really didn't offer much more coverage, only coming a few inches below the bottom edge of the nightie. She stood up and felt the soft carpet envelop her feet. She walked silently down the hallway toward the kitchen.

Standing at the counter dressed in only plaid pajama pants was Anderson. He was standing in front of a waffle iron, making breakfast.

"Hey, sleepyhead," Anderson said with a smile.

"Good morning," Angela said, as she walked into Anderson's open arms.

He kissed the top of her head as he held her close to his body. She could feel the heat radiating from his skin. She tilted her head to meet his lips. Their kisses started slowly and gently, almost as if they were timid. Anderson's hands traced her spine and found her supple ass. He cupped it and gently squeezed the curves.

Angela could feel his cock begin to stiffen and press against her thigh. She had almost forgotten how large his penis was. Their kisses started to become more passionate than they had been previously. It was as if they needed each other, like they would die if they didn't have one another soon.

He started to kiss her neck, sucking and biting gently in the process. As Anderson teased her skin, she started to feel her body respond. It was like his kisses electrified her body and left her begging for more.

Angela felt that it was time. She sank to her knees. On the way down, she gave Anderson's pants a quick yank, freeing his large, swollen cock. She wasted no time. She licked his cock, making it throb as she worked her tongue up and down the shaft. She could feel his cock begin to twitch with the sensation of her tongue traveling down the sensitive skin of his prick.

"Enough. Stand up," Anderson demanded.

"Yes, sir," Angela replied as she carried out the orders.

She stood, just as he had commanded, and was greeted by Anderson taking a fistful of her hair. He brought her lips to his in a forceful way before pulling her head back. She looked at him and saw that the dominant glean had returned to his eyes, making her feel that perhaps this was his normal state of being.

He released her hair from his grip and let his hands wander

over her soft, smooth skin. He pulled her sleep shorts off of her thin frame, and picked her up. He lifted her just as he had yesterday in the ocean. She wrapped her legs around his waist, but this time it was different.

As she formed herself to his body, she felt the swell of his cock enter her. He wasted no time in warming up her wet pussy, but instead began taking her hard and fast. That was exactly what Angel had longed for at that moment. She didn't want any sweet, tender lovemaking; she wanted hard and fast fucking.

Anderson walked to the wall by the refrigerator and held her against the wall. He captured her hands in his and held them against the wall above her hands. It was as if Angela was completely immobilized. She felt that she absolutely could not go anywhere or get away from Anderson even if she tried. Of course, she didn't want to get away. She was enjoying his cock pummeling her pussy far too much to want it to end.

With her pegged against the wall, Anderson was able to get much deeper inside her pussy. Every time he was inside her, Angela felt as though his cock was too thick for her tight pussy. She felt that he would rip right through her.

Anderson let go of her hands and instead held her legs. Angela couldn't remember a time that she had ever been fucked as hard as she was in that moment. Suddenly, she started moaning in orgasm. She hadn't felt it growing inside her, but instead it took her by complete surprise.

Anderson's orgasm followed hers, but it was no less intense. His face wrenched in pleasure as a deep moan resonated in his chest and emanated from his throat. He too felt the sweet release of an orgasm, sending his hot liquid deep inside Angela. He kissed her, both of their chests rising and falling in rapid succession, only to be out raced by their heart beats.

"I'm sure the waffles are burnt to a crisp. Do you want to go out to get breakfast?" Anderson asked as her feet touched the floor once more.

"That sounds good to me," Angela said through her laughter.

16

MAXINE TO THE RESCUE

"Maxine, I have a problem."
"Admitting it is the first step."
"Ha, ha, Maxine, very funny."

Angela felt the hot water surround her feet as the pedicurist filled the basin. She added some soft petals and sweet smelling salts to the bath of hot water and then left Angela and Maxine alone.

"This feels amazing, Angela. It seems like it's been forever since we have had a girls' day."

"It really does, Maxi."

"So, what's this problem you seem to have?"

"I think I am starting to fall in love."

"Ooh, with who?" Maxine cooed.

"Anderson."

"I had a feeling it was him. He seems like a really nice man, Angela, but what are you planning to do about Mark?"

"That's the problem. If I didn't have real feelings for Mark as well, this wouldn't really be an issue. The problem is, I do still have feelings for him. It isn't like I can just choose one or the other, but I really need to, and soon. It's not fair to anyone. I can't keep them waiting in this purgatory-like state. It's not fair. It's not fair to me to be so unsure about which man I want most."

"That's all really true, Angela. I'm glad you're going through this and not me, to be honest."

"Thanks, Maxine. Your words are really sweet," Angela said in a sarcastic tone. She knew that her friend was just being playful, so she didn't take any offense from her words. She knew that her friend really had her best interest at heart.

"Be honest, Angela. Do you favor one more than another?"

"Well, of course I do."

"That's the one you should choose."

"But how do I know that things are really over with Mark?"

"You have to make that decision. Do you really want to keep going around in circles with him? It never seems to end. One minute you're together, and then a few hours later you're crying on the floor, feeling absolutely heartbroken. I really don't want to see you go through that anymore, Angela. You deserve so much better than that. You know you do."

"You're right. I know you're right. You're always right, Maxine. It's just so much easier to listen to advice than to actually follow it."

"I'm sure it's easier than living in limbo."

"I'll let you know when I make a choice."

At that moment, the women doing their pedicures came back. The young woman lifted Angela's foot out of the basin of water and began to scrub away the dead skin and callouses on the sole of her foot. She wished that the woman could scrub hard enough to take her problems away, or at least make the decision easier.

Of course, the pedicurist wasn't a magician, and she wasn't able to make the decision for her. Angela thought about asking the woman, but she thought that the woman might think she was crazy.

Angela had no choice but to try and figure out the answer on her own. She sat in the pedicure chair, and while she was supposed to be relaxing, she could think of nothing but Mark and Anderson. She had actually started to compare them in her mind, as if that would help her make a choice.

Anderson is rich and Mark is just above being broke all the time. Mark is interested in a lot of the same things that I am, and Anderson has expensive tastes that I can't relate to yet. Anderson is new and exciting; Mark is safe and familiar. Mark is an ex-boyfriend, and Anderson is quickly becoming the boyfriend I want more than anything.

Angela fought within herself. Her mind was at war, each side firing invisible cannons at the other.

The woman picked up the gray nail polish that Angela had chosen earlier. As she watched the woman roll the bottle between her palms, she imagined she was inside the tiny bottle. That's how it felt; it was as if her mind and her body were spinning quickly through turmoil.

Her mind raced, quickly shifting between thoughts of Mark, and of Anderson. The choice she would have to make was becoming clearer to her with every turn of the bottle. She knew that she would have to make her choice soon.

She could sense something in her interactions with Anderson that made it apparent that he was getting sick of waiting. She knew he wanted her in every way, in every sense of the word. He wanted to have complete control over her, and she wanted the same thing.

As the woman painted the thick, opaque varnish onto her toenails, it was as if the manicurist was sealing in her decision, making her unable to change her mind. She had chosen Anderson over Mark. Now, she had to find a way to break the bad news to Mark, and to tell Anderson that she was finally his.

17

WHAT SHE CHOSE PART 5

Angela couldn't deny that Anderson was actually showing her a lot of patience. Though she didn't know every little thing about him yet, she did know that in his business endeavors he had never really been what you would consider a patient man. Anderson was a strong, powerful alpha male type of man who was used to getting what he wanted and getting it when he wanted it.

She had to admit to herself that she was starting to feel a bit guilty for keeping him somewhat on hold, and she was afraid to think about what might possibly happen if he decided he was tired of waiting for her to make up her mind be totally and completely dedicated to him and only him.

Angela knew that Anderson was no fool, nor was he blind, either. She had to assume that he knew about her dealings with Mark, and she was impressed by the fact that he had yet to bring up the subject, but she also knew deep down, that no man, especially a dominating billionaire alpha male, would actually want to share his woman with another man—unless, of course, it was a man that Anderson himself had invited into the equation.

Ever since the night that he had introduced Angela to the

alcohol-induced foursome she had experienced with him and that couple he was friends with, he had not yet again invited another man—or woman—to join them in their erotic sexcapades. Perhaps he was enjoying having her all to himself for the time being (well, almost all to himself) as Angela was still fighting with herself over her undying feelings for Mark.

Angela was allowing those thoughts to fill her mind as she got ready for work on Monday morning. She had thoroughly enjoyed the time she had been spending with Anderson, and he was certainly working his way into her heart. She couldn't deny that she was also a little bit scared that her fling with Anderson would end up being just that: a fling.

A part of her was still worried that a man like Anderson, handsome, wealthy, and dominant, could have any woman in the world. Why was he so infatuated with her? What was it about her that attracted him? She had been too afraid to come right out and ask him, as she figured that maybe he did this type of thing with other women. Maybe he would set his sights on one that he was attracted to, and then once he tired of her, he'd move on to a new one.

Deep down, Angela hoped that it wasn't true. She could see herself falling head over heels for him, but their unequal social statuses did cause her to worry about whether or not she was woman enough to keep a man like Anderson all to herself. Could she really keep him happy for the rest of his life? Would he really be completely dedicated to her and only her? Or would he eventually tire of her and move on to a new, more exciting woman as soon as Angela decided to dedicate herself to him completely?

All of these thoughts were swirling around Angela's mind as she headed toward the office. It was really great and exciting to always look forward to work, to look forward to seeing Anderson nearly every day. It was also a bit intimidating to think about how weird things could become if Anderson did someday tire of her. Would he still be cordial and sweet, even if he decided to break things off with her? Or would things get so weird around here that she would have to find another job elsewhere?

Angela shook her thoughts from her mind as she approached the parking area for the building employees. She knew she needed to clear her head and focus her thoughts on work—at least for the time being. She looked around to see if she saw one of Anderson's expensive vehicles parked in his reserved parking spot, but she didn't see any of his cars there. She assumed he wasn't in the office yet, so she grabbed her purse and headed up to her desk.

As she approached her desk, she noticed a new face that she didn't recognize. There was a new receptionist at the reception desk. Anderson hadn't mentioned hiring a new receptionist, so Angela was a bit surprised to see the new young face. As Angela walked past her, the new girl spoke to her.

"Good morning. You must be Angela," the young woman said in a friendly voice, flashing a vibrant smile her way.

Angela, turned to face the young woman and gave her a quick once-over.

"Good morning," Angela replied. "Yes, I'm Angela. I don't believe we've met."

The young woman stood up and came out from behind her desk to formally introduce herself to Angela.

"My name is Mallory. Mallory Watkins," she said, extending her perfectly-manicured hand to Angela.

Mallory was very young looking. She looked to be even younger than Angela, as if she was in her early twenties. She was tall and thin, thinner even than Angela, but she had a perfect set of breasts and a nice round ass behind her as well.

To Angela, Mallory looked as if she could be a model. She had to be at least 5 foot 7 and, in her 4-inch heels, she was standing nearly 6 feet tall in front of Angela. She had long, silky blonde hair that fell down into several thick golden locks around her shoulders. She was a bit paler than Angela, as if she could use a few tanning bed sessions or several hours out roasting under the hot sun. But her skin was creamy and utterly flawless, otherwise.

Her eyes were a beautiful almond color and her lashes were long and thick. They had to have been lengthened with an expensive mascara, Angela thought, because no one naturally had lashes that long and thick. Nonetheless, her eyes were very pretty and alluring, and even though Angela did not consider herself to be attracted to other women, she couldn't deny that Mallory was definitely a stunning-looking young woman.

"Nice to meet you," Angela replied, grasping Mallory's hand and shaking it firmly. Mallory's skin was as soft and smooth as it looked. Her hands felt as if Mallory slept in mittens filled with lotion, they were so smooth. "You have really smooth hands."

"Thanks. I use a paraffin wax on them twice a day," Mallory replied, her wide smile never leaving her face. "It's a pain in the ass, but it works wonders on your skin."

"I see," Angela commented, looking at Mallory's perfect-looking plump lips. Mallory had them covered in a shiny, glistening pink gloss that matched her silky pink blouse. Her blouse was tasteful, yet still sensual-looking. It hugged her firm, pert breasts and her cream-colored pencil skirt accentuated her slender hips and her round little ass. For just a split second, Angela felt a slight twinge of jealousy. She wondered if perhaps Anderson had hired this new young, vivacious vixen because he was growing tired of her. Maybe he was planning to ...

"Good morning, ladies." Anderson's voice broke Angela out of her thoughts. "Angela, I see you've met Mallory, and Mallory, you've met Angela."

Mallory nodded toward Anderson and smiled. Angela

turned around, surprised at hearing the sound of Anderson's voice.

"Morning, boss," Mallory replied.

"Oh, good morning, Anderson. I didn't know you were here," Angela stated. She felt her heart rate start to speed up from nervousness. She felt as if she had somehow been caught with her hand in the cookie jar.

"Mallory, I have some training videos you'll need to watch. You can watch them in the conference room," said Anderson.

"Angela, you and I have a lunch meeting at our usual spot, today" he said sternly, looking her directly in the eye.

Angela felt a twitch between her legs when she thought of Mallory in that same conference room where she and Anderson had had so many hot, erotic exploits. And the bossiness in his voice automatically turned her on. He treated her like a regular assistant in front of the other co-workers, but whenever they were alone, he was a completely different person.

"Yes, sir," Angela answered. She waved and headed to her desk.

She turned back to see Anderson leading Mallory out into the hallway and down toward the conference room. For just a moment, she felt that slight little twinge of jealousy again. She frowned when Anderson and Mallory disappeared down the hallway and then turned her attention back to her desk.

Am I really jealous? she thought to herself. What the hell is wrong with me?

She shook her head again, attempting to shake the jealous feeling out of her mind.

Angela couldn't wait for lunchtime to come around. She wanted to have some time to be alone with Anderson and possibly ask why he had hired Mallory and why he hadn't said anything about to her. She knew he didn't really owe her any explanation as they were not exactly a couple yet. But, for some reason, that fact didn't stop her feelings from getting involved.

She looked at her phone to see if Anderson had sent her a text or a naughty photo, but there was nothing there. She did see a text message from Mark, though.

When did he send that? I didn't see it this morning when I left the house, Angela thought to herself. She swiped her finger across the screen and then tapped the new message icon to see what Mark had texted to her. It read:

Hi Ang. Do you have any lunch plans? I was hoping we could talk today.

"Talk about what?" Angela wondered out loud. There was no way she was about to break her lunch date with Anderson just to meet with Mark. She quickly texted him a message back:

I can't today. But maybe tomorrow?

She pressed "send" and waited to see if Mark would text back. She waited and waited and nothing. Eventually she just went back to completing her work and wishing that the morning would hurry by so it could be lunchtime.

When her cell phone alarm went off at exactly 12:00 p.m., Angela was ecstatic. She shut down her computer in a hurry and headed out to the front lot. Anderson's "lunch meeting" at their "usual spot" meant that he'd have a limo come and meet her in back of the building and they would feed one another exotic fruits and creams in the back of the limo while driving around town.

Anderson would always add something sexual to the meal, whether it was licking strawberry-flavored whipped cream off of his massive cock or him sucking cherry sauce off of Angela's nipples and clit. She wondered what he had in store for them this time around. He was always chockful of erotic surprises.

For a moment, Angela started to wonder if she was possibly mistaking her feelings of excitement and arousal for infatuation and her overwhelming passion and lust for feelings of love. Again, she shook the thought away and focused only on the stimulating lunch task at hand.

She rushed to the elevator and pressed the button over and over again, trying to make the elevator arrive sooner.

"Come on, come on!" she said out loud, to no one in particular. There were a few people in the hallways, likely headed out on their own lunch breaks. She wondered if any of them did the same kinky types of activities that she and Anderson often enjoyed on their lunch dates.

It felt as if the elevator was taking forever, though, she knew she was really in no big hurry. Anderson was her boss, so however late he kept her past the allotted one hour lunch break was completely fine with him. There had been a time or two that they had never even made it back to the office after their lunch date. It all depended on Anderson's schedule and workload for the day.

Finally the elevator dinged and the doors opened. There were about three or four other people on the elevator when Angela got on. All of them seemed to be headed to the ground floor. She noticed that she hadn't seen the pretty, new receptionist around since she'd first arrived that morning. She wondered where little Miss Model Mallory had disappeared off to. Perhaps she had spent the better half of the morning watching training videos in the conference room—the one that Angela and Anderson had christened in more ways than one, more times than a few.

Angela couldn't even hear the babble and chatter of the other employees on the elevator. All she could think about was her lunch date with Anderson. And then suddenly, her cell phone buzzed. She looked down to see that Mark had sent her a reply to her text message from earlier that morning. She swiped her finger over the touch screen to see what his response had been.

Tomorrow sounds good. What time is your lunch break?

Angela thought for a moment. Should she take the chance and go meet him for lunch? What would Anderson think if he or one of his subordinates just happened to see her out in public with Mark during the work day? She paused for a moment, unsure of what to text back to Mark.

Just then, the elevator dinged again and the doors opened up to the lobby level of the office building. Angela stepped out of the elevator and headed outside.

There was a long black stretch limousine sitting just outside of the building and Angela knew it was her lunch ride. Just seeing the vehicle's darkly-tinted windows and knowing that Anderson was inside of it, waiting for her with some type of kinky lunchtime surprise antics, made her instantly moist between her thighs. It still amazed her sometimes, the effect that Anderson had on her.

She had dated Mark for two years, and he had never excited her in the sexual ways that Anderson could so easily. Not that Mark was bad in bed or anything. He was a passionate and attentive lover. But, he was nowhere near as adventurous, aggressive, creative, or dominant when it came to sex, not like Anderson was.

Angela could never imagine herself becoming bored or disinterested when it came to sex with Anderson. But a part of her had to admit, great sex alone did not equal a great relationship. With Mark, Angela would pretty much be guaranteed the long-term, fully-committed relationship she longed for, along with the security of knowing she would have someone there for her whenever she needed them. She longed to have that with

Anderson, but she wasn't quite sure yet if that was what he wanted with her, as well.

Talking to Mark was easy. She could talk to him about pretty much anything, and he would listen and would always take her feelings into consideration. With Anderson, she still felt somewhat intimidated and afraid to talk to him about serious relationship-centered topics. She knew what she wanted with him, but was afraid to bring the subject up. And up until now, he had not yet mentioned anything along those lines, himself.

But, right now was not the time for thinking about such things; right now was time to put her mind into pleasure mode and enjoy the wild, sensuous lunchtime thrill she was soon to be experiencing with her handsome, sexually-arousing billionaire lover. She put a flirtatious smile on her face and walked outside to her waiting ride.

The chauffeur was waiting for her at the rear door of the stretch limo. She walked over to the door and flashed him a pleasant smile.

"Your ride, ma'am," he stated, tipping his hat to her and opening the rear passenger side door of the limo.

"Thank you," Angela replied, and then climbed inside the limo as he closed the door behind her.

Anderson was inside the limousine and he had quite a lunch spread prepared for the two of them in the back of the elaborate limousine.

"Hello, darling," he said in his smooth, melodic sensual voice. "I hope you're hungry. I know I sure I am." He licked his lips in a sexual way that made Angela instantly moist between her legs.

Angela flashed him a sexy smile and batted her eyes at him. It still never ceased to amaze her how he always made her feel like a gushing young girl every time she was in his presence.

"Hello, Mr. Cromby," she crooned, already feeling the ache in her core.

Her body always reacted in an arousing way whenever she was with him. He had a certain power over her—a sexual power—that she could never deny, even if she wanted to. She slid into the seat beside him, greeting him with a firm kiss on the lips.

"Mmm, tastes like the appetizer already," Anderson stated, winking at her flirtatiously. Angela swooned like a blushing schoolgirl.

She looked over at the delicious-looking spread of exotic fruits and creams that Anderson had so carefully laid out for their erotic lunch break. There was a bowl of ripe strawberries and several flavors of whipped cream. There was also a plate of fruits that Angela couldn't name right off the bat, but they looked incredibly enticing and tasty. There was also a bottle of expensive-looking champagne with two wine glasses sitting directly in front of it.

"Oh, wow!" Angela's eyes lit up at the sight the mini-buffet. "This looks amazing, Anderson!" She still wondered how he never ceased to amaze her with his creativity and idealism.

Anderson allowed a small, smug grin to spread across his perfect lips. He thoroughly enjoyed the way Angela reacted to his innovative seduction techniques. He raised his freshly groomed eyebrows at her.

Just then, the limousine pulled off onto the street and begin to head south.

"I know we don't have a lot of room in here, but I want you to put this on," Anderson requested, handing her a red box that was in the shape of a heart. It had a drawn-on bow on the top of it. Angela opened the box and her eyes widened in delight when she saw a red-colored edible nightie inside of it.

"Oh my gosh!" Angela said, giggling in spite of herself. "I think this may turn out to be one of our best lunch dates yet!"

Anderson proceeded to pour the two of them some champagne in the wine glasses as Angela hurriedly removed the dress she had worn to work so she could slip on the edible nightie. She had already stopped wearing underwear to work the day she had started working her new job at Anderson's office building. And, since her breasts were firm and perky, she often went braless as well. Today had been the perfect day to leave the panties and bra at home, and she was very glad she had. She tore off her dress and slid daintily into the edible red nightie.

There was also a pair of edible candy panties underneath the nightie, so she slid those on as well. Anderson had already seen her naked on numerous occasions, of course, but he turned away to prepare their champagne and fruit plates while she changed. He wanted to wait to see her completely dressed up in the sexy edible outfit before he turned back around to officially start their lunch break.

"No peeking!" Angela said with a giggle, as she slid the edible candy panties up around her slender hips.

"I'm not peeking," Anderson assured her. He was already imagining how delicious she would look in the edible gear he had gotten her, and he was also thinking about how delicious she would taste, as well.

"Okay, you can look now," Angela told him.

Anderson turned around to see her posing seductively in her sexy little lingerie attire. His eyes widened with delight at the sight of her. The stringy lingerie hugged her figure with pure perfection. It accented each and every curve of her body from her pert, large breasts to her thin, feminine hips, and when she turned her body to the side, the candy panties aligned her firm, round, ass with precision.

"You, my dear, look more mouth-watering and appetizing than any of these exotic fruits and creams ever could," Anderson crooned.

His voice was oh so soft, sensuous, and tantalizing. He was leaning in so close to her ear that she could feel his warm breath right against the upper part of her neck. It sent a wave of shudders through her entire body. His voice was so deep and gruff that every time he would whisper in her ear, she would feel another twinge between her thighs. He really knew exactly how to turn her on.

Anderson was wearing dark-colored button-down silk shirt and a pair of expensive black slacks. To Angela, he always looked very elegant and sexy, no matter what he wore on any given day. His silk shirts always hugged the muscles of his arms and chest, outlining the flawless definition of his perfectly-chiseled figure through the thin fabric. As he sat there looking at Angela in her edible lingerie, taking in the sight of her while holding his full glass of champagne in his hand, Angela couldn't help but feel a very strong urge to rip his shirt off of him and ravage his sexy body. Instead, she winked at him, barely able to contain her ever-growing arousal.

"Champagne?" he asked, handing her the glass he had poured for her while she had been changing into her lunch attire.

"Why, thank you, Mr. Cromby," Angela said, unable to keep herself from smiling at him. She noticed that she did a lot of smiling, giggling, and laughing whenever she was Anderson. More so than whenever she was with Mark, in fact. And she also did significantly more moaning, groaning, panting and squealing whenever she was with having sex with Anderson—more than what she had ever done while having sex with Mark. But, she didn't want to think about such things right now, so again, she pushed the thoughts out of her mind and focused on enjoying her time with Anderson, for the time being.

The two of them sipped champagne and made a bit of small talk as the sexual tension between them continued to build.

Angela knew that Anderson thoroughly enjoyed building up the suspense of their rendezvouses. It made the end result so much more satisfying and it always left the both of them craving more of each other. He loved to have control over Angela in a sexual way and bring her to the brink of literally begging him for more. Angela couldn't deny that she loved it just as much as he did.

"Open that pretty mouth of yours, Angela," Anderson ordered. She obliged. He dipped a strawberry in whipped cream and placed between her lips. She bit down, tasting the sweetness of the fruit and the cream on her tongue.

"Mmm," she hummed, chewing the fruit and then swallowing.

"You're so fucking sexy when you eat," Anderson told her, reaching for another fruit. "This is what we're going to do today, my love. I want you to taste one of every fruit here, and then I'm going to blindfold you. I'm going to feed you a different fruit and you are going to tell me which type of fruit it is, just by smell and taste alone."

"Okay," Angela answered.

"I'm going to ask you which kind of fruit it is and each time you get it right, I'm going to eat a piece of your nightie off of you. But, each time you guess it wrong, I am going pull down your candy panties and spank you on your beautiful ass."

Angela shuddered again, this time with elevated excitement. She could already feel the goosebumps spreading all over her body, just thinking about being blindfolded and spanked by Anderson. She was already planning to purposely guess some of the fruits wrong so that she could feel the thrill of the intertwined pleasure and pain of his firm, strong palms on the cheeks of her ass.

"Are you ready?" Anderson asked her, finishing the last of his champagne with one final gulp. He reached into the deep left pocket of his trousers and pulled out a black blindfold. Angela swallowed down the rest of her champagne and nodded, eagerly.

Anderson set the blindfold down on his lap right over the large imprint of his already-hardening cock and picked up one of every fruit on the mini lunch buffet table of the limo. He told her what each fruit was and then allowed her one taste of each one. They enjoyed one more glass of champagne afterwards, and Angela could already feel the effects of the alcohol starting to make her feel more relaxed and less inhibited—not that she needed champagne or any other alcoholic beverage to feel that way when she was with Anderson. His presence alone was her natural aphrodisiac, all on its own.

Angela closed her eyes and felt her heartrate begin to increase as Anderson carefully and gently slid the blindfold over her face. And then, surprise! Anderson also had a pair of handcuffs. He cuffed her hands together behind her back.

Angela felt another twinge of sexual excitement between her legs. Her Anderson was always full of surprises, and he never failed to keep her guessing. It excited her to no end, and she enthusiastically allowed him to lock her wrists together behind her back. He then sat her on his lap with her legs hanging just over the left side of his body.

He gently rubbed the back of her neck, massaging her bare, exposed skin, making her want to purr like a kitten in a warm, furry slipper. The anticipation of what was to come was almost too much for Angela to bear. She could feel her clit already beginning to pulsate with desire against one of the candies on her candy panties, as the moistness between her legs started to increase.

"Here's the first one," Anderson told her, as he dipped a small, bite-sized piece of fruit in one of the creams and slid it between Angela's pursed lips.

"Mmm," she said again, savoring the sweet, tangy taste of the fruit as it mixed in with the cream.

"Which type of fruit is this, Angela?" Anderson asked her in a stern voice as his hands worked their way down until they were massaging the area directly in the middle of the small of her back. It was one of the most sensitive parts of Angela's back and she arched it forward in response to his mesmerizing touch. A small sigh escaped her lips as he worked his fingertips around on the surface of her skin.

"Mmm, is it a starfruit? It tastes like a starfruit," Angela replied.

All she could see was the black darkness of the blindfold over her eyes. But it seemed that by temporarily losing her ability to see her other senses had been heightened somewhat. She felt every movement of Anderson's fingers as they worked their way around her neck and back, sending shivers of desire down her spine. The aroma and the tastes of the exotic fruits even seemed to be more intensified, as well.

"Right you are! Good girl," Anderson told her.

He fed her the rest of the fruit and then Angela felt the heat of his mouth against her nipple. With his mouth, he peeled back a part of the edible nightie, the part covering her right breast, exposing her soft, bare skin and fully-erect nipple. Angela hissed in delight at the feel of Anderson's mouth and tongue on her breasts. His tongue circled around her hard nipple, causing her to let out another moan of pleasure.

"Mmm, I was right," Anderson said, in a deep, sensuous voice, his lips barely an inch from Angela's ear. She shuddered again from the sensation of his warm breath against the nape of her delicate neck. "You taste so much better than any fruit or cream on this mini smorgasbord of treats."

Anderson unzipped his pants and released his already half-hard cock. Angela couldn't see what he was doing, but she could hear the zipper of his trousers being pulled down. She immediately knew that he had freed his thick, massive cock from his pants, and the thought of it only heightened the level of her arousal. Behind the darkness of the blindfold, she could imagine Anderson's cock, its huge head swollen and stiff with desire for her. She licked her lips at the thought.

"Okay, Angela, here's the next one," Anderson slid another cream-covered piece of fruit in her mouth.

"This one's an easy one. It's a clementine," Angela stated confidently.

"Smart girl!" Anderson said. He fed her the rest of the fruit and then used his mouth to release her other breast from the edible lingerie. He licked around her left nipple, causing it to harden as if the temperature in the room had dropped down to below 50 degrees. Angela let out another moan as her back arched again, thrusting her breast further into Anderson's face. Anderson took her whole left breast deep into his mouth, suckling hungrily, causing her to pant with desire.

"Oh, Anderson," Angela whispered.

"Okay, Angela, here's the next one," Anderson told her.

This time, Angela was stumped on the type of fruit that Anderson had placed in her mouth. She worked it around her mouth, trying to identify the taste, but couldn't quite place it, specifically.

"Hmm," she said, frowning just a bit. "I don't know. Is it a kiwi?"

Anderson shook his head, though Angela couldn't see it.

"I'm sorry, Angela, that's not right," Anderson said. With one swift movement, he bent Angela's thin body over his lap with her round ass poking up in the air. He ripped the candy panties off of her with one quick gesture, sending the little candies flying around the back of the limo. Angela could feel his cock now throbbing hard against her midsection as Anderson began to prepare her for her spanking—her punishment for guessing the wrong fruit.

Angela could barely control her excitement as she felt the candy panties being torn from her crotch. With her bare, naked ass in the air, lying across Anderson's lap, she felt her crotch grow wetter from her elevating arousal. She braced herself as she felt Anderson's warm, smooth hands rubbing, caressing and massaging her ass cheeks, squeezing and kneading, making her shudder in anticipation.

"You guessed the wrong fruit, Angela. You know what your punishment is, right?" Anderson asked her in a soft, almost soothing tone of voice.

"Yes, I know what my punishment is," she replied in a hushed voice, barely louder than a whisper.

"What is your punishment, Angela?" Anderson demanded sternly, his voice still soft and calm. His hands were still massaging and caressing the cheeks of her exposed ass.

"My punishment is a spanking," Angela answered.

"Are you ready for our punishment?" Anderson asked, his squeezes on her buttocks becoming a little rougher.

"Yes, I'm ready for my punishment," Angela affirmed.

"Louder, Angela," Anderson commanded, his voice a little sterner, now.

"I'm ready for my punishment!" Angela said in a much louder voice.

"Good girl," Anderson said.

Just then, his large, heavy hand came down on the right cheek of her ass with a loud "smack!" sound. Angela winced in pain and let out a small yelp. Though the right cheek of her ass was stinging, a rush of arousal and excitement surged throughout the rest of her body.

"Don't you move, Angela," Anderson warned. Angela lay as still as she possibly could, trying her hardest not to react to the stinging pain that had been left behind from his hard slap.

She felt and heard another loud smack as Anderson's hand came down on her other ass cheek. She let out another small yelp and bit down on her lip, fighting the intense urge to react to the stinging pain his slap had left on her exposed left buttock with every ounce of her will. Again, the pain of the hard smack sent another rush of desire racing all throughout her body, causing her to shiver, ever so slightly.

"Good girl," Anderson commended her, his firm, strong hands now back to rubbing and caressing her stinging buttocks, massaging away the pain they'd just caused. Angela felt her pussy grow even wetter between her legs. She was extremely turned on and her ever-moistening crotch was yearning for some attention—some stimulation—from Anderson.

"One more, for guessing the wrong fruit, Angela," Anderson cautioned her. Once more, Angela braced herself for the smack. This time, his hefty hand came down with a powerful, hard smack against both of her buttocks simultaneously.

Angela couldn't help but let out another yelp as both of her ass cheeks began to sting with pain, yet the rush of desire that followed was even more immense. She felt Anderson begin to caress and rub the stinging pain away right after that last hard smack and her body was on fire for him.

"You should see your beautiful ass, Angela. It looks like it's blushing right now," Anderson said with a small smile on his face. Angela couldn't see it, but she could tell by the tone of his voice that he was smiling. "Good girl! You took your punishment well, Angela. You've earned a reward."

With that, Anderson lifted her small body with another swift movement and lay her down on the seat of the limo. He spread her legs wide and maneuvered his body between them, her hands still cuffed behind her back.

He slowly slid both of his hands down her smooth, soft legs, making his way down her thighs and closer down toward her swollen, moist, fully-exposed, pulsating clit. Angela was breathing deep and sighing, anticipating the touch of his hands on her yearning womanhood.

"Yes, relax, Angela. I'm going to give you a reward for being such a good girl. Do you want it?" Anderson asked her, his voice raspy with his own arousal.

"Yesss," Angela hissed, raising her hips up toward him to invite his touch. "I want it. I want it so badly, Anderson!"

She shuddered as he grazed his fingers over her clit, causing her to emit a sigh of passion.

Just then, she felt a cool, light sensation on her crotch. She realized right away that Anderson had sprayed a bit of one of the flavored whipped creams on her clit.

He wasted no time diving in and sucking the whipped cream from her clit, licking it all away and then flicking his tongue against it, just the way he knew she liked it. Angela writhed and rocked with pleasure, moaning and sighing in response to his oral stimulation. Being unable to see somehow intensified the feeling of his mouth and tongue on her clit and she felt herself already getting close to climaxing. She knew that Anderson would bring her right to the edge and then stop, making her weak with desire and ready to beg him for her orgasm.

"Oh, yes! Yes, Anderson, yes!" she cried, her hips gyrating against his face, her orgasm building and getting closer and closer.

"Mmm, Angela, you taste so good! I'd rather eat you than anything else in this limo," Anderson mumbled between licks and tongue flicks.

He knew she was almost there and he stopped abruptly, knowing she was right at the edge.

"I have one more fruit for you to try, Angela," he told her, licking the taste of her crotch from his lips.

He knelt down in front of her face and turned her head toward him. He stroked his hard, throbbing cock with his hand, making sure it was nice and stiff before he commanded her to open her mouth. He squirted a bit of one of the flavored whipped creams onto the head of his dick and then inserted it into her open mouth with a deep groan and a sigh of delight.

Angela realized immediately that the cream-covered fruit was Anderson's large, thick, rock-hard cock and opened her mouth even wider to receive it. She savored the taste of the flavored cream intermingled with the taste of his dick and sucked all of the cream off of the tip. Anderson groaned his pleasure in a voice barely louder than a whisper.

"Ooh, shit, Angela," he hissed, sliding his cock further into her mouth, forcing her to take it deeper down toward the depth of her throat. Angela moaned as she sucked his cock hungrily, taking it deeper and deeper into her mouth until the tip was almost completely in the back of her throat. Fortunately, she had become so used to sucking Anderson's massive cock that she no longer had any kind of gag reflex whatsoever, and she sucked it with precision, hoping that if she did a very good job, he would give her the orgasm he now had her aching for so desperately.

"I'm going to fuck your pretty little face with my huge cock, Angela," Anderson told her, grabbing her head with his hands and throwing his own head back to close his eyes as he completely and thoroughly enjoyed the feel of her lovely mouth wrapped around his dick, sucking energetically, eagerly and passionately. He held her head steady and began to thrust his hips toward her face, forcing his cock even deeper into her mouth, increasing the speed and the rhythm of his pumping, fervently.

Angela moaned and groaned enthusiastically with her

mouth full of Anderson's dick as he literally fucked her face, plunging his cock deep into her throat, over and over again.

"Ahh, yesss, Angela! That's a good girl. Suck this big, thick cock like you want it," he said in a hoarse whisper between his sighs and pants of pleasure.

He reached down and began to fondle Angela's exposed breasts, rubbing and squeezing them and gently pinching the nipples, causing Angela's moans and grunts to increase and grow louder. Soon, he felt himself getting closer to shooting off his huge load, and he wanted to feel the walls of Angela's tight cunt around his dick, dripping wet with her desire for him. Just the thought of it almost brought him all the way to edge of his own orgasm, and he abruptly pulled his cock from Angela's mouth, stopping himself before he exploded deep into the depths of her throat.

"Do you want this cock, Angela?" he asked firmly, in a dominating voice.

"Yes! I want your cock, Anderson! I want it so badly!" she replied, begging for him to fuck her and bring her over the edge.

"Are you gonna fuck this cock until I cum deep inside your tight, wet cunt?" he asked her, in a louder, more commanding voice.

"Oh, yes, Anderson! I want to fuck you until you fill my pussy with your hot, juicy cum!" Angela cried, writhing with desire, wanting to be free of the handcuffs that bound her, but only so she could grab Anderson's cock and push it deep inside of her cunt, which was yearning to for Anderson to fill it up, completely.

But Anderson did not release her from her handcuffs, just yet. He pulled his pants down to below his knees and took another surprising little device out of his other pocket. Though Angela couldn't see what he was doing, she could hear that he was shuffling around. She assumed he was taking his pants down or off, which was correct, but what she wasn't expecting was the little device he took out and turned on. She could hear a buzzing sound and she instantly knew he had some type of small vibrating device.

"I'm going to fuck you, Angela. I'm going to give you the orgasm you so deserve for being such a good girl today. But I'm not going to free you from your handcuffs just yet. I'm going to fuck you with your hands bound behind your back and your face blindfolded, but I'm going to make you cum nice and hard. Do you want that, Angela?" he asked her, intently.

"Ooh, yes, Anderson! I want it! Please! I need it right now!" Angela cried out to him with desperation in her voice. She was so aroused that she could barely contain her excitement any longer. Her entire body was on fire for Anderson and she wanted to feel every inch of his cock inside of her.

All of a sudden, Angela felt a vibrating sensation directly on her clit, and she instantly knew it was Anderson using the vibrating gadget on her. It felt like a vibrating egg or a bullet device, and it was definitely a powerful one. She let out a whimper of pleasure at the sensations the vibrator sent through her core. She could feel herself getting closer to an orgasm as small beads of perspiration began to form around the outer edge of her forehead. She arched her back, writhing against the vibrator, wanting to reach that peak that she was oh so close to reaching. Just then, Anderson took the vibrator away.

Angela sighed, raising her hips as if trying to signal Anderson to resume the sensation.

"Ah, ah, ah," Anderson taunted her, in a deep, sing-songy tone of voice. Angela could picture him shaking his finger at her as if chastising her like a small, young child. "Not yet. When you cum, you're gonna cum all over my cock, Angela."

Angela shuddered as she felt Anderson turning her body over, leaning her over the seat with her ass up in the air. She knew he was about to fuck her and the anticipation was driving her mad with desire.

"Mmm, Angela, your pretty ass is still slightly red from the spanking I gave you. It looks so sexy." He was whispering in her ear again, causing her to shiver, slightly.

"Please Anderson, I can't take it anymore! Please, fuck me right now! I need to cum! I need to cum so badly!" Angela was begging for his cock, and that's exactly what he wanted to hear.

Anderson looked down and saw her slightly-reddened, perfectly round ass up in the air and her cunt was juicy and wet with her arousal. Her clit was swollen and moist and just looking at her in that state turned him on to no end. He grabbed his stiff, throbbing cock in his hand and rubbed the head of it against Angela's dripping wet snatch, teasing her with the tip, soaking it in her juices.

Angela moaned and arched her back, panting with anticipation. She backed her ass up into his cock, trying to slide her pussy onto it. Anderson grabbed her ass with one hand and with the other, he slid his hard dick into her tight, wet pussy with a groan and a hiss of sheer pleasure. Angela moaned her delight loudly, backing up into him until his cock was completely swallowed into her cunt. He was so deep inside of her that she could feel his balls bang against her swollen clit. She writhed with pleasure and shuddered with delight, sighing and crying out in passion.

"Oh yes, yes, Anderson! Fuck me!" she cried out as she began to move back and forth, backing her ass up onto Anderson's cock harder and faster and harder and faster. "Ohhh!! Yes!!"

Anderson groaned as he felt his own climax building. He knew Angela only needed one more good thrust to completely send her over the edge. He wanted her orgasm to be mind-blowing. She had definitely earned it.

He took the vibrator and placed it directly on her pulsating clit and turned it up on full blast. At the same time, he slammed his cock into her, hard and deep, while reaching around and squeezing her right breast, pinching the nipple with his finger and thumb. The combination of sensations sent Angela over the edge.

"Oh GOD!!!" she screamed out loudly, as her orgasm peaked and shook throughout her entire body. "GOD, Anderson! FUCK, YESSS!"

Her whole body tensed up and her hips began to jerk uncontrollably as the intensity of her climax engulfed her in an overwhelming wave of ecstasy. Anderson tossed the vibrator aside and his fingertips replaced it, applying just the right amount of pressure to Angela's clit as her orgasm continued to peak, her hips jerking against his cock and the hand that was between her legs.

After a brief moment, Angela's climax finally began to subside and she let out a long groan and a deep sigh of blissful satiation. With his huge, hard cock still deep inside of her pussy, Anderson felt the spasms of her walls tightening around his dick as she orgasmed, and the sensation sent him over the edge, as well. He grabbed her entire pussy and pulled her back onto his cock hard and deep, shooting his load off inside of her with a loud groan of ecstasy. His cock throbbed and pulsated inside of her as spurt after spurt of his hot cum shot out of him, deep inside of Angela's soaking wet cunt.

Anderson collapsed on top of Angela with a deep, satisfied sigh. The two of them basked in the afterglow of their hot, steamy session for a brief moment, and then Anderson slid his cock out of Angela and freed her from her handcuffs. Angela removed the blindfold from over her eyes and turned her body around so she could hold Anderson close to her. The two of them embraced one another for a few moments and Anderson kissed her softly on her mouth.

"That ..." Anderson began, breathing heavily into Angela's right ear, "was absolutely AMAZING."

Angela smiled at his acknowledgement.

"Oh, yes, Mr. Cromby! It was incredible!" she agreed.

Just then, the limo slowed down to a complete stop. Angela wasn't sure where they had arrived at, but she knew she needed to get cleaned up before she could go back to work. Anderson rolled down the darkly-tinted rear driver's side window of the limo and looked outside.

"We're at my place, love. How about we go inside and get ourselves cleaned up and get back to finishing out this lovely work day?" Anderson suggested, before planting another soft, gentle kiss high on the top of Angela's perspiration-covered forehead.

ANGELA KNEW that her time was running out and she was going to have to make a decision between Anderson and Mark. It was really starting to nag at her—seeing both men behind their backs. She knew neither of them was blind or stupid, and she was starting to feel a bit guilty about not being 100% committed to either one of them. She decided that it was time to have a serious discussion with Anderson about their relationship the very next time they were together. She knew that Anderson usually liked to have dinner with her on Tuesday evenings, so she made a promise to herself to talk to him about things, then.

As she got dressed for her dinner with Anderson, she could feel her heartrate beginning to increase with a combination of nervousness and anxiety. She had never brought up the status of her and Anderson's relationship before and she was unsure about exactly how to go about doing it.

What if he rejects me? she thought to herself. What if I really am just a fling to him and he plans to move on to a newer, younger model as soon as he grows bored with me? What if that's why he hired that hot new young receptionist?

Angela knew she had to prepare herself for whatever he might say. She was hoping with everything inside of her that he would feel the same way as she did and that he would want a full-blown, committed, long-term relationship with her. But if that wasn't quite where his mind was, she needed to mentally prepare herself for heartbreak—just in case.

Even if he wasn't interested in the type of relationship she was interested in, she intended to let him know that she would still be interested in carrying on their passionate, exciting fling, because honestly, Angela couldn't see herself being completely without him. If she could only have him this way for a while, she felt like it would still be much better than not having him at all. If he did end up rejecting her, she wondered if she would be able to continue working for him.

Would things become weird and/or awkward at Anderson's office? Having to see him nearly every day, knowing that she could never be with him that way again—or worse yet, having to see him with another woman, and having to work face to face with that other woman, each day—would be an absolute nightmare in her opinion, at least as far as her feelings were concerned.

She shook all of her thoughts from her mind as she checked herself out in her full-length bedroom mirror. She had just finished putting on her make-up and was almost ready to head out to the limousine that Anderson had sent over to her house to pick her up, when her cell phone rang, snapping her from her swarm of silent thoughts that were playing loudly inside of her mind.

Angela picked up her cell phone up from its current location laying on the bed beside the small blue purse she had selected to match her dinner dress and shoes. She looked at the number on the LCD screen and saw that it was Maxine.

"Hey, girlie," Angela answered with a cheerful voice. She was happy to be hearing from Maxi.

"Uh uh! Don't even try to give me that hey, girlie bullshit! Where have you been, stranger?" Maxine teased. Angela could hear the mock sarcasm in her friend's voice.

"Oh, Max, come on! I'm so sorry! I have been a little bit preoccupied, I admit. But I was going to call you tomorrow if you had not called me first," Angela explained. She wasn't lying. In fact, she really had been thinking about Maxine lately and had made a mental note to give her a call or maybe even pay her a visit on the following day.

"So what's been keeping you so damn busy that I haven't heard from you in so many days? Is his name Anderson or Mark? Or perhaps a little bit of both?" Maxine asked.

Angela let out a small giggle at her friend's blunt question.

"Actually, I haven't really talked to Mark lately. I was supposed to meet him for lunch yesterday, but I told him that something had come up and I was unable to make it."

In a way, though, Angela hadn't lied to Mark. In fact, what had actually come up was her billionaire plaything, Anderson Cromby's, thick, humongous cock. And when it came up, Angela wasn't interested in anything else other than taking advantage of the situation. Something about Anderson's dick had her completely hypnotized every time she even so much as thought about it. He had her utterly "dicknotized."

"So have you decided which way you're going to go, yet?" Maxine asked. Her intentions were definitely good. She only wanted her bestie to be happy and to have a healthy, blissful relationship with whichever man she chose to be with.

"You know what, Max? I think that I have. I am going out dinner with Anderson tonight. Though I have been somewhat afraid of asking him about our relationship, I've decided that tonight's the night. I am going to spill the beans and let him know exactly how I feel and what I want. If he feels the same way, I am going to take that chance and completely dedicate myself to him."

Maxine could tell by the tone of her best friend's voice that Angela was serious. She was in love and she was going to let the man she loved know it. She had a deep respect for Angela. She knew that it couldn't possibly be easy for her to have to make such an important and difficult decision between two men she clearly had deep, unfathomable feelings for. Maxine couldn't deny that she was very proud of her friend, and she hoped more than anything that Angela's love life would end up working out for her for the best.

ANGELA STEPPED out of the luxury car that Anderson had sent over to her apartment to pick her up and take her to the restaurant they were meeting at for a nice romantic dinner. The restaurant was called Chez LaFre' and it offered an exquisite selection of top-of-the-line French cuisine. Angela thanked the limousine driver and walked into the front entrance of the huge, fancy, 5-star-rated French restaurant.

Her eyes lit up with wonder as she entered the lobby area of Chez LaFre'. It was one of the most beautiful restaurants she had ever set foot inside of. She looked around in awe as the host, who was dressed in a stylish black tuxedo, led her toward an elegantly-decorated private VIP booth up on the veranda area of the large venue.

Angela saw Anderson sitting in a comfy little VIP-area dinner booth, talking on his cell phone. He looked incredibly handsome in his three-piece teal-colored silk suit. His shirt was a multi-colored one, form-fitting, accentuating the well-defined muscles of his toned arms. He had the jacket lying beside him on the seat of the booth and his hair looked extra-thick and shiny in the dim lighting of the restaurant. The well-dressed Hispanic-looking restaurant host led her to the table and motioned for her to sit down in the booth across from Anderson.

"You look ravishing, darling," Anderson said, standing up to greet her with a kiss on the cheek. He pulled out her chair and she sat down. Anderson sat back down across from her.

"Thanks. So do you! As usual," Angela replied, flashing him a smile

"I took the liberty of ordering us a fine bottle of imported white wine and I also ordered an absolutely scrumptious appetizer I think you will like," Anderson told her. He opened the bottle of wine and proceeded to fill their glasses.

"I'm really glad you invited me out to dinner tonight, Anderson. This place is incredible," Angela commented, her eyes wide with impression.

Anderson loved the way Angela always expressed her appreciation to him.

"Anything to keep a smile on that beautiful face of yours," Anderson stated with a grin. Angela blushed like a school girl, in spite of herself.

"There's something I want to talk to you about, Anderson," Angela said. She felt her heartrate begin to increase as the feeling of nervousness started to take over. "And I have to admit, I'm really nervous about it."

Just then, the waiter brought over their appetizer and set it down on the table. The aroma of the food made Angela's mouth water.

"Are you ready to order?" the well-dressed waiter asked them.

"Give us just a few moments, please," Anderson told him.

"Sure, monsieur," the waiter replied and walked off.

"What is it, Angela? I would like to think that you would be able to talk to me about anything," he said in a soft, comforting voice. His face showed genuine concern.

"Well ... I ... um," Angela stammered, fidgeting uncomfortably in her seat. Anderson reached across the table and took her hand.

"Angela, please. What is it?" His gorgeous eyes were searching hers. It made her heart melt.

"Well, I was just ... um ... wondering. What are we? You know?" She looked at him with questioning eyes. "I mean, I always enjoy myself in ways I never have before when I'm with you. I've never felt so alive, so free, and so happy. But I want you to understand that if I am only a phase, only a passing fling, I am okay with it, as long as I get to spend as much time with you as possible while it lasts."

Anderson grew quiet for a moment, as if allowing her words to fully sink in.

"How do you feel about me, Angela?" he asked her with a soft, but serious look on his face.

"Honestly? I am in love with you, Anderson. I have been for a while now. I just wasn't sure how you felt about me, so I didn't want to bring it up. I didn't want to make things weird between us, you know?"

"Are you still seeing that Mark guy?" he asked her.

There it was. He knew about Mark. Actually, Angela wasn't all that surprised that he knew. She knew Anderson was no dummy and that he had friends and associates all over the area. She just hadn't been sure whether he cared or not. Angela lowered her head, feeling just a tad bit ashamed for some reason.

"Mark and I have a past. He wasn't the worst boyfriend in the world, but he wasn't the best either. He came back into my life right before you and I met. I never thought that you and I would end up where we are, and I wasn't sure if we were going to be a serious 'thing' or just a passing 'fling.' So, I guess I was sort of keeping him around as ... insurance of some sort, kind of a back-up plan."

"Just in case things between you and I didn't work out," Anderson added. It was more of a statement than it was a question. He said it as if he had known all along.

"Please understand, Anderson, I have never met anyone like you before. You are a man who has everything in the world and you could have any woman you wanted. I was just scared that whatever you saw in me would eventually wear off, you know? I was afraid you would get bored with me and move on to the next new and exciting young woman who happened to catch your eye."

Anderson listened to her quietly, allowing her to completely state her piece.

"If you could have your way, what would you want us to be?" he asked her.

"If I could have my way, Anderson, I would want to be with you for the rest of my life," Angela answered.

"I want to tell you something that I probably should have told you a while ago," Anderson began. "I have dated plenty of different kinds of women in my lifetime. Models, actresses, dancers, you name it, women from all kinds of different backgrounds and social statuses. You see, it's easy to find a woman, but it's very hard to find a woman like you." He emphasized the word "you" and looked directly into Angela's eyes. "You are beautiful, intelligent, driven, independent, yet still so submissive, and you are also sweet, kind and amazing in bed. You are the kind of woman I could see myself settling down with.

"You are happy whether we go to a 5-star restaurant or a have a turkey sandwich picnic in the park. You don't need any of the things I choose to do for you, but you appreciate all of them. I can trust you with my business, and I feel like I could also trust you with my heart. I just didn't understand what it was about that Mark that you just couldn't seem to let him go. So I wasn't sure if this was where you truly wanted to be. So I just never pressed the issue."

Angela's eyes filled up with tears of happiness that threatened to spill over and run down her cheeks.

"So what are you saying, Anderson?" Angela asked in soft voice, barely louder than a hoarse whisper.

"I'm saying that I want you to be my woman and my woman, only. If that's what you want as well," Anderson replied, giving her hand a little squeeze.

"Oh, Anderson! That's exactly what I want! I've never wanted anything more in my entire life!" Angela allowed her tears of joy to run freely down her cheeks. She was overwhelmed with emotion. She reached out and grabbed Anderson's other hand and squeezed them both.

"These are the only tears I ever want to see in your eyes," Anderson said, reaching up to wipe one of them away. Angela smiled at him as another tear replaced it. He leaned in and kissed the other tear as he placed something in her hand.

"What's this?" she asked him, wiping away a stray tear.

"I want you to go in the ladies' room and put it in your panties, right up against your clit. I have the remote in my hand. When you come out, you're going to call this Mark character and tell him it's over."

Angela's heart began to race again. This time, it was with excitement. She grinned at Anderson and leaned in to give him a kiss on the mouth.

"Order for me, will you?" she asked with a wide smile and then hurried off to the ladies' room.

THE END

SIGN UP TO RECEIVE FREE BOOKS

Sign Up to Receive Free E-Books and Audiobook Codes.

Would you like to read **The Unexpected Nanny, Dirty Little Virgin** and **other romance books** for **free**?

You can sign up to receive these free e-books and audiobooks by typing this link into your browser:

https://www.steamyromance.info/free-books-and-audiobooks-hot-and-steamy/

Or this one:

https://www.steamyromance.info/the-unexpected-nanny-free/

PREVIEW OF MAELSTROM COMPLETE SERIES 1-4

An Alpha Billionaire Romance Boxed Set

By Michelle Love

Blurb

Young coffee-house owner Sarah Bailey has finally got over the mysterious disappearance of her husband two years previously and is looking forward to her new life as a single woman. She doesn't count on meeting Isaac Quinn, billionaire tech magnet, who sets out to seduce the beautiful Sarah. Unable to resist the incredible connection between them, they soon begin a passionate and sensual relationship that soon becomes headline news in the gossip columns.

Their happiness is marred when Sarah attracts a jealous stalker who sends her threats and Isaac begins to wonder if his fame and status has put the woman he is falling in love in terrible, terrible danger....

SINCE YESTERDAY PART ONE

If she hadn't been thinking about the letter, Sarah Bailey wouldn't have started so violently when Molly shouted her name across the busy coffee house. Sarah felt her balance slip away from her. She landed hard on her backside and laughed, embarrassed. She felt hands slide under her arms and lift her to her feet. She turned to face her savior and her stomach flipped. Her rescuer was tall, and broad, his dark hair cropped close to his head. He was dressed casually in jeans and a t-shirt but she could tell that they were artfully distressed to look vintage. Expensive, and exclusive. Sarah couldn't help but stare into his dark green eyes, which were crinkled at the corners in a crooked smile which softened his perfectly sculpted face. His smile widened as he took her in, and as she wobbled, his big hands moved to her shoulders to steady her. He was so tall, she had to tilt her head right back to gaze at him and suddenly she felt vulnerable in his presence.

"You okay, sweetheart?"

Oh god, his *voice*. Chocolate and sex. *Damn*. His hands on her felt so good. *Get a grip,* Sarah shook herself and smiled at him.

"Thank you."

His smile widened. "It was absolutely my pleasure, beautiful."

Sarah flushed at the compliment and stammered through another thanks before scooping her bag up from the floor. Molly met her at the counter.

"Sorry, honey." Molly grinned, her green eyes amused.

Sarah hugged her friend. "Not your fault. Just me being clumsy."

"How are you?"

Sarah held up her left hand and Molly's eyes widened.

"You've taken your wedding ring off."

"I decided that today is the day I move on. Dan is either dead or he left me. Either way, I know he's not coming back." Sarah took a deep breath and smiled. "New day, new life. He's been gone two years on Saturday. It's time, is all."

Molly hugged her. "I'm glad." She went to serve a customer and Sarah went into the backroom. She pulled the envelope out of her bag. *Sarah Bailey.* It was the same handwriting as the others and she guessed that it would contain the same repulsive, spite-filled messages as the last few. Her stomach clenched with fear, her skin breaking out in a sweat under her clothes. She wanted to share the letter with Molly, to ask her best friend's advice. She closed her eyes and swallowed down thinking of the vile threats and words of the last letters. This one would be no different. Her entire body started to tremble. *No. Not now, please.* She shoved the letter into the pocket of her jeans and went to work.

At twenty-eight, Sarah Bailey had known most people on the

island since she was a child and living in the now-closed children's home down on Dogwood Street. When the Jewell family had moved next door the two kids, Molly and Finn, had claimed Sarah as their own. They were drawn to the shy young part-Asian girl; her dark hair tumbling to the middle of her back, the almond eyes so dark and big, fringed with thick lashes. Her beauty was offset by her tomboyish nature – never out of her flared blue jeans and beloved sneakers, her knees and elbows forever grazed from running and climbing. It was a childhood spent climbing trees, swimming, camping out in the county park.

Unable to stay away from the island, after college and newly married to Daniel Bailey, Sarah had rebuilt the derelict movie house into the Varsity coffee house, mostly with just an instruction manual and the help of Dan, Molly and Finn. The locals watched in admiration – their local girl done good - and when the coffee house finally opened, it became the heart of Main Street. Grizzled fishermen would sit at the counter and order throat-strippingly strong coffee, next to the tourists who enjoyed their tea from the most delicate of china cups. When Dan had disappeared, so shocking, so unexpected, they had rallied around her, not letting her fall apart, not letting her feel the desperate guilt that consumed her when she was alone. She thought about moving away but this place, this little haven of an island an hour away from Seattle, was the only place she'd ever felt like she belonged.

The day was sultry with humidity. From the coffee shop window, ferries could be seen pulling into the small dock. The Varsity was full, humming with the music of conversation, crockery and Sarah didn't have a chance to tell Molly about the letter.

Late afternoon and the rush eased. Sarah opened the till to

change some notes. Molly was at the counter flirting with one of their customers. Sarah pulled out the cash tin. She heard a low soft voice across the restaurant and her stomach flipped. She glanced up. Her savior from earlier was chatting with some of the regulars, leaning back in his chair, relaxed, his long denim-clad legs stretched out in front of him.

"George makes an incredible chocolate mud pie that I practically drool over."

"Huh?" Sarah looked at Molly in confusion and her friend grinned.

"I'm just saying." She nodded at the guy who was now walking towards them. "That's how you were looking at that demi-God just then."

The demi-God came to the counter. Sarah flushed and scowled at Molly.

"I was not and shut up. Go wash a cup or something," she hissed at Molly then turned her burning face to greet him. "Hey."

"Hey yourself, beautiful."

She flushed again. God, she was *divine*...

Isaac Quinn studied the scarlet blush that colored her cheeks, the dark, lovely eyes. He'd seen her name tag earlier... *Sarah*. It suited her, soft, feminine.

"What can I get you?" Her voice was gruff and the sound of it made his groin tighten.

"Now let me see." He picked up a menu and studied it. Slowly, deliberately he moved his hand so it was next to hers, almost touching. He could feel the heat of her skin, smell her perfume, fresh air, and clean laundry.

"Okay, you ready?"

"I'm ready." She waved her notepad and smiled.
"You sure?"
"Sure."

Isaac grinned "Fine purveyor of all things drinkable... "I would very much like to partake of a fine cocktail called "A Tea Garden"."

Sarah laughed and he saw her eyes start to dance, enjoying the joke.

"Ok, your wish is my command, what is it?"

"Okay. It's one-third vodka, one-third apricot brandy, one-sixth..."

Sarah started giggling. Isaac mock-scowled at her.

"I'm not done. One-sixth vermouth and wait for it...one-sixth Tiffin."

"Tiffin?"

"Tiffin."

Sarah wrote this down.

"Just one question... what the hell is a Tiffin?"

"How should I know? I was kinda hoping you'd tell me."

Sarah raised her eyebrows at him, eyes wide and amused. "Well, you've got me there. I hate to disappoint."

He grinned at her. "Well, you'll just have to make it up to me... somehow."

The blush was back – the air between them electric. She cleared her throat and swept a shaking hand through her hair.

"Okay, so this cocktail... coffee black, yes?"

He sighed and shrugged good-naturedly. "You already know me so well. I'm Isaac."

She shook his outstretched hand. "Sarah. Sarah Bailey."

He held onto her hand. "Well, Sarah Bailey – " he grinned at her, "I'm delighted to meet you."

Sarah looked up from her paperwork just after seven o'clock. The coffee shop was almost emptied - a couple of teenagers hanging out, laughing, glued to their phones. The man who had helped her up earlier was standing near the bookshelves at the back of the room, looking through the racks of battered paperbacks. He glanced up and smiled at her and it was so infectious that Sarah couldn't help but return the grin.

"Can you recommend anything?" He called out and she went over. His voice was deep and mellifluous. He was so tall. He dwarfed her five foot five.

"What kind of thing are you looking for?" Her question was innocent but when she looked up at him, he merely smiled and his eyes locked onto hers in a way that made the blood in her veins become scorching hot. He reached out a finger and lightly brushed her cheek, just briefly before turning back to the shelf. Sarah's skin burned where he'd touched her.

"Something new..." he murmured then smiled. "I'm new to the island, actually, thinking of buying a house on the northern point."

"Really? I live there too.... just the other side of the boy's school."

Almost imperceptibly he moved closer. Her breath caught in her throat as she gazed up at him. *Touch me...* Her senses were hyperactive, every nerve ending on fire in the presence of this man. He smiled down at her. Sarah was suddenly aware that the coffee house had emptied out and they were alone.

"Then we'll be neighbors, Sarah Bailey," he said softly. His hand moved to cup her cheek, his big thumb stroking across her skin.

"Are you free for dinner tonight, Sarah Bailey?"

The way he said her name made her weak and she nodded.

"Come to my place. I'll cook." She didn't know why she had said that - all she knew was that she wanted to be alone with this man. Alone, naked, helpless with desire... all she was feeling she could see reflected in his eyes. He grinned, confident.

"Write down your address for me... or I could give you a ride home..."

She had driven into work this morning but to hell with it. "I finish in an hour."

Had she lost her mind? She felt almost delirious with desire, knowing without a doubt that if they went home together, they would be naked and writhing and fucking.

She had to bite back a moan as he slid a finger under her t-shirt and stroked her belly. She closed her eyes and felt his lips against her temple.

The spell was broken when they heard Molly shouting from the kitchen. She glanced over to the door, almost guiltily, and stepped away from Isaac, still burning from his touch. "An hour, then..."

Their gazes locked and he nodded. "An hour," he said, lowering his voice, "an hour, beautiful Sarah and then I'm going to strip you slowly and kiss every part of your glorious body. Then I'm going to fuck you all night long."

She *did* moan then, softly and she tilted her head up to his. His lips brushed against hers.

"I want to kiss you so deep, Sarah, but I'm afraid that if I do, I'll lose what little control I have left."

She nodded and stepped away.

"An hour."

He touched her cheek. "One hour...I'll be back to pick you up."

Molly stuck her head out of the kitchen and saw her boss standing alone, seemingly frozen in place. "Hey... you okay?"

Sarah turned to her, her face red and excited, her eyes wide and filled with wonder. "Yeah, I'm good... more than good."

Molly glanced out of the window and saw the back of the guy that had been in the coffeehouse. The one who flirted with Sarah. Molly started to grin.

"Oh, I see. Someone got a hot date?"

Sarah laughed and drew in a shaky breath. "You have no idea..."

Isaac came back for her forty minutes later. "I'm sorry I'm early... I couldn't wait."

"Molly?" Sarah immediately hollered for her friend. "I'm taking off early, you okay?"

She and Isaac grinned at each other, then the way his eyes swept over her body made her feel naked, desirable and wanted.

Molly stuck her head out of the kitchen door. "Of course." She saw Isaac and her smile widened. "Definitely. Go... *go*..."

They were still laughing as they walked to his car, Isaac holding the door open for her. She directed him towards the road to her house and as he drove, he reached over and took her hand. She laughed softly.

"I kinda feel like I'm dreaming," she confessed and Isaac smiled at her.

"I know what you mean but this *is* happening, Sarah." His hand slid under her dress and brushed against her inner thigh, making her gasp. Then he began to caress her, feeling her warm dampness against his fingers as she became aroused.

"I don't do this.... *god*... I mean, this is not something that happens to me. *Jesus,* Isaac, that feels so good...."

Isaac gave a low chuckle. "You have no idea the things I'm going to do to you tonight, beautiful."

She rolled her hips, grinding against his hand. "Get home quicker," she laughed breathlessly.

She barely had time to open the door before they were tearing each other's clothes off. She reached into his pants and felt the hot, huge length of him against her palm, rock-hard and trembling.

"I want to be inside you." He tumbled her to the floor, tearing her panties off and hitching her legs around his hips. Sarah moaned as he teased her with the wide crest of his cock, sliding it along her slick sex then crying out as he drove the diamond hard length into her. Hard, thrusting, pinning her hands above her head.

"Look at me…"

She met his gaze, saw how intense his green eyes were; completely focused on her as they fucked. Isaac thrust harder, pressing her legs further apart as he rammed into her.

"Christ, Sarah… I want you, *I want you*…"

She felt her limbs liquefy under the assault on her senses, her clit pulsing, her cunt gripping his cock, urging him deeper.

She came; her entire body vibrating, crying out his name, losing herself in the utter bliss of her orgasm, feeling his cock shooting hot semen deep inside her as he climaxed.

"God, Sarah, Sarah, Sarah…"

They shuddered and shivered their way to calmness, catching their breath, him still inside her as they calmed down. They looked at each other and started to laugh in disbelief. He brushed a damp lock of hair away from her face and pressed his lips to hers.

"That's one way of being welcomed to the neighborhood."

Sarah chuckled, still breathless. "That was incredible."

Isaac smiled down at her. "And you know what? We're going to do that all night long. Show me to your bedroom, my Sarah."

Her stomach dropped with pleasure. *My Sarah.* They disconnected and, leaving their clothes where they'd fallen, Sarah led him upstairs.

He had watched the car pull up to her house, saw the tall stranger take Sarah's hand and walked with her into the house. Before they'd kicked the door shut, he'd seen them kissing, clawing at each other.

Fucking *whore*. Who the hell *was* this guy? Did she just meet him? She was his, and his alone. These last two years he'd watched over her, kept her safe and now... the fury at her betrayal ripped through him and he wanted to kick his way into the house, drag the guy off of her and beat the shit out of him. To show her. To show her how much *he* loved her.

Then, when she understood, he would take his knife and show her over and over how much he loved her...

Sarah woke up early, feeling a happiness she hadn't felt in a long time. Beside her, Isaac slept on his stomach, his face soft with sleep, his arm flung across her stomach. They had made love long into the night, finally falling asleep as the sun began to climb into the Washington sky. She turned onto her side, propped her head up on her arm and studied him. There was something familiar about him, something she couldn't define. His arm, so massive, felt good curved around her. She bent her head and kissed him softly, the stubble rough against her lips. Isaac murmured and smiled in his sleep.

Sarah slipped carefully from the bed and tugged her jeans and t-shirt on. Going down to the kitchen, she put the coffee pot on and opened the back door. The day was already warm and she sat down on the porch steps to think. Her head was spinning from the last twenty-four hours – and the man asleep in her bed.

He was undeniably gorgeous but as well as that, she'd discovered that he was also funny, kind and an incredible lover. The way he'd fucked her in the hallway last night, so masterfully, so expertly... god, she'd never felt like that before. Not with Dan, not with anyone. She'd never known sex could be like that: animal, feral, almost violent. The way his huge cock plowed her into delirium, his mouth on her clit – she drew in a shaky breath. Damn, she was getting wet again just thinking about it, despite the fact her thighs still ached from last night. She didn't even know this man, just went with her instincts. *I guess I moved on then,* she grinned to herself. It was strange – for two years she had been trying to find out what happened to Dan but lately, a resentment had been building. Her relationship with her husband had always been up and down but before he'd gone, it had started to feel alien. Like she didn't know who that person was anymore. He was different. She'd started to suspect he was having an affair but the day she had planned to confront him, she'd gotten home to find him gone. She'd wandered around near their home, looking to see if she could find him, if he'd taken their dog Wilson for a walk. She'd called out for her husband, and for her beloved Labrador but had found nothing. When she climbed up to the abandoned lighthouse on the edge of their property, she found Dan's keys, phone, wallet, shoes laid out in a neat line at the edge of the cliff. Wilson had been tied up and whined when he saw her.

That's when she'd panicked.

Sarah pushed the memory away. *No. No way.* Nothing was going to spoil her mood today. Whatever happened now between her and Isaac, last night had been the most erotic in her life. Nothing would change that, even if it turned out to be a one night stand. Sarah pushed away the quick rush of pain that idea brought her.

She shifted and felt a rustle in the pocket of her jeans and pulled out the letter she'd received the day before. The latest letter, she thought. Isaac's presence had made her feel weirdly safer and she steeled herself and ripped it open.

I'm always watching, I see you, Sarah, don"t let me down...

She screwed it up and threw it aside. It was the third strange note she'd received but she figured it was some jerk trying to freak her out. She thought she might have an idea who it was too – the ever charming Caroline. *Hateful woman.*

Eager to expunge the bad taste the letter had left, she scrambled to her feet, went inside to make the coffee. Taking them upstairs, she saw Isaac sitting up in bed, stretching. He grinned when he saw her.

"Good morning, beautiful."

She put the cups down on the nightstand, leaned over to kiss him.

"Good morning yourself, handsome."

He slid his hands into her hair as he kissed her. "God, you taste so good."

She chuckled her lips against his mouth. "Even with morning breath?"

"Especially that. I do have one complaint. You have too many clothes on."

Sarah grinned and stood up, peeling her t-shirt off slowly, then her jeans. Isaac's eyes moved over her body appreciatively. She sat down next to him, bending to kiss his hard chest.

Isaac trailed a finger down her spine and she shivered with pleasure. She stood and moved toward the bathroom, beckoning him.

"Wanna join me in the shower?"

Isaac grinned. "You know I do."

As they stood under the cool spray, Sarah took him into her mouth, hollowing out her cheeks as her warm, wet mouth enveloped his cock, sucking at him, teasing the tip with her tongue. Isaac sucked in a deep breath of pleasure, his fingers tangling in her dark hair. She brought him to the edge of climax before he lifted her easily and plunged into her, pressing her back against the cool tile, his mouth hungry on hers.

"God, Sarah. I could fuck you all day."

She laughed, gasping as he thrust hard into her, his cock unrelenting as it drove her towards orgasm. "Fuck me harder, Isaac...." She gasped as, grinning, he did as she asked, and ramming his hips against hers until she felt her body melt and shudder.

Afterward, they dressed and Sarah cooked them breakfast; scrambled eggs and maple bacon, fresh fruit, and juice. They ate on her porch, looking down to the small cove at the end of her garden.

"It's beautiful here," Isaac said thoughtfully, munching on a strip of crispy bacon. "The island, the Sound... the coffee house owners." He grinned at her as she rolled her eyes and smiled.

"What made you decided to move here?"

Isaac sipped his coffee.

"I wanted somewhere out of the city. I love Seattle but sometimes it can get claustrophobic."

Sarah ate a forkful of eggs. "What do you do?"

For a second, his eyes were amused. "I own a tech company."

"Cool." Then she stopped. "Wait..."

"Yep."

"You're Isaac *Quinn*?"

"Yep."

She grinned sheepishly. "Sorry, you must think I'm a dumbass. It's just I'm not very technological minded. I can work my iPad but that's about it."

Isaac smiled. "No problem – at least you won't bother me about your lost passwords... although you can *totally* bother me about your lost passwords."

Sarah laughed. "Now that you mention it..."

Isaac reached over to touch her face, running the back of his finger down her cheek. "Sarah?"

"Yes?"

"Would you spend the day with me?"

Sarah walked through the storeroom into the kitchen, into the wave of noise sweeping in from the open door to the shop. Sarah drew in a great lungful of air and blew it out slowly, feeling the happiness in her flood through her body.

Going out into the coffee house, she grinned at Molly in greeting, trying to hide her joy. Molly wasn't fooled for a second.

"What's up? You look weird."

Always the silver tongue. Sarah smiled despite herself.

"Weird is right. There's a new man in my life."

Molly's eyes lit up. "My brother finally did the decent thing and left the witch?"

Sarah rolled her eyes. "Will you ever stop trying to fix me and Finn up?

"Not ever," Molly smiled, a wicked grin. "Oh, I know..."

Sarah waited.

"Is it that guy? The computer dude?"

Sarah gaped at her. "Am I the only one who didn't recognize him?"

Molly sighed dramatically. "And you such a geek, as well. Shame on you. So...?"

It was Sarah's turn to grin. "Oh look, customers."

Sarah went to serve the new customers as Molly grinned to herself. Sarah looked out of the window. She saw Finn, dressed in his cop's uniform, walking out of his front door with Caroline at his heels. Caroline was smiling. More like a rictus, Sarah thought. She saw Molly looking at them too. She grimaced

"Ignore her, she's a hideous troll."

"What *does* he see in her?" Sarah slammed the register with a little too much force. A stand of muffins fell off the counter. She went round to pick them up. Molly leaned over to watch her.

"Well, what did you get up to with Mr Robot then?"

Sarah stood, hands full of ruined cakes and dumped them in the trash. Despite herself, she was enjoying tormenting the ever curious Molly.

"We, um, *connected*."

Molly's mouth was hanging open. "You slept with him?"

Sarah leaned on the counter. "A lot. A lot, a lot." She grinned at her friend's astonished face and knew what she was thinking. Sarah didn't have affairs or flings or whatever. Not until now.

Molly started to smile. "Well, hallelujah. Was it good?"

"Yup."

"Wow. Wow."

Sarah nodded. "Mols, honestly, I never knew...well, let's just say it was never like this with Dan. That's not to say it was bad," she added hurriedly, "Just with Isaac... well."

Molly came around the counter and hugged her. "I'm so pleased. I'm so, *so* delighted for you, Sars. You deserve to be happy."

"Thank you."

"Did you tell him about Dan?"

Sarah felt her chest hurt. "Not yet. I don't know where this is going yet and I'm not ready to see that look in his eyes, the one I always get when I tell someone Dan disappeared."

Molly rubbed her friend's arm in sympathy. "I understand, honey."

Sarah was quiet. Molly gave her a minute and went to clear some tables. Sarah looked out of the window, over to Finn's house. Now Caroline was yelling at a departing Finn and his face was set in a grim line as he walked into the coffee house "Hey."

Sarah rolled her eyes at him sympathetically. "Hey, dude."

"Hey girl." He said, his eyes softening. Molly might want Finn and Sarah to be together but both of them knew that was never on the cards. They were too close friends now to ever cross that line.

"Yo, bro." Molly slapped. "What did the dragon yell at you today for?"

Finn shrugged. "Who cares?"

"Why the hell are you still with her?" Molly asked the question Sarah was thinking.

"Fuck knows. My shift doesn't start for an hour but I just had to get out of there."

Sarah tugged one of his blonde curls. "Stay and chill out with us, dude. We'll feed you all the basic food groups – sugar, coffee, butter."

Finn grinned at his friend. "You make it sound so good and so dirty at the same time."

Molly cleared her throat and nodded at her boss.

"Talking of which... Sarah's had an interesting twenty-four hours."

Sarah blushed and Finn raised his eyebrows at her. Sarah half-smiled, feeling strange at telling her old friend about the new man in her life.

"I'm seeing someone. Sort of."

"She means she got laid. Properly laid." Molly's grin was wide and wicked.

Finn choked on his coffee as Sarah laughed in shock at Molly's pronouncement

A half hour later and with the coffee shop empty, the three of them sat at one of the tables. The heat outside had become oppressive and stormy.

"Well." Finn pulled his tie down.

"Yeah."

Finn took a slug of coffee. "I think I should meet him. You know, for security. Make sure he's not a con artist."

Molly grinned into her coffee. Sarah raised her eyebrows at him.

"And how will you ascertain that, Colombo?"

"I shall say... are you a con artist? From his answer, I shall make a judgment call."

"You mean if he says yes, then..."

"Exactly." Finn tried not to grin. Sarah started laughing.

"Our tax dollars hard at work." She got up, squeezing his shoulder. "Thank you, though, you're sweet to think of it." She moved away to the kitchen. She called back over her shoulder. "Anyway, you'll meet him tonight if you're still here about eight. He's picking me, we're going to George's."

He nodded and stood up. "I'll try and come back and meet... what's his name again?"

"Isaac. Isaac Quinn."

"Got it."

Sarah smiled at him.

"Later then?"

"You bet."

"That woman is very unpleasant." Isaac turned back from staring at Caroline. Sarah looked over at Finn – he looked so unhappy that she ached for him. She felt Isaac watching her and turned back to him with a smile.

"Sorry."

They were seated at dinner across the restaurant from Finn and his wife. George's restaurant was full to capacity and the room was buzzing with conversation. Above it all was Caroline's nasal screech, arguing with a morose Finn. Caroline shot daggers over at Sarah who responded with the cheesiest of grins, making Isaac chuckle.

"Not friends then?" He asked after a particularly poisonous glare.

Sarah grinned. "Nope."

Caroline suddenly stood up, scraping her chair against the stone floor.

"Fuck you, Finn!" She stormed out. Finn buried his head in his hands. Sarah's hands tightened on her napkin. Isaac was watching the redhead cross the street and slam into her house. Sarah sighed.

"You're right, Isaac. She is unpleasant. And Finn is one of my best friends, he deserves better."

Isaac covered her hand with his. "Let's change the subject. You look breath-taking."

Sarah grinned, embarrassed. "It's the dress, not me. How are you settling into the hotel?"

"Very well. I travel pretty light so I didn't have to bring much."

"A Nomad."

"Yes. Something like that."

She cleared her throat softly. "You know, you don't have to stay at the hotel."

Isaac smiled. "Is it wrong that I've been sitting here wishing you might say something like that?" He leaned over to kiss her, his lips brushing along hers in a way that made her head swim.

Trying to calm herself – and the frantic quiver between her legs - she studied the menu. "I can never decide what to have in here."

He laughed. "Surely you must have worked your way through the entire menu by now. For our next date, I'll take you to the city and take you to my apartment."

She smiled. "Our next date?"

"And the many, many more to follow."

"Well, how-de-doo." George sang his greeting and Sarah giggled at Isaac's surprised face. She stood and embraced the newcomer.

"Hello George. Isaac, this is George, my pops for intents and purposes. George, this is Isaac Quinn."

"How are you, Isaac?" George offered Isaac his hand. "How are you liking our little island?"

"Hoping to see a little more of it, if Sarah will be kind enough to show me around."

She smiled and nodded. "George, won't you join us?" She looked over to Isaac, who nodded enthusiastically.

"Ha, no, sweet girl, I just came to say hello. Great to meet you, Isaac. I'm sure we'll see you again soon." George patted her shoulder and moved away. Isaac smiled at Sarah.

"Your father?"

Sarah nodded. "Sort of. Very long story and one for another time. He's the only family I have except for Mols and Finn. They're my adopted siblings."

Isaac looked over at Finn, who was still sitting at the bar.

"You know, we could ask Finn to join us. He looks like he could do with a friend."

Sarah was touched. "That's sweet of you but I know Finn, he'd just be embarrassed."

As if on cue, Finn slid from the bar stool and moved to the door, disappearing into the night, without glancing back to see them. Isaac turned back to Sarah.

"Can I ask? Why did you and Finn never... um... I'm presuming here, of course, but growing up together, it never crossed your mind that it could be more?"

Sarah shook her head. "No, really, it didn't. I mean, I love Finn of course, but a relationship? It would feel weird."

Isaac smiled. "So, I don't have to be worried about the competition then?" His tone was light but there was something beneath that she couldn't fathom.

"Definitely not."

"Good."

She smiled. "Are you ready to go? I told Molly we'd stop by the coffee house."

"Hey, dudes." Sarah, followed by Isaac, patted Finn on the back as they made their way into the coffee house. She walked behind the counter and grabbed the coffee pot. She filled three mugs and passed one to each of them. She grabbed a soda from the cooler for herself. Isaac sat down at the counter.

"Finn Jewell, meet Isaac Quinn."

Finn eyed him, offered his hand and without hesitation, Isaac shook it.

"Hey, Chief, good to meet you."

"Likewise."

Sarah beamed.

"Be right back."

She gave them both a smile and disappeared. Molly went to clear the tables and close the door.

Isaac grinned at Finn. "Sarah tells me you're like her big brother. You going to give me the speech?"

Finn laughed. "Let's just say it's implied and leave it at that. You've made her light up, that's for sure, and that's good enough for me."

Isaac beamed. "She rocks my world even after this short a time."

"It's worth it," Finn grinned at his sister who had come back to the counter, "I haven't seen her like this since way before Dan disappeared."

Molly stopped and threw a murderous glare at her brother. Isaac didn't notice.

"Dan?"

Sarah chose that moment to return to the main room. She stopped when she saw their faces – Molly and Finn embarrassed, Isaac confused. She smiled at them.

"What happened? Were you two being socially awkward again? They're twins, you know," she added as a joking aside to Isaac. He smiled and took a deep breath in.

"I think they're worried because they just mentioned someone called Dan. Is it a secret or do I get to know who that is?"

Finn ducked as Caroline threw the glass at him. What he'd done to deserve this, he didn't know. He'd walked in the door and she'd flipped out on him.

"Woah!" He reached over and grabbed her arm before she could pick up another weapon. "What the fuck are you doing?"

Caroline ripped her arm free. "You're an asshole, Finn. I saw you earlier. In that goddamned coffee house. With her."

Finn's shoulders slumped. This again. "Also, with my sister but I suppose it's more convenient for your little story if it was just me and Sarah."

"Don't say her fucking name." Caroline spat at him. "*Sarah-Sarah-Sarah-Sarah-Sarah-fucking-Bailey*. It's all I ever hear about."

She sat down in the armchair and lit a cigarette. She leaned her head back on the chair, looking at him. "Are you screwing her? Just tell me."

Finn sighed. "This again. How many times, we are just friends, we have always *been* just friends. I'm married to you."

"But you love her."

"What do you want me to say, Caroline?"

She laughed. "You can't even deny it, can you?"

"Do we have to do this every week? It's like I could schedule into my diary. The same fight, the same questions and you'll never get a different answer to the one I always give you. Sarah is my *sister*." He looked over to where the glass had shattered. "The glass was new, that was nice, made it kind of special." Finn knew he was goading her now but he didn't care. "If you're so convinced I'm in love with Sarah –," Caroline hissed and he grinned " – why don't you leave me?"

Caroline smirked. "Why don't *you* leave *me*?"

Finn turned to her, defeat in his eyes. "Go to bed, Caroline. You've made your point."

She smiled and stubbed her cigarette out and got up. "Are you coming?"

"No." Finn stepped away from her.

She gave a short laugh and walked off. "Suit yourself."

He heard the bedroom door shut and sighed. He picked up the glass on the floor, tempted to step on it with his bare feet so he could feel something else than the utter hopelessness he felt this night. Why the hell had he married Caroline? *Because she'd faked a pregnancy, dumbass.* He slumped into the armchair and closed his eyes. This nightmare was of his own making – and he had no idea how to leave it.

They'd gone back to her house and were sitting on the porch. Sarah couldn't believe how much had happened in such a few short days. She'd spent a blissful weekend with Isaac, making love.... *fucking like animals*, she grinned to herself, but now it was time to get back to reality. He needed to know about her.

She snagged two beers from the fridge and they settled in the comfortable chairs out back, watching Wilson playing with his ball in the yard. The Labrador and Isaac were already fast friends.

Isaac hadn't pressed her after the incident at the coffee house when she'd asked him to wait until they were alone to explain. She loved him for that.

Now, she turned to him. She was constantly amazed that every time she looked at him, she saw something new and glorious about his handsome face. Even after such a short time, she felt he belonged in her life – and she in his.

"Dan was my husband. He went missing two years ago. It was a Friday, a normal workday. I was at the coffee house, Dan was at his work. Nothing was wrong, we hadn't argued and he showed no signs of depression. All that had happened was that, two days before, I asked him, calmly, if he was having an affair. He denied it and I let it go. I got a call from the school saying he hadn't shown up for work. I went home – and he was gone. Just gone. He'd taken the dog so I thought he'd just gone for a walk but it was odd that he hadn't called anyone. I never saw him again. I found Wilson tied up near an abandoned lighthouse at the edge of our property, Dan's wallet, phone and keys lined up neatly along the cliff."

"He jumped?"

Sarah shrugged. "More like, I think he wanted to give the impression he had."

Isaac studied her. "You sound angry more than sad."

Sarah hesitated. "I was upset for a while but the more I thought about it...Dan wasn't the type to kill himself. I think he wanted out and couldn't face telling me."

"You *are* pissed."

She nodded. "We were happy when we first got married but things changed. He changed. Became.... I don't know. It wasn't as if we argued or he was abusive just, controlling. He got upset easily." She sighed. "I don't know, he might be dead for all I know."

She studied Isaac's expression but he looked interested with no trace of the sympathy she dreaded. "That's rough."

She nodded. "Anyways, I divorced him in absentia. They couldn't find a body and we hired detectives to find him. Nothing. I'd gone from upset to pissed to - and I'm ashamed to admit this - relief."

"What did he teach?"

She was startled. "Music. He taught music. When he was young he used to win prizes, all the time, for piano."

Isaac looked behind him. "Do you have a piano here?"

She nodded. "In the drawing room."

"Do you play?"

She nodded. "But not since."

"I understand."

A somber mood had fallen and Sarah felt uncomfortable. "I would have told you, I promise. I just thought it might be too soon and I didn't want to presume, and I didn't want to burst the bubble I've been in since we met."

Isaac reached out and pulled her onto his lap. "I get it. This is all new. But, Sarah, listen. I'm in this. I want "us". I've never felt this connection with anyone before. If you'll let me, I want to give you everything he never could. You deserve all the love in the world."

Her eyes filled at his words and she pressed her lips to his. "I'm in this too," she whispered against his mouth and felt his mouth curve up in a smile.

"Good." He stood, lifting her with him and carried her into the house. "Guess what we're going to do now?"

Upstairs, he laid her gently on the bed and began to unbutton the front of her dress, pushing the soft cotton aside to expose her bare skin, pressing his lips down on the velvety silkiness. He popped the front clasp of her bra and let her full breasts into his hands, plumping them, taking each nipple into his mouth, his tongue teasing, his teeth grazing them until he felt them harden. He kissed down the line of her stomach, circled the deep hollow of her navel with his tongue, feeling her belly quiver and contract under his touch.

His fingers slid under the sides of her panties and he slowly pulled them down, kissing the soft mound above her sex then, as his mouth found her clit, his tongue lashing around it, he felt Sarah's body tense and her breath quicken. God, she tasted like heaven as he plunged his tongue deep inside her, listening to her moan of pleasure. His cock lay hard against his stomach and soon he was clambering up her body, needing to be inside her. Her legs clamped around his waist, his cock, rigid under the sheer weight and length of it, nudged at her opening then slide all the way in, right to the root. His hips rotated, thrusting as deep as he could into her, his mouth covering hers, his tongue massaging hers. Sarah moaned, a shuddering velvety sound and Isaac smiled down at her.

"I love fucking you, beautiful Sarah...."

In reply, she tilted her hips up, taking him in deeper, her fingers twisting in his dark curls, her cunt hungrily squeezing and contracting around his cock. Their eyes locked as Isaac began to thrust harder, faster, ramming mercilessly into her, urged on by her cries and moans.

He came explosively, his entire body jerking with the force of the semen being pumped from him, shooting deep inside her. His mind was a delirious whirl, consumed by her, the silky skin, and the heady scent of her, her beauty. He murmured her name over and over as she came, his fingers rubbing her clit as his still hard cock plunged in and out of her. She shuddered and cried out as she came and he gathered her to him as they caught their breath.

"Sarah...beautiful, beautiful Sarah..."

There were tears in her eyes and he brushed them away. "What is it, love? Is everything all right?"

She nodded, smiling through her tears. "Everything's perfect, Isaac, it's just....I never knew it could be like this, I never knew I could be this happy..."

Isaac brushed his lips over hers. "I know, baby, I know. I'm falling for you, Sarah Bailey, falling so, so hard..."

He sat in his car, watching Sarah through the big windows at the front of the coffee shop. She looked happy, her dark hair messy, her cheeks flushed as she flitted around, chatting to the customers. Her smile made his stomach twist with desire. The pretty white blouse she wore rode up every time she reached for something from the coffee shop's shelves, he noticed. He imagined the delicate cotton soaking through with her blood, her dusky skin cleaving under his blade.

She'd been fucking that rich asshole for weeks now and looked so happy, so radiant it made his prick harden and twitch. He wanted her in his bed, fucking her into submission, before finally ending it the only way that it could end...

By killing her.

"Hey, geek."

Sarah, mired in accounts and bored out of her mind, looked up and saw Finn coming into the coffee house, obviously ducking out of work to come see her and she was grateful for the interruption. She shoved her glasses up her nose and studied him. His police uniform was crumpled as if he'd been sleeping in it.

"Hey, weirdo." She automatically poured a large Americano for him, sliding across the counter. He grinned his thanks and took a huge slug.

"How's the boyfriend? Gotta say, I like him."

Sarah beamed at him. "I'm glad."

"A definite upgrade."

Sarah peered over the top of her glasses at him and tried to look disapproving. "Finn..."

Finn shrugged unrepentantly. "Truth, sorry. He's treating you well, yes?"

She nodded, feeling uncomfortable. Since Dan's disappearance, Finn had often alluded to the fact he'd never really liked her husband and had never thought him worthy of her. Something came back to her; Isaac asking why and Finn had never hooked up. She pushed the thought away. That wasn't why Finn had disliked Dan... was it?

She found that she couldn't look him in the eye then.

"Yes, he is. Actually, we're going to his place in the city for a few nights."

"Nice."

"Yep."

"Hey, you know how much this guy's worth?"

She frowned at him. "None of my business – or yours either, Finn Jewell."

He grinned. "Hey, the info's right there on the internet. Besides, as a cop and your friend, I had to check him out. Don't worry..." He added hurriedly as she opened her mouth to complain, "Squeaky clean. Guy's worth seven-hundred billion, though."

"Finn! I don't want to know that." Sarah clamped her hands over her ears. She really didn't need to know that; it was bad enough that she couldn't hope to be on equal financial terms with Isaac, let alone knowing exactly what the difference was.

Finn chuckled. "Relax, I'm kidding. More like half of that."

Sarah reached over and picked up a muffin, lobbing it at her friend. "Shut. Up."

Finn caught the cake and took a big bite of it. "Thanks. Seriously, though, bubba, I am happy for you."

She hugged him. "If only you could be as happy."

Finn rolled his eyes. "That is entirely of my making, Bubs. And mine to sort out."

Sarah chewed on her lip, wondering whether to tell him about the letters. Caroline was the only one who hated her enough to send them, the only person she knew was spiteful enough. She and Caroline had loathed each other since childhood; Caroline had been a bully even then and when the headstrong Sarah had failed to bow down to her playground majesty, Caroline had made her a target.

But she didn't want to give Finn more stress. She smiled at him. "One day, I know you'll be happy. I just know it."

Finn finished his coffee and gave her a high-five. "From your lips to God's ears, sweetheart. Better go, poorly performed policing to be done."

Sarah watched Finn cross the street to the police station. Caroline was walking towards him, still haranguing him but he ignored her. Caroline stopped in the middle of the street and looked over to the coffee house. She scowled as she caught Sarah's eye. "*Bitch,*" she mouthed. Sarah, wearing a wide grin, cheerfully gave her the middle finger, laughing as Caroline flounced back to her house.

Isaac looked up as his brother and business partner Saul knocked at his office door. Saul, at forty-two, was Isaac's elder by three years but stood half a foot smaller than Isaac's six-five. Since their parents had died, Isaac and Saul had built the business up into a global endeavor thanks to Isaac's genius and Saul's solid and shark-like business nous.

Along the way, Saul had managed to find himself a wife and now he was the father of two children. His wife, Maika, was a Professor of Chemistry at the local University and Saul had been taking a back seat in the Quinn business for the last few years.

He'd been delighted when Isaac told him about Sarah. "Damn, at last! I was beginning to think we'd have to refurbish our basement for you in your old age."

Isaac grinned. "Very funny. Listen, she's coming to stay with me in the city for a week, think you and Maika could be free for dinner?"

"Sure thing. Let me know when."

After his brother had gone, Isaac attempted to answer a few overdue emails but in truth, his mind was across the water, on the island, wrapped around the image of the beautiful brunette whose bed he'd left this morning. He could call her... then changed his mind. *You're supposed to play it cool, man.* But he couldn't be bothered with childish games. At thirty-nine, he'd thought himself a bachelor for life and he'd been okay with that. The day he'd walked into that coffeehouse had changed all of that.

Isaac got up and walked to the window that looked out over the city and Elliott Bay. He couldn't get the story Sarah had told him about her absent ex-husband out of his head. Why the hell would anyone want to get away from her? He agreed with Sarah – even though he hadn't known Dan, there was something hinky about the way Dan Bailey had gone missing. Why take the dog with him unless he wanted someone to find him and his carefully laid out possessions? It was all too staged.

Be honest, he told himself, *you want to be sure he won't come back for her.* He admired Sarah for divorcing Dan, for not being a victim. There was more she hadn't told him yet, he was sure but that was up to her, he wouldn't push it. Wouldn't hurt to check out Daniel Bailey, though, would it?

Isaac reached for his phone and made a call. "Jake? Yeah, it's Isaac. Listen... can you do a background check on someone for me?"

Molly took over for Sarah in the afternoon and Sarah went home, eager to do her laundry and get packing for her week in the city. She could barely wait to see Isaac; he was coming to pick her up over her protestations that she could drive herself.

"I'm trying to show off," he'd told her with a grin, "I have my own chopper."

Sarah had giggled at him. "A big one?"

"A huge one just for you."

That had stopped the protestation as suddenly, her mouth was busy kissing him, giggling over their silliness.

Now, she gathered clothes from all over the house, where they'd been discarded as Isaac had taken them off her. She loaded the washer then cleaned the house quickly. She remembered when Dan was here, the house had always looked pristine; Dan had hated clutter. Over the last two years, the house had become more homely, books everywhere, records and cds shoved into piles on the living room floor. *More relaxed, more me,* Sarah thought now.

She walked back into the hallway and saw an envelope on the wooden floor. It hadn't been there when she came home. She picked it up and opened the front door, walking out onto the porch and looking to see if anyone was around. All she could hear was the breeze through the trees and the distant yell of schoolchildren from the private school that bordered their land.

She glanced at the envelope and her stomach knotted. Another one. Steeling herself, she ripped it open.

You will make a beautiful corpse...someday soon.

Fury tore through her. "Fuck you, creep," she yelled out into the woods around the house. Only the breeze answered her.

Angry now, she slammed the front door. Wilson came trotting up to her, sensing her distress, and stuck his nose in her hand. Sarah took a couple of deep breaths and tried to smile at the dog.

"It's okay, buddy." She looked at her watch. It was another couple of hours before Isaac was due and she was antsy now.

After a storm the previous evening, the air was fresher but still warm and after she hung the clothes out, she changed into her swimsuit, throwing her jeans and tee over it and headed out the back door. Much to the Wilson's disgust, she tied him up in the barn, using what she called the party leash – the rope tied to his collar that allowed him to roam within the barn and a short way out into the yard. He began barking and whining, his usual song of self-pity and psychological manipulation whenever he was sent to the barn. Luckily, his singing carried to the beach rather than the school, sheltered as it was by the house and woods that surrounded it. Giving him a last pat on the head, Sarah made her way to the little sandy path that led to their tiny beach.

At the water's edge she stripped down to her suit, ran lightly along the little wooden jetty and dived into the cold water.

"The feel of the water streaming past her limbs was glorious. Cold as it was, it made her skin feel fresh and clean, and the weightlessness relaxed the taut muscles of her shoulders and neck. Sarah dived and swam beneath the surface for a few moments then, as she surfaced, pushed her hands over her face to clear her eyes, smooth back her hair.

A surge of angry adrenaline made her strike out again, swimming until she was exhausted. Stopping to catch her breath, something caught her eye. Her head whipped round and her eyes raked the tree line. The skin on her neck prickled. Nothing. Nothing... wait. Movement. Someone was there.

Someone was watching her.

At four o'clock, Isaac couldn't wait any longer. Saying goodbye to his brother, he headed to the helipad on the roof of the building and got in. The piloting lessons he and Saul had taken had proved their worth over and over – none more so than now,

Isaac thought, a little smugly. In a quarter hour, he'd be with her. He thought about calling her but decided to surprise her.

She got out of the water, pulling herself up onto the jetty, never taking her eyes of the woods where she'd seen the movement. She raked the trees with her eyes, searching, seeking anything, any figure. Nothing. She let out a deep breath. *Paranoia?*

She tugged on her jeans over her wet swimsuit, ignoring the way her t-shirt clung to her damp skin and set of for home.

She hadn't gone ten yards before she heard it. An inhuman scream of absolute pain, a scream that faded into a long mournful wolf-like howl.

Wilson.

Finn got home to find Caroline absent. He relaxed then, taking his time in the shower then grabbing a bottle of Jack and flicking on the t.v. It crossed his mind that Caroline was with another man. *God, I hope so.* Finn smirked to himself. *Dude, you are so messed up.*

But he truly didn't care.

Her breath came in ragged, panicked gasps.

Sarah ran through the trees that separated the beach from the house, the thinner limbs whipping her as she scrambled her way through, away from whoever was watching her. As the woods thinned, she stumbled into the yard. Still no sound. Wilson should be going crazy by now. She yanked the barn door open, calling Wilson's name. To her horror, she heard a pitiful whimper, followed by a hacking, vomiting retching. She cast around desperately and saw a hind leg sticking out from one of the stalls in the barn. She dashed over to where Wilson lay and cried out in despair. The dog lay on his side, a fit sending spasms through his body, blood, drool and vomit hanging from his slack jaw.

Wilson groaned in agony as Sarah scooped him up into her arms and ran for the truck.

Isaac landed the chopper expertly on Sarah's land and got out. He frowned. Her truck was missing and the front door to the house was wide open. He walked to the house and inside.

"Sarah?"

He walked from room to room only to find them empty. Returning to the hallway, he saw a balled up piece of paper and picked it up, smoothing it out.

His breath froze in his lungs.

You will make a beautiful corpse...

Isaac cursed to himself. Going back outside, he called her name, searched through the woods and down at the beach. Finally, he got back into the chopper, remonstrating with himself for not driving, and headed into town.

Dead-eyed and exhausted, Sarah sat in the coffee house wrapped in a blanket while Molly and Finn cast worried glances at each other. A quarter hour before, she'd walked into the Varsity, tears pouring down her face.

Molly had rushed to her side as she sobbed. "Sarah, what's wrong? I thought you had plans with Isaac tonight..."

Sarah interrupted her. "I was swimming. In the cove, I was swimming and I saw someone watching me. And then there was this scream and..."

"Someone was watching you?" Molly was incredulous. "What the hell?"

"It was Wilson, he was screaming and... god..."
Molly shook her head, not understanding.

"There was no... I ran, Molly, I ran... the trees, whoever it was had gone but Wilson..." Sarah started to cry. Finn came in and stopped, his face a picture of confusion. Molly waved him closer, as she tried to comfort her friend.

"What's wrong, what's happened?" Finn put a hand on Sarah's back and as she turned to him, he wrapped his arms around her, his eyes full of concern. Sarah sobbed out something but he just shook his head.

"Sarah, I don't understand, just tell me, honey."

"Wilson...he was lying down in the barn and having fits, there was blood and vomit..."

"Oh my God," Finn pressed his fist to his forehead, realizing what she was about to say.

"He wouldn't stop, the spasms, so I picked him up and I just ran for the truck. The vet said... I had to say..." Sarah was sobbing now,"...goodbye, but I couldn't... he was in so much pain, Finn."

He pulled her into his arms and she sobbed against his chest. He held her while she cried herself out, rocking her gently.

"He was poisoned. The vet said there was no doubt. Someone poisoned my dog. Why would anyone do that?"

There was a commotion outside and the three of them looked up to see a helicopter land in the middle of the street. Sarah's eyes widened. "God... Isaac... what he must have thought."

Molly patted her shoulder. "I'll go get him, fill him in." She went out into the street and Sarah could see her talking to Isaac. Finn's arms were still locked around her and as Isaac come in, she saw his eyes flicker with something as he took in the scene. Finn released her and walked to Isaac and she heard them talk in low tones. Isaac's shoulders slumped and he came over.

"I'm so sorry, Sarah." He pulled her into his arms, pressing his lips against her forehead. Sarah sank into his embrace, feeling her energy drain out of her. After a moment, Isaac held her at arm's length and stared down at her. "We need to talk."

Dumbly she nodded and sat down at the nearest table. Isaac turned to Molly and Finn, who were discreetly giving them space, and waved them over. "I think we all need to talk about this – and, Chief?" He nodded at Finn. "We might need you in a professional capacity."

All four settled at the table. Isaac took Sarah's hands. "Darling.... I was at your house, as you know. Sarah, I found the note."

He pulled it from the table and smoothed it out so Finn and Molly could read it. Finn cursed viciously and got up, his hand in his hair. Molly covered her mouth with horror. Isaac rubbed his thumb gently on the back of Sarah's hand.

"There have been more, right? Am I right?"

Sarah nodded, resigned. "Yes."

"How many?"

There was a long silence. "Twenty seven."

Molly gasped and Finn pounded his fist down on the table. "Jesus. H. Christ, Sarah, are you crazy? How did you not tell us?"

Sarah looked at Isaac, who was blank-faced. "It's just a crank. A sicko trying to scare me."

Finn cursed again and Isaac shook his head slowly.

"No, sweetheart. This is a death threat. I assume the others were along a similar vein?"

She nodded. "Yes."

"For how long?"

She lowered her eyes. "Six months."

"And now someone killed your dog." Finn was almost wild with anger. She looked at him.

"Calm down, Finn. Do you want to know why I didn't tell you? Because I thought the letters were a sick prank – and we all know the only person spiteful enough to do that is..."

"...Caroline." Finn gritted his teeth. "Well, we'll soon find out." He stalked out of the coffee house. Sarah sighed and put her head down on the table.

Isaac stroked a finger down her face. "Look, why don't we get your things and go back to my place? We can't do anything tonight. You need to rest."

She smiled at him gratefully and Molly got up. "Look, I have my car, let me drive you back home to get your stuff. Isaac, why don't you stay here and talk to Finn?" She locked eyes with him and he nodded. He kissed Sarah, brushing his lips over hers.

"Come back soon."

"I will."

Molly and Sarah left and Isaac waited in the coffee shop for Finn to return. He didn't have to wait long. The police officer came back with a disgusted look on his face.

"She's denying everything, of course. And I don't think she'd go as far as poisoning Wilson. She hasn't the brains to think of that."

Isaac studied the younger man. "Can I ask you something?"

Finn tried to smile. ""Is it why am I married to such a bitch"? Because I haven't got an answer for that, buddy, I really don't."

Isaac nodded then sighed. "Listen, I take these threats seriously. Sarah's a beautiful woman and any freak could have fixated on her. I just want her safe."

Finn nodded. "Preaching to the choir, Isaac. These last two years have been pretty…strange."

"You didn't think much of Daniel Bailey, did you?"

Finn looked uncomfortable and Isaac held his hand up. "Strictly between you and me."

Finn sighed. "I thought he was too in love with himself. He could be very charming, even genuinely friendly and I do believe he loved Sarah but conditionally. He hated anyone else looking at her and if she talked to any other man for too long, he would sulk. Like a two-year-old. I think he was dreadfully insecure at the same time as being totally narcissistic. It was all about *him*."

Isaac nodded, taking his words in. "Can I ask you something?"

"Shoot."

"Are you in love with Sarah?"

Finn gave a genuine laugh then and he leaned forward, clapping Isaac's shoulder. "You been talking to my wife? No, Isaac, me and Sarah are family, sure, but nothing more, I promise you."

"Okay, just needed to hear it from the horse's mouth."

"Fair enough. Look, let's work together here – get what you can out of Sarah about the other letters and ask if anything else has happened that we should know about. I'll investigate here, go to the house and make sure that it's secure."

Isaac offered his hand to Finn. "Deal. Sorry for asking… you know."

"I do. Look, man, take care of her. She could do with someone to look after her – although, don't tell her I said that, she'll kill me."

Finn grinned and Isaac laughed. "Our secret, I promise."

He opened the door to his apartment and stood aside to let her in. She'd changed into a pale blue sundress, brushed out her hair and was now looking brighter than earlier. She smiled at him.

"I'm almost afraid to look. Will there be gold taps and animal print bed sheets?"

Isaac pretended to look affronted. "But of course – and carpet on the ceiling."

"Fancy."

He was glad she seemed more like herself. "Come on in then, your palace awaits."

He was more nervous than he would admit. He wanted her to like his place, to approve of his taste. In the short time they had known each other, she had become more, much more to him than just someone with whom he enjoyed amazing chemistry and had incredible mind-blowing sex. She had become his friend, his confidant, his buddy. It was a new sensation for him to let someone get this close.

Sarah walked into the living room. "Huh. I kind of expected a minimalist nightmare but this is kinda like my place."

Isaac grinned. It *was* like her place, a place of enjoyment, of comfort, bookshelves stuffed to full, an admittedly top range music system, huge, over-stuffed couches. Sarah turned to smile at him, nodding to the huge flat screen.

"Boys with their toys, of course."

"Of course. Look, why don't we order a pizza and stay in tonight?"

She sighed. "That sounds heavenly. Have you got a big tub?"

Isaac grinned. "Oh yes, enough room for two. Plenty room for splashing too."

Sarah grinned. "You know what?" She caught the spaghetti strap of her dress between her fingers and pulled it slowly down her shoulder, followed by the other.

Isaac grinned. "Wait..." He sat down in one of the couches and got comfortable. Sarah laughed as he gestured grandly. "Continue."

She stood in front of him, stripping slowly, enjoying his obvious admiration. "You like what you see?"

"God, yes. Unclasp your bra, beautiful, let me see those spectacular tits."

Sarah grinned at him. "If I'd have known you like the dirty talk..." She eased her dress down, letting it fall to the floor and unhooked her bra, freeing her full breasts. Isaac sighed happily.

"Christ, have you any idea how beautiful you are?"

Sarah smiled, a scarlet blush coloring her cheeks. "As long as you think so." Naked except for her panties, she straddled him, bending her head to kiss him. Isaac spanned her waist with his big hands, cupped her breasts in his hands. He grinned up at her.

"I am going to fuck you senseless tonight, Miss Bailey."

"Damn straight."

He took a nipple into his mouth as she unzipped his pants, reaching and freeing his cock from his underwear. She stroked the length of it, her hands moving gently at first then as it swelled and hardened under her touch, she began to pull gently, urging it to thicken until it stood ramrod straight. She pulled open his shirt, revealing the smooth chest and hard pecs. In one swift movement, Isaac flipped her onto the floor and she smiled up at him as he tore the rest of his clothes off, and tugged down her panties. He kissed her mouth and moved down her body; kissing the hollow of her throat, the valley between her breasts as his fingers caressed her clit then slid inside her, pressing hard, making her wet and slick. Sarah ground her hips against his hand as she pressed her lips against his skin.

"Tell me what you want to do, Isaac," she whispered in his ear as his long fingers spread her labia gently and the crest of hic cock nudged tantalizingly at the entrance of her sex. Isaac groaned.

"I want to fill your sweet little cunt with my cock, make you scream, make you never want to leave my bed." With one hard thrust, he sank deep inside her and she moaned so beautifully he nearly came right away. They moved together, mouths hungry, hands gripping each other's, fingers digging into skin fiercely, bruising and clawing. They fucked hard and long, driving each other into a pitch of screaming frenzy. Isaac gave a long moan as he came, his cock spasming as he shot into her, burying his seed deep inside of her. Sarah tightened her legs around him, her arms twined around his neck, whispering his name over and over.

Breathless, he gazed into her deep brown eyes. "Sarah... my Sarah..."

She smiled up at him, her eyes soft. "I love it when you say my name like that..."

Isaac traced her bottom lip with the tip of his finger. "I love *you*, Sarah Bailey."

She grinned delightedly. "And I love you, Isaac Quinn and just so you know, I *never* want to leave your bed."

"Glad to hear it." He pulled her in the crook of his arm, his leg hitching over hers, curled around her. "Let's not move from here for a while."

"Deal."

For a few minutes, they lay in silence, listening to their breathing, skin-on-skin. Sarah tilted her head up to him. "Thank you. For making this day better. You make everything better."

Isaac was touched. "That's nice to hear. Sarah, I only want you to be happy and safe. Whoever is doing this to you, we have to find out who it is. For now, can I ask you to stay with me while Finn checks it out?"

Sarah sighed but nodded. "I hate to be run out of my own home."

"I know. And you're probably right, it's probably a spiteful, jealous person looking for cheap thrills but just to be safe, okay?"

Sarah nodded but stayed silent. He studied her expression. "You really think its Finn's wife?"

Sarah rubbed a hand over her eyes. "I don't know. We have never gotten along, not since we were kids."

"Still, why would she do something so spiteful?"

"Because that's who Caroline is. Can we talk about something else now?"

He kissed her forehead. "You got it, beautiful."

Later, in his bed, with Sarah asleep in his arms, Isaac lay awake, his mind whirling. It wasn't the notes or the poisoning of Sarah's dog that had him worried. It was what his private detective had found out. Or rather, what he hadn't.

"I've found marriage records, five years ago to Sarah Hannah Li but before that nothing. Literally nothing. No employment records, no medical records, no birth certificate – at least nothing legal. Nothing. Guy's a ghost."

Isaac had been unsettled by the detective's incredulous tone. It *was*, he told him, possible to disappear into the vastness of the US, but usually there was always some trace, some footprint.

Whoever he was or had been, Daniel Bailey was not who he told his wife he was.

Sarah stirred in his arms. He smiled as she muttered something inaudible and snuggled deeper into his arms. He had no regrets, no doubts about telling her loved her. It was more than true; he'd known for weeks, hell, had known almost from the beginning. He loved her easy manner, her wicked sense of humor, her intelligence and warmth. He loved the way she would shove her glasses up her nose when she was reading, or she would laugh at the stupidest jokes – the sillier the better. He loved that she loved her food and didn't pick at a garden salad like so many of his vapid ex-girlfriends. He loved the fact her butt jiggled when she washed her hair in the shower and that she didn't care.

Sarah opened her eyes as if aware of his scrutiny and smiled sleepily at him. "Hey, you."

In reply, he moved his body over hers, his erection already growing and she hitched her legs around his waist.

"I like sleepy sex," she said and he chuckled, sliding into her gently and moving slowly. Her mouth sought his and their tongues met and caressed as they made love, tenderly, taking their time and savoring the connection. She was still slick from his come, a thought that made him feel good. He wanted her to carry part of him always.

After they'd come, he spent a long time just touching her, stroking his hand over the curves of her, the full breasts with their dark red nipples, her belly which curved out slightly and was soft rather than hard muscles like his own. Her skin was like silk to him.

Sarah stroked her finger down his face. "Isaac?"
"Promise me something."
"Anything."

"Promise me you'll never stop touching me like that."

Isaac smiled, his sculpted features softening. "I promise you unconditionally."

He gathered her to him and they made love long into the night.

Molly rolled over onto her stomach and looked at the clock. Ten past four in the morning. She groaned softly and dropped her face into the pillow. Looking up, she saw that her husband Mike was deeply asleep, occasional snores rumbling through his chest. Molly smiled and kissed him gently, contemplating waking him. Deciding to let him sleep, she pushed the blanket away and swung her legs over the side of the bed. She regretted the action as the fierce cold of the early morning hit her. She pulled her robe around her and padded into the little kitchen. Dumping a spoonful of hot chocolate into a mug, she waited for the kettle to boil. Outside the window, she could see rain running in rivers down Main Street. When the kettle whistled she poured the hot water into the cup and took her drink into the living room. Her tabby cat Pigeon opened one eye and contemplated her as she perched next to him on the window seat. She scratched the top of his head, smiling at the meow he mouthed silently. His eye closed and he was immediately asleep again.

Molly could feel a headache buzzing around her skull and pressed her hot forehead against the cool window. The first ferry to the city left at four and already she saw the odd commuter head blearily down to the harbor. A light went on across the street at Finn's place. She watched as her brother walked to his car, got in and drove past the Varsity, heading for the west coast road. She frowned. Weird. Was he working? Molly rubbed her head, trying to ignore the idea that popped into her head. He was going to Sarah's house. But why in the middle of the night? Molly quelled the sudden panic and then remembered Sarah was in the city with Isaac. The cool window had eased her headache a little and she shivered, chilled now. As she was about to step away from the window when a movement opposite caught her eye. Outside the Varsity, a figure stood staring into the darkness of the empty coffee house. Molly watched, frowning, as the man – she was sure it was a man from his outline – stayed there for a while then as he turned away, the streetlight illuminated his face briefly and Molly gasped.

His face was a mask of anger, of hatred, of purest vitriol and Molly recoiled from the window at the sight of his twisted, contorted face. But it wasn't the waves of evil that came from the man that shocked her to the core. It was because she knew the face. Knew the man.

It was Daniel Bailey.

Sarah sighed as the hot bath water soothed her aching limbs. The tub was three times the size of her own tub at home – come to think of it, the entire apartment was bigger than her home. Home, she thought guiltily. She had to admit she hadn't missed being there at all these last few days. Molly had assured her that they were coping, that the coffee house was running fine but still, Sarah knew that in a day or two, her bubble would burst and she'd have to go back.

"You don't have to," Isaac said later when they were at dinner. "You can have anything you want, stay here and live with me. Start over if you want."

Sarah smiled. "You are sweet but no. As much as I love you, I don't want to be a kept woman."

Isaac shrugged, grinning good-naturedly. "I knew you'd say that but the offer is there. I *would* like to talk about where we go from here. I know it's fast."

Sarah considered. "It *is* a little fast but neither of us is a teenager, we know the risk and rewards of a relationship. We can talk about it, certainly."

"Moving in together?"

She nodded. "Talking about is the first step. But not tonight, tonight I just want to have fun. There's a wonderful cover band who play up at the Paramount on Thursday nights, I wondered if you would…"

"Count me in." Isaac was smiling but she could see there was something else bothering him.

"What is it, my love? What's bugging you?"

Isaac shifted in his chair, not meeting her eyes. "I've done something and I need to tell you about it."

Her chest clenched up immediately…*he cheated on me….he wants to end it*…but she forced herself to keep her face blank. "Oh?"

Isaac took a deep breath in. "Before that day, the day Wilson died and I found one of the letters, what you had been telling me about Dan had been bothering me. His disappearance. So I ask a private detective to look into it. I know I should have told you, it's just what he found, I couldn't get my head around."

Sarah felt the tension ease. "That's fine, Isaac. I'd be as curious as you if the tables were turned but I told you, we couldn't find anything."

He nodded. "Same here. Nothing. That's just it. As far as Daniel Bailey goes, he didn't exist before your marriage."

Icy cold shock hit her. "What are you talking about?"

"There was no Daniel Bailey born when he said he was, where he said he was. Did you ever meet any of his family?"

Sarah shook her head. "His parents were dead, no siblings."

"No cousins, no aunts and uncles?"

She shook her head slowly. "It was one of the things we had in common, no family." Her voice was gruff, uncertain. "This is crazy, why would he say.... why would he?" Her eyes filled with tears and she slumped in her chair. "What does it matter now, anyway? He's gone."

Isaac let her think about what he said while they ate. After their entrees had been cleared, she looked at him and he was sad to see the hurt in her eyes.

"Why am I surprised?" She said, then sat up. "Isaac... there's a lot about me, a lot about my marriage that I haven't, well, we haven't had a lot of time to get to know each other so perhaps it's not surprising that I haven't told you."

He took her hand. "Tell me."

Sarah rolled her shoulders trying to ease some of the tension. "I met Dan at college – he was teaching a music program. We met in the cafeteria – he started to talk to me one day and we became friends. One night, when he was walking me home from the cinema, he kissed me and that was that. We got married after I graduated and then came back here to open the coffee house and for Dan to teach at the school. Our life together wasn't... there were times when we spent a great deal of time apart and to be honest, it seemed to suit us both. The friendship we had kind of just went. Suddenly, I was his wife and therefore his property. He even resented me spending time with George and the twins, trying to isolate me from them. That's how he started to behave for a while until I reached my limit. He was controlling to the point of ridiculousness but he'd always turn it around saying I was oversensitive until I was convinced I was."

She saw the muscle in Isaac's face clench in anger and tried to smile. "I asked him to go to counseling and he agreed and everything seemed to change for the better. Then I found out he was watching me at work. All the time. He'd put security cameras in the coffee house and had actually made a note of every time I spoke to a man – especially Finn – and quizzed me on what was said, and how long they were talking to me. As far as I know that's as far as it went but I'd had enough. I told him I wanted to spend some time apart. He begged me to stay with him. After a couple of months, I became convinced that he was having an affair. So I asked him, straight out. No reproach, no shouting. I just said to tell me if he wanted out. He said no, the only way he would leave me is if I wanted out. Then two days later, he disappeared."

Isaac cursed softly under his breath. "I'm sorry, Sarah, what a fucking manipulative…"

"Quite. After I'd got over the shock of him going missing, thinking he was dead, thinking he had killed himself and it was my fault… that's when I got angry. I'm still angry."

"Good. Stay that way."

"He's alive somewhere, doing the same thing to someone else. Probably under a different name." She smiled then. "What a tool. I seriously am happy he's gone. "

Isaac burst out laughing at the expression on her face. "No more walking on eggshells."

"Nope. And thank god for you, showing me what a real, *healthy* relationship should be."

He toasted to that with his champagne but as they drank, a ribbon of unease curled in his stomach. Was Dan somewhere else?

Or was he here and still watching her?

"It wasn't Dan."

Molly scowled at her brother. He was so sure and so annoyingly smug about it. "You don't know, you weren't there."

"Mols, you're projecting. Dan is gone, and to be honest, good riddance. It's just because Wilson died and because of the letters that you're imagining boogeymen. And anyway, Dan never showed any violent tendencies. Yeah, he was a douche but he genuinely loved Sarah, he would never have hurt her or killed her dog."

Mols shivered. "You didn't see his face."

Finn rolled his eyes. "Whoever it was, it's nothing to worry about."

Molly got up then and made herself busy washing the breakfast stuff. Her children and Mike had left together just because Finn came to waste some time with her, rather than Caroline, before he went to work. Molly couldn't help feeling that Finn was being too blasé about what she thought she saw. She knew Daniel Bailey's face. It *was* him.

"Okay think about this," she turned to her brother who was sneaking some cold toast from one of the kids" discarded plates. "What if he came back and was going to see her but saw her with Isaac? Maybe it pissed him off."

"Sarah hasn't been with Isaac for six months. Also, Wilson was Dan's dog too."

Molly muttered to herself and Finn grinned. He stood and put his around his sister's shoulders. "Look, let's not make trouble where there is none. Wilson could have eaten something left for a raccoon or something."

"And the letters?"

Finn shrugged. "Sarah's convinced they are just sent out of

spite. I don't know, I want to believe that, I even want to *know* it's Caroline. Nothing we can do about it until…well."

"Someone hurts Sarah?"

Finn looked uncomfortable.

"Not going to let that happen. Anyway, better get to work."

As he opened the door to leave, Molly called him. She fixed him with a stare. "Finn… she's our family, our sister."

He nodded. "I know."

After he'd gone, Molly finished clearing the kitchen and went to get ready for work. Her cell phone beeped. A text from Sarah.

Hey gorgeous, see you at work this afternoon. Missed you xxx

Molly smiled. Finn was right. Sarah was happy at last and nothing was going to get in the way of that.

"I don't think I'm going to let you out of this bed." Isaac covered Sarah's naked body with his, using his weight to pin her down, feeling her pillowy breasts against his solid chest, her soft belly against his. Sarah grinned up at him as he wound his fingers through hers.

"You can keep me prisoner whenever you like but my business may suffer."

He nibbled her earlobe. "Maybe I'll quit my job, come work with you."

Sarah chuckled, enjoying his kisses. "I guess at this point you can do just about anything."

Isaac grinned wickedly. "Damn right. Now, beautiful Sarah, you gonna wrap those amazing legs around me or am I gonna have to do it for you? Because my cock needs to be inside you right now."

Sarah sighed happily as she curled her legs around his waist and then moaned as Isaac plunged his rock-hard cock into her. It was the morning that she was going home but Sarah didn't want to think about that, laying here in Isaac's massive bed, being thoroughly and expertly fucked by him. This gorgeous, funny, alpha man who owned her body so completely. Isaac smiled down at her as he thrust.

"You're so beautiful, baby, I can never get enough of looking at you, especially like this."

She lifted her mouth to his, caught his lower lip between her teeth for a playful nip, then ground her lips against his, exploring his mouth with her tongue. "Isaac Quinn... I love you so much."

"I love you, schmushy face, and then there's this..." He thrust hard and she gasped with pleasure as her senses exploded. She tightened her pelvic muscles, gripping his cock, making herself as tight as she could for him, eager to make sure she gave him as much pleasure as he did her. From his groan and the way his eyes closed, she could tell she did.

"What do you like, Isaac... tell me... I'll do anything for you, with you... tell me..." She whispered this in his ear, felt his teeth biting down on her neck as he moaned with pleasure.

"You. I want to fuck you forever, in every way. Sarah, I want to take you against a wall, fuck you in a rainstorm, feel your sweet mouth milking me dry... *god,* Sarah. There's nothing I wouldn't do to you if you let me..."

His words made her pulse quicken until it was a furious rush of blood through her veins and she clung to him, riding him hard. "Do it, do whatever you want..."

Isaac came then immediately turned her on her stomach.

"I'm going to fuck you in your perfect ass, Sarah, but you want me to stop, you say so straight away and we'll stop..."

She nodded, unable to speak in her excitement. Once she consented, she heard him reaching for something – the sound made her realize that he was applying lube to his firm cock. She shuddered and gave a low moan as he also teased her asshole by slowly rubbing it with a lubricated finger. As he pushed slowly into her, his fingers caressing her clit as he did, she gave a long, shuddering moan. She'd never done this before, not with Dan, not with anyone and the pleasure was so intense she felt her head swim, her limbs liquefy. She came again and again, heard Isaac telling her over and over how much he loved her.

Afterward in the shower, they were messing around, soaping each other up and laughing.

"My legs are still wobbling," she told him, "That was incredible."

Isaac grinned. "We can do so much more if you like... anything."

Sarah pressed her breasts against him. "God, yes, please..."

Isaac smiled, smoothing her hair with his big hands. "Sarah...I'd like you to meet my brother, his family. You'd like them."

"I'd love to... you know more about me than I do about you at this point. Time to redress the balance."

"Good. I'll set up dinner plans – not too scary, huh?"

"Not at all." She was distracted. His erection was hard against her belly and she stroked it gently as she smiled up at him. "You know what?"

"What?" He was obviously enjoying her touch, smiling, relaxed, turned on.

"I never enjoyed sex before you. I didn't hate it, but it was always a chore, always so "let's just get this over with". I never knew what the fuss was about."

Isaac bent his head to kiss her. "That's because we fit together. We belong together."

"You betcha. Now, put this incredible cock back inside me..."

As they flew back to the island, Isaac took her hand in his. "I have a few meetings today but I can be back over here by about ten tonight. If you're not sick of me."

"Hah, would never happen. God, it's beautiful out here today."

The Washington day had broken bright and warm and the sun sparkled off the waters of the Sound as they flew out over the bay. Sarah squeezed Isaac's hand.

"Hey, listen, I was thinking of having a cookout at the weekend. You, me, Molly and Mike, Finn and some friends. You could invite your brother and his family, your friends. Might be less stressful for everyone to meet like that."

Isaac nodded. "Sounds perfect, although you mean I have to share you for a whole day?"

She grinned. "Just for an afternoon and early evening. Afterward, I'll fuck your brains out in every room of the house if you'd like."

Isaac chuckled at her dirty talk. "I'll hold you to that. And keep talking like that, sexy girl, and I'll land this bird right here."

Sarah peered out of the window. "We'd sink."

"But what a way to go."

In a few more minutes, they were over the island and soon Isaac was landing the helicopter gently on her land. Sarah leaned over to kiss him. "Hey, Cap'n, do you have to go straight away?"

Isaac slid his hands onto her cheeks. "I'm the boss, I can play hooky for as long as you need me."

Sarah grinned, her mouth curving up in a smile against his. "Good, because I think I need to be fucked again."

Isaac laughed, unbuckling his seat belt. "I've turned you into sex maniac."

"Yes, you have."

Isaac got out of the chopper and walked around to her door, pulling her up into his arms as she laughed, pressing her lips to his throat. Easily, he carried her up onto the porch and let her down as she searched her purse for her key. His lips were on her shoulder as she unlocked the door, his hands pulling up her skirt. She turned in his arms and cupped his thickening cock through his pants. "God, you're big...."

He smiled, his eyes sleepily turned on. "For you, always." He slipped his fingers into her panties and stroked her. She shivered with desire and sighed. Isaac grinned. "I'm just gonna fuck you right here against this door." He slid two fingers into her and she gasped as his thumb stroked back and forth against her clit. "Tell me what you want to do, beautiful...."

She kissed him ferociously, grinding her hips against his hand. "I want to suck that big cock until you come in my mouth, handsome."

With a growl, he ripped her panties from her as she freed his cock, already so engorged that it strained against her hand. He lifted her and impaled her onto it, her soft, wet cunt stretching to envelop him. "Fuck me hard, Isaac."

He did, ramming his hips against hers, grinding his lips onto hers. They moved together hungrily; feral, clawing at each other until their movements made the door open and they tumbled, still fucking, onto the hallway floor.

Sarah knew something was wrong the moment that the door opened. A cold draft blew through the house from the kitchen at the far end of the hallway.

"Sarah? Is everything okay?"

"I don't know."

She disengaged from him, pulling her dress down and walked towards the kitchen, Isaac behind her. She saw at once that the back door was open. She let out a shaky breath. It had been busted open with something, she guessed a tire iron, a crowbar. Then she saw it. Reflected in the window. It made no sense. Something painted on the wall behind her. She turned and put her hands over her mouth in horror. Isaac looked at her face and turned with her.

WHORE

Red paint, dripping. Sarah gasped, humiliated, shaking.

"Oh my God." Isaac was shocked. He put his arms around her and coaxed her onto a chair. She couldn't say anything. Isaac crouched beside her.

"I'll call Finn. Get him over here." He stood to go to the phone but she grabbed his hand.

"No." She whispered. "No. I don't want him here, I don't want him to see this."

"But I really think – "

"No." Her voice was stronger, determined. "Please, Isaac. I couldn't bear it. Please."

He looked uncertain then nodded. "Okay, but on condition that you let me deal with this. Go into the other room. I'll fix you a drink and then I'll clean this up. You have cleaning products here somewhere?"

She nodded and pointed to the cupboard under the sink. He

put his arm around her and steered her into the living room. She let him tuck her into an armchair. She put her head into her hands. A few moments later, she heard him come back into the room.

"Here."

Isaac was offering her a glass. She took it and sipped it, wrinkling her nose. Scotch. Isaac smoothed a hand down her hair.

"It'll help. Sit here and relax. I'll be in the kitchen."

She wanted to protest, to ask him to stay with her but she couldn't speak. Hurt, shock, humiliation, anger flowed through her. *Whore.* Whoever it was that was tormenting her had just upped their game. She hadn't realized it was that easy to get into her house, to get to her. Was she in actual danger? From whom, though? She shook her head and stood, the irritation outweighing the shock now. She went into the kitchen to see Isaac, stripped to the waist, his expensive shirt and jacket hung over a chair, a bucket of soapy water at his feet. He looked up as she came in.

"You okay?"

She nodded. "Yeah, I'm sorry about freaking out. Listen... let's take a couple of photos, just to have a record."

Isaac stopped, his fist clenched around a sponge. "You sure you don't want me to call Finn? There might be fingerprints."

She hesitated then her shoulders slumped. "Okay."

Finn sighed. He recognized the writing immediately and cursed out loud. "Fucking, fucking woman..."

Sarah, by now calm, and with Isaac's arms around her, watched him. "Dude... I'm kind of relieved if it is Crap-o-line.... sorry, I mean, *Caroline.*"

Finn grinned and she heard Isaac's soft chuckle. Finn looked at Sarah. "You wanna press charges?"

She shook her head. "I cannot be bothered with all that – just make her pay for the door if you can."

"I'll pay for it."

Sarah frowned at her old friend. "You will not." She knew Caroline's family were rich – not that it had done Finn any good – he was too proud to take her money. "Caroline can pay – unless she wants her mom and dad to know about this."

Finn scrubbed his hands through his short blonde curls. Isaac cleared his throat.

"Any idea why she's doing this?

Finn shook his head. "I really don't but I'll talk to her about it. Look, guys, I'm sorry, if it is her, my relationship with her isn't helping."

"Not your fault, buddy."

Sarah smiled gratefully at Isaac as he clapped her friend on the shoulder. Finn nodded and bade them farewell. Sarah sighed and leaned against Isaac.

"Well, look. I'll clean this up and get to the coffee house. You should go, this nonsense shouldn't interfere with your day."

Isaac put his arms around her. "Forget it, I'm staying."

"Iss', really. I'm just going to go on as if nothing's happened."

Isaac looked unconvinced. "But I'm coming back this evening. I don't want you alone here."

"She returns!" Molly threw herself dramatically across the counter as Sarah entered the coffee house, and feigned a faint. "God bless us everyone, we are saved!"

Sarah, laughing, hugged her friend. "You are a lunatic."

"And you – let's see you properly – "Molly held her friend at arm's length and studied her then nodded satisfactorily, "have been screwed good and properly. I can tell."

Sarah rolled her eyes while going scarlet but she joined in with her friend's high spirits. It felt good to fool around. "You are correct, Ms. Jewell. I have been fucked good and properly, right into next Wednesday. In fact, I need to sit down so you'll have to do all the work."

Molly shrugged. "What else is new? I'm just kidding." She hugged her friend. "Good to have you back."

"Glad you think so... don't think everyone will be."

Quickly she filled Molly in on the vandalism to her house. Molly listened with growing annoyance.

"That bitch," she hissed when Sarah had finished.

"Yep. Just when you think that she couldn't get any lower."

Molly chewed this over while Sarah put on her apron and began to work. "Hey, Sar, you absolutely sure it was her?"

Sarah shrugged. "Finn recognized her handwriting. Besides, I don't think I've pissed anyone else off."

"Okay."

"Why?"

"No reason."

Sarah nodded then went out into the kitchen. Molly mulled over what she'd been told – and what she herself was keeping secret. Finn had finally convinced her that she hadn't seen Dan Bailey that night but the thought had kept nagging away at her. Then there were the letters that had come to the Varsity while Sarah was away. Molly had them in her apron pocket for three days – she didn't want to give them to her friend, not after everything.

"Oh hey..." Sarah stuck her head out of the kitchen, "I'm having a cookout at my place on Saturday – Isaac's brother and his family are invited. Wanna come? Bring Mike and the kids, it'll be a family thing."

Molly smiled. "Now that sounds like fun. Want some help setting up?"

Sarah grinned. "Oh hell yes."

"Are you two actually here to help or are you just too much in awe of my twinkle lights?" Sarah grinned down at them from the loft. Finn and Molly were gazing at the hundreds and hundreds of tiny white lights she'd strung up around the barn next to her house.

"It looks like Tinkerbell threw up in here." Finn ducked as she hefted a piece of wood at him. He grinned and started up the ladder to join her. Sarah grabbed the top of the ladder and pretend to push it over.

"Give it up, woman." He hoisted himself onto the loft beside her. "Hi." She smiled at him and handed him a staple gun.

An hour later, they went into the house and Sarah fixed sandwiches and lemonade for their lunch. The kitchen smelt of freshly baked bread and cookies, food for the party on every available surface. Finn looked around in astonishment.

"When do you have time to, I don't know, sleep?"

"It's not much, George's bringing most of the food." She passed him and Molly a plate of cookies then sat down heavily. "I am pretty beat, though. Hey, do you to mind if I skip out for ten minutes? I need to go to the drugstore, get some aspirin."

"Headache?"

"Yep and I have a full evening's.... how can put this..."

Finn demolished his sandwich in two bites. "Heavy fucking?"

Molly spat a mouthful of coffee out as Sarah laughed. "Yeah, so I have to be on top form."

"When's your boo arriving?"

"An hour or so. His brother and his family are following him here. Some of his friends are coming too. Look, I'll be quick at the store."

"Go on, go," Molly shooed her away.

The grocery store on the far side of the island was almost empty. Despite having been to the drugstore for aspirin and swallowing two with some water, her head throbbed with the beginnings of another migraine, her vision blurred, and she was nauseous. Sarah grabbed a cart and headed towards the bakery aisle. She stopped, closed her eyes, trying to ride out the wave of dizziness. She swallowed, the bitter taste of bile in the back of her throat. It took her a moment to realize someone was talking to her. Todd, the trainee baker, greeted her.

"Hey Sarah, we don't see you over here often. Hey... you okay? "

She smiled weakly at the young man, his clear features clouded with concern. His carefully gelled hair stuck up in a Mohawk. He had been one of Dan's favorite students.

"I'm fine, Todd. Keeping up with your piano practice I hope?"

Todd grinned, sheepish. "Ah, I got a guitar now. Me and Zane started a band. Maybe we could play at the coffee house sometime?"

Sarah nodded. "Sure thing. Come see me, okay?"

She waved goodbye at him and steered the cart around the rest of the store, still trying to shake the nausea.

She turned into the breakfast cereal aisle and almost collided with Caroline. She let out a groan before she could stop herself.

Caroline grinned. "Hey, slut. Fucked any helpless billionaires lately?"

Sarah wondered if she could batter Caroline senseless with a roll of frozen cookie dough and get away with it. "Drop dead, dumbass."

Caroline's eyes brightened and she smiled, a strange grimace, almost triumphant.

"Oh you first, Sarah. You first."

Sarah pushed past her, irritation making her skin itch. She shoved the cart too hard against the checkout, smiled an apology at the girl behind it as she jumped. A couple of lanes over, she could see Caroline talking to two women. They were glancing over and laughing. Sarah gritted her teeth.

Then she saw it.

The shock was icy cold, constricting. Sarah couldn't look away. She breathed in short gasps. The front page of the *Bugler*. A child, covered in blood, being carried out of a trailer by a cop. Blinded, shell-shocked in the glare of flashlights. Tears. Her tears. Sarah felt her knees give way and she clutched the side of the checkout for support. More photos – the body of a woman with her throat cut. And another picture of Sarah, grown, from the other day. Looking tired and worn down. She couldn't breathe.

"Hey, are you okay?"

Somewhere in the turmoil in her mind, it registered that the question was one she had been asked too much lately. She couldn't stop looking at the photo of her mother, her eyes staring and mouth screaming silently. Sarah pushed herself away from the checkout, abandoning her cart and staggered out of the door. Behind her, she heard the catcalls and hysterical laughter of Caroline and her friends.

She made it to the door of the store before she threw up.

At Sarah's house, George's face made Molly rock back as the elderly man jumped out his car, waving a newspaper.

"Hey, hey what's up?" Molly went to greet him. He was out of breath, and she guided him into a chair. He caught his breath but without a word, handed her the newspaper. Molly took it. Her hand flew to her mouth.

"Oh my God..." A whisper. She met George's gaze.

"Where's Sarah?"

A squeal of tires answered them. They looked up as she saw Sarah's truck appear from the wrong direction, weaving wildly along the road to her house.

"What the hell?" Molly dashed for the door to see the truck slam into the streetlight at the end of the road. The impact crumpled the truck's hood, the metal screeching against the concrete.

"Sarah!" George and Molly sprinted over to her truck, seeing out the corner of her eye, Finn, bursting out of the barn at the sound of the crash, followed behind. Molly, her breath coming in short panicked breaths, wrenched open the cab door to see Sarah slumped over the steering wheel. Finn flew around and opened the passenger side and slid in next to his friend.

"Oh God...sweetheart?" Molly touched her friend's shoulder, felt her shift. She sighed with relief as Sarah sat up, obviously dazed, but unharmed.

"You maybe shouldn't move, sweetheart." Finn's brown eyes were serious as he pressed two fingers to her neck, feeling her pulse. He shared a concerned look with Molly. Sarah shook her head slowly, her face set, angry.

"Have you seen the paper?" Her voice was flat, dead. She didn't look at them, staring straight ahead.

George and Molly exchanged a look. Finn cleared his throat.

"Sarah, maybe you should come and lie down."

"No." She looked at George, more focused now. "Did you see it?"

"Yes," George answered her at last. Molly had gone back to the house and now returned with the paper, handing it to Finn.

"These are crime scene photos," Finn hissed, "what the hell?"

"How did they get hold of them?" George"s voice shook with anger, with pity for Sarah. He touched her arm but she shook it off.

"I know exactly who gave them to the paper," she said, suddenly glancing in her rearview mirror. They all turned to where she was looking, and before they could stop her, she was out and sprinting.

Caroline Jewell – infuriatingly invited to the party because Finn would be there - drove up to the house and got out of the car. She turned just as Sarah launched herself onto her, crying out in surprise as the two women tumbled to the ground. She tried to grab Sarah's hands as the smaller woman whaled on her, cussing and shouting.

"You fucking, fucking bitch! I know it was you, you piece of human shit."

George and Finn hauled Sarah off, arms hooked under her shoulders. Caroline got up, grinning maniacally despite the blood pouring from her nose. Sarah struggled against her captors" grasp.

"Sarah!" George's sharp voice finally broke through the madness and Sarah calmed herself, never taking her eyes off Caroline.

"George, I know she's the one who gave them all that..." she trailed off as Caroline laughed again.

"Prove it, psycho," she wiped her nose with her hand. "Ain't nothing people didn't already know anyways."

Finn nodded to George, who locked his arms around Sarah, as Finn stepped over to Caroline. He picked her bag up, shoving it at her.

"Is it true?"

Caroline sneered at him, brushing the dirt from her pants. "I couldn't say. Nothing to do with me where they get their stories from. Like I said, everyone knows she's trash. As far as I'm concerned, The Bugler's just saying it runs in the family."

"That's enough," said Finn and Caroline quelled under his hard stare. "Those photos were police property. If I find out they were stolen..."

Caroline gave up her simpering. "Like I said, prove it."

"What the hell is going on?"

They all started and turned. Isaac was standing behind George, Sarah, and Finn. A man, who had to be Isaac's brother and a tall, elegant Asian woman stood by his side, looking wide-eyed and concerned. In the car behind them, two children stared out at them. Sarah started to tremble. Isaac raised his arms towards Sarah and she went straight into them. He held her close and looked up at Finn.

"What's going on?"

Caroline smiled nastily. "I don't think we've met. I'm..."

"I don't give a shit who you are. I asked what was going on." His voice was like ice and Caroline balked. She scowled.

"I'll tell you. *Sarah, Sarah, Sarah Bailey, got all chopped up by her mo-ho-mmy,*" she sang out of tune and cackled. Sarah lost her temper again and they all reached for her. Caroline turned towards her home. "Lock that bitch up. Oh actually," she swung around again and spoke directly to Finn, "I'd like to press charges. Assault charges."

Molly gave a squeak of disgusted alarm but Finn winked at her. "For what?" he said calmly, looking at Caroline. Caroline waved at Sarah.

"She attacked me, of course. Christ, how did I pick someone this stupid for my husband?"

Finn looked at her steadily. "Attack you? I didn't see anything of the sort." He turned to the others. "You?"

Various shakes of the head and murmurs greeted his question.

Finn stared his wife down. "Go home, Caroline, no-one wants you here."

Caroline huffed in irritation, getting back into the car. George sighed and turned to Sarah, still locked in Isaac's arms.

"You okay, bubs?"

She nodded, a strange expression in her eyes. "I'm fine, pops." She extricated herself from Isaac's embrace. "Thanks, baby. " George saw Isaac smile down at her.

"Anytime. Now, you going to tell me what's going on?"

Sarah looked out at the people on her lawn, in her barn. She could see Saul, Isaac's brother chatting with Finn, his kids, Christopher and Rosie, running around with Molly's kids, Becky and Mike Jr.. Molly and Maika were chatting and laughing at the food table, George playing host.

"They're basically doing my job for me," she fretted but Isaac drew her into his arms.

"They're okay, baby. Now, do you want to tell me what happened?"

She looked at him, a sad smile on her face. "I come from a very different background to you, Isaac. There was no family estate, no happy family. I grew up in a trailer park just south of the city. My mother was a prostitute. She was an illegal immigrant from Shanghai. Barely spoke English, didn't bother to learn. I spoke Mandarin until I was five. Never knew who my father was, could have been any one of her clients."

"What happened to your mother?"

Sarah sighed. "When I was six, I came home from school and found her happy. Believe me, it was unusual. She barely even noticed me anymore. But this one day, she seemed almost giddy. She had made dinner – just sandwiches and juice. We ate together. I started to feel odd. She was watching me, smiling all the time. I couldn't keep my eyes open. Just before I feel asleep, I felt her take my arms. There was a stinging pain I didn't recognize and then nothing. When I woke up, she was lying next to me. Dead. She had cut her wrists. And mine. What she hadn't realized was that by giving me a sedative it had slowed down my pulse and the cuts on my arms weren't deep enough. I crawled through all the blood and got help."

Isaac didn't say anything just kept watching her. She looked away, over the field to the school.

"George was the one who found me – he was the police chief at the time. Because of his age, his marital status, and his profession, they wouldn't let him adopt me formally. So I went to live in the children's home. No one wanted to adopt a damaged mixed-race kid. Not with that history. The children's home was okay, food and lodgings. But lonely – George came most days and would take me out when he could." Sarah was matter-of-fact.

"Then when I was thirteen, a family moved next door." She grinned at Isaac. "You can guess who."

"Molly and Finn?"

She nodded. "It was the family I never had. They were funny and loud and argumentative. But the love, Isaac, man, I never knew what it was until the Jewell family came into my life. They taught me to trust again. Everyone except myself. It all caught up with me when I went to college, I went through some pretty tough times."

Isaac blew out a long breath, his arms tightening around her, his lips against her hair. "Jesus, Sarah. I'm so sorry. What a messed up start to life. It does explain one thing, though…"

"How I ended up trusting Dan? Because he said all the right things?"

Isaac looked down to see her smiling at him and he grinned good-naturedly. "Yep."

Her face clouded over. "It doesn't change things between us, I mean?"

He looked surprised then upset. "God, no, why would it?"

She smiled but pulled away from him a little. "We can't be naive. You're a pretty high-profile guy. When it gets out, the press will eat it up. The billionaire and his psycho crazy girlfriend."

Isaac frowned. "You are not crazy, or a psycho or anything I could ever, ever be ashamed of. I love you. I'm *in* love with you, Sarah, the for-better-or-for-worse kind of love, the –til-death-do-us-part love."

Sarah froze. "What?"

There was a pause. "You heard me."

"Are you asking…?"

Isaac sighed. "No. Not yet. Not like this. But I will ask you that someday. Someday that's happy and without all this stress. Some day when you'll believe it's out of love and not out of sympathy."

She smiled daily. "You know me so well already."

Isaac reached for her. "We're meant to be together, I know that."

She tilted her head up to kiss him. "I know that too and later, I'm going to show you how much."

He grinned. "You bet your cute little butt you will. Now, before my trousers become something "tent-like", let's go meet my family."

Molly sidled up to Isaac as he sat back, relaxed in the porch swing. The party had died down, the sun was beginning to set. His brother and his family had left ten minutes previously, hugging their new friends. Saul had taken Isaac aside. "Sarah's lovely, bro. I'm so happy for you."

Isaac was grateful to his brother for not holding the earlier drama against Sarah, but he knew he'd have to explain it to him Monday morning at the office. He smiled at Molly now as she slunk into the chair next to him. "So..."

She grinned. "I may have a huge girl crush on your sister-in-law."

Isaac laughed. "Fair enough, but don't tell Sarah you're cheating on her."

Molly mimed zipping her mouth then her smile faded. "She okay?"

She nodded towards Sarah – who admitted was being corralled by Becky and Mike Jr, who were clambering all over her.

Isaac nodded. "I think so."

"She tell you about her mom? Crazy, huh?"

Isaac nodded grimly. "I can't even imagine."

She studied him. "You get the picket fence?"

Isaac shrugged. "Not always but a lifetime better than what Sarah got. Our parents pretty much hated each other but they both loved us. I cannot imagine why a parent would do that to a child."

"Not every parent loves their kids, but no, me either. How far she's come is amazing to me."

"How far who's come?" A breathless Sarah staggered up to the porch, carrying a child under each arm. They collapsed in a giggling pile on the porch.

"Hillary Clinton," said Molly smoothly. She got up and

dragged her kids of Sarah. "Right you monsters, go wash your hands and find your dad. George?" She called over to the older man who was tidying the food table. "Can we give you a ride into town?"

George hesitated but Sarah waved him over. "Pops, leave that, I'll clear up."

An hour later, Sarah and Isaac were alone and lazing in her tub. Sarah lay back against his solid chest and closed her eyes as Isaac's fingertips drifted lazily up and down her stomach.

"Did you have a good time today?" Isaac's deep voice, low and sexy, rumbled through his chest, his lips at her ear. Sarah nodded slowly.

"Despite everything, yes. I really liked Saul and Maika and the kids are adorable."

"They thought the same of you. We'll get together with them again soon."

"Good."

They lay in silence for a long time before Sarah sat up and turned around in the bath, managing to straddle him. Isaac slid his hands around her waist and smiled at her.

"Hey, beautiful."

She searched his eyes for a second. "Isaac, I want you to be honest with me. If everything that's been going on with me is more than you signed up for, I'll understand."

He frowned. "Are you kidding me? Do you honestly think that little of me that I'd run at the slightest hint of baggage?"

She shook her head. "No, I didn't mean that. *At all.* You are the best thing that's ever happened to me. I just don't want you to feel obligated to deal with my shit."

He kissed her fiercely. "I'm all in, Sarah, whatever comes our way."

She relaxed. "Thank you." She slid her hands down between his legs and cupped his cock but he grabbed her hands, made her look at him.

"Is anything scaring you? About the story, about the letters? Because you can tell me, no matter what it is."

Sarah considered. "Actually, all I'm concerned with is how this affects you. Now that I know it was Caroline who sold the story, I'm convinced she's the one sending the letters. Yeah, it's upsetting but no, I'm not scared.

He released her hands and pulled her to him, his fingers sliding under her hair at the nape of her neck, as he kissed her slowly this time, deeply, savoring the feel of her. Sarah sighed into the kiss. Isaac nuzzled her neck, then with his lips to her ear, he whispered.

"Let's get out of the tub, sweetheart, because you promised me a night of supreme fucking..."

Sarah moaned at the honey of his voice and in a flash they were tumbled from the tub, sloshing water everywhere, onto the wooden floor of the bathroom.

Isaac moved down her body, pushing her legs apart gently, and burying his face in her sex, his tongue lashing around her clit, along the soft peachy folds of her, feeling her labia swell and engorge. His teeth graze her clit before he bit down on it gently, grinning when he heard her sharp intake of breath, felt her fingers knot in his hair. He sucked, tasted, teased her until she was panting, begging him to fill her. His cock was straining painfully, so heavy it bobbed under its own weight as he climbed her body and scooped a hand under her buttocks as she wound her legs around him. His cock slid into her, filling her sweet cunt, and gratified, Isaac watched her eyes roll back with the pleasure he was giving her.

"I'm gonna fuck you so hard, baby..." Her cry of ecstasy spurred him on and he slammed into her over and over and over until they were both crying and laughing.

Sarah woke in the morning feeling so sick that she had to scramble to the bathroom to throw up. Afterward, she brushed her teeth and washed her face. Looking in the mirror, she saw the dark circles etched around her eyes, her skin yellow and sickly and the deep crease of stress between her eyebrows. Her eyes, usually so expressive, were dead and flat.

"Hey, you. Are you okay?" Isaac, just in his boxers, stood at the door frowning then, when he saw her wan face, he stepped into the room and swept a hand onto her forehead. "Jesus, you're burning up."

He made her get back into bed despite her protestations and brought her tea and aspirin. Despite herself, Sarah fell asleep for half an hour. When she woke, she heard Isaac on the phone.

"No, surely someone else can deal with this? I need to be at home today. Saul, yes, yes, okay." She heard him end the call. "God."

"Is everything okay?" She tried to sit up but Isaac pushed her gently back down.

"You need to rest, beautiful. Look, I have to go into the city for a meeting, I tried to cancel it but Saul's being a hard-ass."

"It's okay, go. I'll be fine here. I'm not working today anyway."

Isaac hesitated then nodded. "Okay, look, I'll be a couple of hours tops. You need anything, you call me or Molly, promise?"

After he'd left, Sarah fell back asleep, her head pounding. She was so soundly asleep that she didn't even hear the front door open and the creak of the stairs outside her bedroom.

He looked down at her, so still, so beautiful. Her skin looked damp, a flush of heat in her cheeks. Fever. He smiled. An easy reaction to manufacture if you knew the right drugs to hide in her vitamin supplements. Now, though, he needed to make sure she stayed unconscious. He flicked the plastic cover of the syringe he had in his pocket and eased the needle into the vein in her neck. She stirred at the quick pain but then settled. He waited five minutes before drawing back the covers. It all took less than a minute to snap the photos of her glorious body, so vulnerable. He smiled to himself. Let them know that they couldn't stop him, that he would get to her whatever they did. He pulled the covers back over her body and left the bedroom. His next task would take a lot longer.

Sarah woke just after three, just as Isaac's helicopter landed outside. She heard him taking the stairs two at a time and then he was there. She smiled at him. Isaac sat next to her.

"How are you feeling?"

She sat up in bed. "Much better, although pretty sweaty and gross."

"Are you hungry?" Isaac started to take his tie off. "I'll make you some eggs if you like?"

Suddenly she was starving. "God, yes, please. I'm just going to take a shower, change the bedsheets."

He leaned over to kiss her. "See you downstairs."

After a blissful shower, she pulled the bedsheets from the bed and gathered them into a ball to take downstairs. She heard something fall from the comforter and bent to see what it was. She frowned as she picked up the small plastic cap. A syringe cover? She scanned her memory. She didn't think she'd ever used a syringe in her life.

"Yo, sexy, your meal awaits."

She grinned at Isaac yelling up the stairs, then, shrugging, she threw the cap into the trash and went downstairs.

Finn had fallen into a routine of sleeping in his office at home, showering when Caroline was still asleep and then only emerging for meals and to change for work. Caroline didn't object. They avoided each other; being together only led to rows. He could hear her watching a dumb soap in the living room.

He dressed for work and went into the kitchen. Caroline was making herself some lunch.

"Do you want some?" She indicated the sandwich fixings. He shook his head.

"No thanks." He grabbed his keys.

"Finn?"

He turned. Caroline gave him a half-smile. "Have a good day."

He blinked. This Caroline, he hadn't seen for years. Conciliatory. Friendly.

"Thanks." He returned her smile. "You too."

She nodded and turned back to her sandwich.

Finn walked around the block to the station but changed his mind at the last moment and headed over to the coffee house, In the Varsity, Molly was on her own. She looked up, grinned, and waved him over.

""Sup sis?" He hugged her and immediately reached for the coffee pot. She rolled her eyes and pushed the plate of muffins towards him.

"An invitation. Mike and I would like to invite you and the *Gorgon*, I'm sorry, Caroline, to have drinks with us tonight. Nothing fancy, just at Hanks. I know Caroline does"t drink, perhaps they'll have Virgin Mary's – hey! She could finally, legitimately, have the blood of a virgin."

Finn grinned. "You done?"

Molly pretended to think for a second then nodded. "I'm out. Well?"

Finn picked at a muffin. "Yeah, sure. As far as I know Caroline's free, I'll have to check. What's the deal?"

"You mean apart from spending time with me, your wonderful sister? And the fact we finally have a babysitter we trust not to lead the kids down a path of devil worship and Taylor Swift fandom?"

Finn rolled his eyes at his sister. "You are certifiable, you know that?"

Molly grinned but then her expression sobered. "Look, I figure if we at least try to be pleasant to Caroline, she might lay off Sarah."

Fin shrugged. "Worth a shot."

Molly grimaced. "Mike's idea. Do-gooder." But she grinned. Finn got up, shaking his head in amusement.

"So you'll come?" She called after him.

"Yeah, yeah what time?"

"Eight. See you there."

Molly watched her brother cross the street to the police station. It has been the first time that she had seen him smile in quite a while. His face was drawn, his pallor pale, clammy. He looked so much older than a few months ago, she realized with a pang. Maybe tonight he'd relax, have some fun. A nub of guilt settled in her chest. She knew why Mike wanted this evening, this get-together – to make peace between them all. She'd happily gone along with it and now she questioned herself. Finn was her family and Caroline made him miserable. Still, if it helped... shrugging, Molly sighed and went back to work.

The evening sun faded and was about to drop below the horizon. After a light supper, they sat outside, talking, listening to the quiet evening, the faint lapping of water from the beach at the bottom of the garden. Sarah, her feet in Isaac's lap as he rubbed them, studied him. At work, in his exquisite suits, he looked every inch the powerful billionaire businessman but here, sitting on her porch swing, in his artfully faded t-shirt and his long, long legs in blue jeans, he looked at home. She told him that and he smiled.

"I feel at home, babe. Anywhere with you would feel like home."

She flushed with pleasure, stroked a finger down his cheek. "Maybe we should talk about where we go from here?" she suddenly got nervous but Isaac leaned over to kiss her.

"Sarah, would you be as kind as to move in with me?" He said in a formal English accent that made her giggle.

"Sir, I would be delighted," she replied, waving her hand in a flourish.

"That's the worse accent I've ever heard," he teased. She stuck her tongue out at him.

"So, we're doing this then?"

He pulled her onto his lap. "Hell yes, we are. I can't wait any longer. We just have to work out the logistics but that can wait for later. Right now, I think we should celebrate." And he swung her up into his arms and went inside.

He stood back from the tree line as Isaac carried Sarah into the house. He had watched them for the last few minutes, talking, being so easy and relaxed with each other. It made his rage threaten to burst out of him.

Now, he back-tracked through the wood to his car and drove back across the island. He had somewhere he needed to be.

The bar was crowded and noisy so Molly bent her head, her mouth next to Mike's ear.

"I'm going kill her. I'm going to kill her with extra death. I'm going to hang her entrails from a tree and dress her corpse up like a goat. With sprinkles."

Mike snorted with laughter. "Inventive." He couldn't blame Molly, he was regretting extending the drinks invitation to Caroline Jewell.

The evening had begun promising enough. Finn and Molly were a tag-team, busting each other's chops, making Mike laugh. Soon enough, though, Caroline had tired of them hogging the spotlight and had butted in. Mike felt Molly tense beside him immediately, watched Finn's shoulders slump. Caroline appeared oblivious, and worse, was fawning over both Finn and himself. Mike was reminded of a faded small-town pageant queen, once glossy and used to male attention. He wasn't fooled by Caroline any more than Molly or Finn or anyone else was. Caroline was telling about her plans to have a baby.

Mike caught Molly rolling her eyes at him and he grinned. Finn shifted in his chair.

"I can see us having a whole bunch of kids," Caroline was saying.

"Half human, half spawn of Beelzebub," Molly muttered under her breath. Mike grinned. Finn was looking at Caroline, a strange expression on his face.

""A whole bunch"?"

Caroline smiled and patted his knee. "Of course. I want at least four."

Finn threw back his drink. "You never mentioned *four*." His voice was tired, defeated. Caroline's face fell the tiniest amount, but then a nasty smile started to form around her mouth.

"Well, I do. I want us to be a family. You know you could be more enthusiastic, I thought we were trying."

Finn shrugged but this time Molly couldn't hold back. She grinned wickedly.

"You're always *trying*, Caroline."

Caroline bristled, Finn smirked and Mike put a warning hand on Molly's knee.

"I wouldn't expect you to understand," Caroline narrowed her eyes at Molly, "but I was born to be a mother."

"One word, couple of syllables missing from the end of that," Molly shot back with a syrupy smile. Mike couldn't help the bark of laughter that escaped him then and even Finn chuckled.

Caroline's face set with spite and she turned back to Finn. "Anyways, my point is, you should be grateful that you're with someone who can provide you with an heir. A legacy."

Molly rolled her eyes then. "Yeah 'cos anything getting half its DNA from you…"

"Molly." Finn's warning was soft and low. She grinned, shrugged.

Caroline's nose went in the air. "Any DNA from me is surely better than the fetid gene pool that spat out that half-bred bitch."

"Shut the fuck up." Finn stood up suddenly, slamming his chair back. He looked down at his wife, oblivious to the alarmed looks of his sister and her husband. "You don't say one more word about Sarah, you understand?"

Caroline laughed. "It's not my fault you *still* get a hard-on for that skank."

Mike started to stand as Finn stepped towards his wife. "You don't get to talk about her like that. Ever. Do you understand me? She's worth a million of you, Caroline. Don't forget it." His voice was rigid with anger, with contempt. Caroline made a disgusted noise, pushed her old chair back and stalked out. Finn struggled to get control of his temper. Molly stood and tried to put her hand on his arm but he shook it off. After a moment, he reached into his pockets, pulled a couple of bills out and dropped them on the table.

"I'm sorry." He didn't look at them again before walking out. Mike blew out a long breath and drew Molly in for a hug. He could feel her trembling.

"I'm sorry...I started that," she muttered into his shoulder. He tightened his arms around her and stared out of the window, watching as Finn's car disappeared from view.

'Light the touch paper', he thought, unease curling his stomach. He looked down at Molly, kissed her gently. "Wanna get out of here?"

At the small hotel set at the corner of the island's golf course, he threw down his keys and looked around. Everything he owned was in this room. He smiled, he liked his compact way of living. The apartment on the island was perfect. He'd already figured out he could see into the coffee house from the large picture window; even better, that there was a network of alleyways behind both buildings that would come in handy.

He grabbed his laptop and fired it up. Soon he had the camera feeds up. Her kitchen. Her living room. Her bathroom. Her bedroom. His anger snarled through him when he saw them, naked, kissing, touching, fucking. He watched as Sarah, on top of Isaac, rode his cock hard, throwing her head back as she came, watched Quinn's hands on her tits, squeezing, saw him go down on her, watched as Sarah sucked his cock.

Whore

But it made him unbearably hard to watch them. Later, he

watched them asleep in her bed, Quinn curled around her tiny, beautiful body, her dark hair clouded around that face. God, that *face*. It haunted him the way her dark lashes swept down onto her cheeks. His eyes moved all over her body, the full, ripe breasts, the softly curved belly, the legs that were longer than her height would suggest. Quinn's big hand was splayed across her belly and it made the watcher want to throw up. How would Quinn feel when she was dead? When her blood stained her beautiful skin, when her eyes would close for the last time?

He lay on the bed and thought about what his next move would be. The rich asshole was definitely a problem but he knew how to deal with that. In that, he had assistance. He grinned to himself. Caroline. Her repugnant vanity and her absolute hatred of Sarah made her so malleable. With only the slightest show of affection on his part, she had bent to his will, given him her trust. Yes, she'd been invaluable over the past year but... his lip curled in distaste and he sat up. When they had broken into Sarah's home, he had been furious when she had painted that obscene graffiti in the kitchen but later, thinking about it, it had been advantageous – they would know it was Caroline – but Caroline working alone, never suspecting that he was her puppet-master. They would be upset but not scared. *Yet.* He was free and clear for the moment.

He began to collect his possessions; his suitcase, his photography equipment. He loaded up his car and went back in for his final bag. Pausing, he unzipped and pulled out the heavy canvas roll and unfurled it. His knives. He pulled out the one he planned to use on Sarah – long and thin. He imagined it slicing into her tender flesh, visualize her terror, her pain as he murdered her. It made him hard just thinking about it and he went into the shower and began to jerk off. Maybe it was time he gave them a taster of what he had planned for her, and at the same time, fuck with Quinn's head, and destroy Sarah's peace of mind.

And he knew just want to do.

A week later, Sarah didn't see Isaac when he came into the coffee house, her head was down, concentrating on the account books. He smiled to himself, picked a flower out of the arrangement on one of the tables. She was sitting facing away from him. He touched the flower to her neck, the lightest touch. She didn't turn, just swatted at herself, distracted. He grinned and ran the bloom down her skin. She turned and smiled delightedly. She moved around the counter into his arms and he kissed her.

"Hey you, I wasn't expecting to see you until later. You playing hooky again?"

"Yep. You're a terrible influence." He grinned and bopped her nose with the flower. Your corsage, ma'am." He stuck the flower in her hair. She laughed.

"You want coffee?"

"Always." He sat down and studied her as she grabbed the coffee pot. He'd been away on a business for the last two days and now he drank in the sight of her. "Is it possible you got more beautiful than ever since I last saw you?"

She made a face and made him laugh.

He reached over to take her hand. "I missed you," he said, grinning at her, "this working thing is really inconvenient. What are you up to later?"

"I have to drop some paperwork off at George's place. He still refuses to join the technology age and get a computer so I had to print some stuff off for him. After that, I'm free for whatever you want." She grinned lasciviously and he smiled.

An hour later, Isaac nodded and turned the car around, heading out of town. He glanced over at her. "So what do you feel like doing after?"

"You."

"Damn, you keep talking like that, we're never going to get to George's place. Hey, not to ruin the moment, but any new letters or anything weird?"

She shook her head. "Nothing. Maybe Caroline's finally got the message. Finn must have threatened her with arrest for stealing the crime scene photos to get her to stop. I think she's done, the stupid idiot."

Isaac sighed. "She has definitely lived up my first impression of her." He looked over at her and smiled. "Remember that? Our first date at George's restaurant?"

Her eyes were soft. "Of course, I do. God, was there ever a time when I didn't know and love you?"

He pulled her hand up to his mouth and kissed it. "I know what you mean, sweetheart."

They drove in silence and a few minutes later Isaac drew the car up to the sidewalk outside George's house. Sarah started to open the door but Isaac stopped her.

"Are you mine forever?" He whispered.

"For all time." She answered simply and when she looked up at him, he could see the love in her eyes. He smiled.

"Guess I better go make nice with my future father-in-law."

She laughed slightly as she got out of the car. "One thing at a time, buddy. Besides," she gave him a sly smile, "I need to be wooed first."

He laughed out loud. "Wooed?"

"Hell yes." She rummaged in her purse for the key and opened the door. As she was stepping into the house, Isaac's phone buzzed.

"I'll be right behind you, darling."

The downstairs was in darkness, the drapes pulled. In the hallway, she thought she smelled cooking, or food and wondered if George had prepared something for them.

"Hey pops," she called. No answer.

She went into the kitchen and stopped. The blinds were down and the room in absolute darkness but the smell of... something... was strong in here. She felt her gag reflex kick in. *Jesus*...Her heart began to thump unpleasantly. She felt her way over to the window, almost slipping in something wet on the floor. She pulled the blinds up, letting the sun stream into the room, and turned.

Everything in her world stopped. Everything in her world ended.

Her knees gave way, and every bone in her body went soft. A sound, a scream, a howl ripped its way from the center of her being. Her knees hit the floor, splashing still warm blood over her clothes, her face. She sat there, panting, all human thought gone. Unthinking she crawled through the blood to the front door and somehow managed to get it open. Still on all-fours, she managed to make it to the middle of the front lawn before collapsing. Isaac's face was a mask of horror as he took in her blood-covered form. She curled into a fetal position, her mind shut down. Catatonic.

"Christ, Sarah.... what? What happened?" Isaac's voice, frantic sounded hollow to her, an echo in an empty hall. She didn't even feel it when Isaac lifted her into his arms and took her to the car.

Finn came out of the house, his face white, shocked. He pulled

Isaac away from the ambulance as he argued with the paramedics. Sarah was refusing to be taken to the hospital and the paramedics were trying to persuade her otherwise.

"Isaac, let them look after her. You need to see this."

He followed Finn into the house, the smell of the blood, of flesh starting to decompose hitting him. He balked at the entrance of the kitchen, and when he did take a step into the room, he clamped a hand over his nose. George was laid out on the kitchen table, his eyes open and staring, his face contorted in unimaginable agony. His torso was split from his throat down to his groin and his organs, his intestines spilled out over his body, his blood covered the floor, congealing, the stench of iron and death. There were stab marks all over his body, his face, and his head.

Isaac gagged. "*Jesus.*"

Finn nodded. "I know. But that's not what I need you to see. The killer left a message for Sarah." He nodded to the far wall. From his position, Isaac couldn't see what he was indicating. He moved into the room a little more, wincing as his shoes squeaked in the blood, looked up at where Finn was pointing and his heart stopped.

Photographs of Sarah. Hundreds, maybe thousands, layer upon layer of them. In most of them, she wasn't looking at the camera, some obviously taken from a distance, some from awkward angles. She was smiling in most, oblivious to the camera, or talking to someone else. Photos of Isaac and Sarah together. In one they were holding hands, laughing at one of their silly jokes, aprons on, lording it over the barbecue as if they were cordon bleu chefs. That one was at the house, her house. He tried to figure out the angle the picture was taken from. It wasn't hard.

The photographer must have been in the tree line. Photos where he could see members of his own family in the background.

Then he saw the photos in the center of the collage and his heart began to thump, a wave of nausea rising in his throat. Sarah. Dead. Murdered. Stabbed, shot, strangled. They were obviously photo-shopped images of her head on the bodies of murdered women but it didn't lessen the horror of imagining her like that. It would have been clear what the threat was even without the most damning evidence.

In George's blood, smeared in dark gobs across the wall.

You are next...

If you want to continue reading this story, you can get your copy from your favorite vendor by searching for the title:

Maelstrom Complete Series 1-4

An Alpha Billionaire Romance Boxed Set

You can also find the e-book version by typing this link in your computer's browser:

https://www.hotandsteamyromance.com/products/maelstrom-an-alpha-billionaire-romance

OTHER BOOKS BY THIS AUTHOR

Saving Her Rescuer: A Billionaire & A Virgin Romance

I was just trying to get away from my crazy ex for the weekend when I ended up in a giant pileup on the highway up to Gore Mountain.

https://geni.us/SavingHerRescuer

Sensual Sounds: A Rockstar Ménage

Lust. Lies. Double lives.

The rock and roll industry is full of people who are looking out for themselves and willing to do anything to rise to the top.

https://www.hotandsteamyromance.com/collections/frontpage/products/sensual-sounds-a-rockstar-menage

---

On the Run: A Secret Baby Romance

Murder. Lies. Fraud. Just another day in the lives of billionaires and women on the run.

https://www.hotandsteamyromance.com/collections/frontpage/products/on-the-run-a-secret-baby-romance

The Dirty Doctor's Touch: A Billionaire Doctor Romance

I am a master. An elitist. I am at the top of my field, and I know what I am doing.

https://www.hotandsteamyromance.com/collections/frontpage/products/the-dirty-doctor-s-touch-a-billionaire-doctor-romance

The Hero She Needs: A Single Daddy Next Door Romance

He's the only man I've ever wanted...

https://www.hotandsteamyromance.com/collections/frontpage/products/the-hero-she-needs-a-single-daddy-next-door-romance

You can find all of my books here:

Hot and Steamy Romance

https://www.hotandsteamyromance.com

Facebook

facebook.com/HotAndSteamyRomance

ABOUT THE AUTHOR

Mrs. Love writes about smart, sexy women and the hot alpha billionaires who love them. She has found her own happily ever after with her dream husband and adorable 6 and 2 year old kids.
Currently, Michelle is hard at work on the next book in the series, and trying to stay off the Internet.
"Thank you for supporting an indie author. Anything you can do, whether it be writing a review, or even simply telling a fellow reader that you enjoyed this. Thanks

 facebook.com/HotAndSteamyRomance
 instagram.com/michellesromance

©Copyright 2020 by Michelle Love - All rights Reserved
In no way is it legal to reproduce, duplicate, or transmit any part of this document in either electronic means or in printed format. Recording of this publication is strictly prohibited and any storage of this document is not allowed unless with written permission from the publisher. All rights are reserved.
Respective authors own all copyrights not held by the publisher.

 Created with Vellum

www.ingramcontent.com/pod-product-compliance
Lightning Source LLC
LaVergne TN
LVHW021656060526
838200LV00050B/2385